About the Author

Ade Tokunbo [Full name: Adetokunbo Oluwadamilare Sanni] is British born. His parents are from Nigeria. He grew-up in Lagos, Nigeria. He came back to the UK to live at the age of nineteen. He graduated from London South Bank University, studied BA (Hon) Business Administration.

Ade Tokunbo enjoys telling and writing stories he sees as vision. After graduating from the university, Ade Tokunbo decided to have a change of career. He decided to follow his passion, his wide imagination, and what he believes he knows how to do best – telling and writing fiction.

Solomon and the Dark-gods is one out of many. Many more stories are to come from Ade Tokunbo.

Solomon
and the
Dark-gods

Ade Tokunbo

 New Generation Publishing

Book dedicated to my Mother;

Chief (Mrs) Sophia Wuraola Sanni
(Nee Okubule)
The Yeye-Oge of Ilisan
1951 – 2009

May her sweet and gentle soul rest in perfect peace
(Amen)

Acknowledgements

I would like to give a special thanks to the almighty God for guiding me through out the entire story and giving me wisdom, inspiration, knowledge and understanding.

The Good Message I

People, LIFE is short.
To live it full, you need to be GOOD.
Being good to one another is the key factor of a GOOD LIFE.
It's not about what you have but who you are and what you represent.

> *"Good is what I represent and proud to be."*
> *"It feels good to be good."*

So my dearest brothers and sisters;
Let us for the sake of LOVE and for GOODNESS sake, be good.
God bless you.

...be good.

Message from
Ade Tokunbo:
Crown from across the sea.

Contents

Chapter One

Egitee Land

A small land, located on the south coast West African border, flourished with forest and mountains, beautiful birds, lagoons and streams, demarcated round by a river crossing Togo, Benin, and Nigeria. A small West African country colonised by the British, became independent on May 8th, 1946 - a year after the Second World War, making it the first Western African country to gain independence. It's the land of the Dark-gods. It's Egitee Land.

Egitee is one of the West African countries blessed with natural resources like cocoa, coal, gas, and oil - which is the country's main resource. It's also among the twelve biggest oil exporters but due to corrupt governance, it's classified amongst the poorest who are frustrated with poverty, corruption, and injustice. The country has been going through agony ever since the year 1967 when a ferocious military man took over to lead the nation. The good suffers while the bad enjoys.

The people from Egitee known as 'Egite' strongly believe in spiritual powers such as voodoo, just like many other Western African countries. Sixty percent of the people practice voodoo. It plays a large part in the cultural understanding and awareness of the people. It is real. Voodoo in Egitee has had recognition as an official religion ever since 1947. The people consult different types of gods like; Eeyemojaja (The God of Yemojaja), and many other unknown gods. People consult these gods for different reasons such as; to get protection over evil ones, to cure sickness/illness, for money rituals, to cast spells or curse their fellow citizens. However, many Egite claim to be Christians, and a few are Muslims. But some of the ones that claim to be Christians or Muslims still most of the time practice voodoo.

Despite the voodoo practice, life isn't really enjoyable for the good and innocent people in Egitee. Killing, kidnapping, rape, and armed-robbery are everyday experiences they suffer. Egitee is practically a lawless country ever since the military took over. People in government take advantage of the power. They never lack anything; they have security, wealth, and power. They're always protected by armed forces. Since 1967 up to this present day, Egitee is still under military rule; ferocious soldiers everywhere. The present leader has been ruling for almost fourteen years now. He's a powerful, feared and well-respected man in Egitee, so is his father (the military man that took over in 1967). His name is GENERAL (Gen.) FAHRUK AGAJA. No one can stop him. He's put his son MUSIAH AGAJA as his head security just the same way his father made him his head security during his time. Anyone that tries going against the Agaja's ruling will be severely dealt with, or probably get killed. Their words should be final.

Both Gen. Fahruk and his father's rulings are bad. Gen. Fahruk overthrew the power from a man his father appointed to be the interim president. His father, an ex-dictator of Egitee, killed and overthrew the power from the first man (first leader) the British appointed and handed over authority's power to rule the nation. But after so much turmoil, rioting, and fighting in Egitee against Gen. Fahruk's father to leave the presidential seat, he got spiritually ill and couldn't go further after twenty-one years in power. So he made a plan with his son - Gen. Fahruk - to put a very humble, honest, and naive man into power. A civilian the people would

14

prefer to see as their president/leader. And after just three months of this man as the interim president of Egitee, Gen. Fahruk overthrow.

"We need a stronger man to lead us. Egitee needs me. The country is collapsing and according to our military rules, I, as a General, need to make a right move to rescue the country. It's my job as head of the army to rescue my country. Only I, General Fahruk Agaja can put Egitee together," part of the statement made by Gen. Fahruk after hijacking the power fourteen years ago.

Since the ruling of Gen. Fahruk's father and Gen. Fahruk, things hasn't really been getting better but getting worse. Gen. Fahruk is a man of war. He wouldn't mind going to war. He's been warned by his spiritualist adviser that in some years to come, there will be a big WAR in Egitee. The Americans supply the country guns and ammunitions regularly. Gen. Fahruk's idea is to store loads of guns and ammunitions. *"Should in-case anyone tries to start a war with us, we should be ready!,"* Gen. Fahruk always alerts his men. His father many years ago formed a cult group called - CULT BOYZ to work alongside with the police force. Gen. Fahruk also trained and made a lot of youth to join this group; where they carry guns and fight for him. They're part of his army. He provides them food and shelter. Most are hooligans that have no homes. Apparently, most of these boys commit most of the crime in the country. They misuse the power given to them. Gen. Fahruk spends more on guns than anything else for the country. According to recent reports, gun crime is terribly high, and economically the country is collapsing.

Things aren't really going-on well for the poor, innocent, and good people in Egitee, not until…

Chapter Two

Solomon Gondi

A man called SOLOMON GONDI in his mid-forties, one of the ministers in Egitee, is incredibly sick and tired with the whole situation of his country. He's had enough, wants a change, and wants to fight. He wants to get things done. He's determined and focused, but the thing is, no one dares to challenge/step-up to Gen. Fahruk's ruling.

Solomon is a married man with two beautiful daughters. He wouldn't want anything bad to happen to them. He loves them dearly. Stepping up against Gen. Fahruk can be dangerous and wouldn't bring any good to his dearest family. *"But something has to be done. There must be a way,"* words from Solomon. He's a man that believes he can make a difference, and a man of vision. He believes no one should be above the law. He's a man of his word.

Solomon is also a very religious man. He goes to the same church as Gen. Fahruk, a church meant only for the top government bodies. Ministers, senators, governors, and their families all attend this church. Occasionally, a world-famous pastor - PASTOR NICOLAS JAMES from the United Kingdom ministers in this church. He is well respected and honoured being a famous man of God, and also being from the UK. On several occasions, Pastor Nicolas has preached the good wisdom of God, faith and belief. *"Yet most of us seem not to practise or carry out any of this Good, Faith and Belief,"* thought Solomon.

Solomon felt unaided. His country, his people needs help. *"But something has to be done. There must be a way,"* Solomon keeps saying to himself. He's desperate to help. The one person he thinks he can call for rescue is Pastor Nicolas. Pastor Nicolas is the main person on his mind he thinks perhaps can try convincing the bad people in his country including Gen. Fahruk & co to change for good and not get hunted or killed. Pastor Nicola is well respected like that. Also, Gen. Fahruk is God-fearing when it comes to dealing with a true prophet of God, and wouldn't dare do anything horrific to U.K. or any western country's representatives. Also, Pastor Nicolas is white.

On most visits of Pastor Nicolas, he's enjoyed dinner with Solomon and his family. Solomon amongst all in the government is closer to Pastor Nicolas. They're good friends. They read, discuss, and go through the Bible together. Pastor Nicolas always tells Solomon three phrases: *"Be good, have faith, and always believe in yourself."*

Solomon is known to be a good man even though he's a part of Gen. Fahruk's government. He has tried all he could to make peace and stop corruption but there's only so much he can do. He can't do it all alone. He needs back-ups but he isn't getting any from anyone. And as for faith and belief, Solomon is from a religious family. He very much believes in himself and has faith in God. He's also trying to keep faith in Christianity and not believe in other gods since he's a Christian. He truly believes one day things will get better. *"At least, am good, faithful, and a true believer,"* thought Solomon.

Solomon has in the past tried talking smoothly to Gen. Fahruk but Gen. Fahruk wouldn't listen. All he ever said at the end of the conversation is, *"Why don't you just enjoy your post and stop crying. You really do not want to see the dark side of me."* Solomon has also tried talking to close pals of Gen. Fahruk but it seems there is nothing they can also do than to enjoy their post. Solomon has had enough of this and thought he should speak to Pastor Nicolas instead. He has to intensely think of what to do to make this work. He came-up with a PLAN.

Solomon eventually made up his mind. Part of his plan is to call Pastor Nicolas to arrange for another divine preaching of God to his people, as it's a new beginning of a new year. His plan is to also broadcast the preaching on national TV because Pastor Nicolas preaching has never been broadcast on national TV in Egitee. Solomon's plan is to make sure the good message from a man of God is reached to everyone in the country and not just top bodies in the government. It will also be free to attend. Solomon also plan for a live TV talk show with Pastor Nicolas by him to be broadcast the following day. He wants this to happen as soon as possible but at this moment, Pastor Nicolas' schedule is pretty-much stretched. He's already planned on going on a holy-crusade (a preaching and praying mission for God) around the world. He will be visiting Egitee anyway for a divine preaching of God which is good news for Solomon. But the bad news is, *"Egitee isn't among the first few countries I will be visiting,"* Pastor Nicolas says to Solomon on the phone. The time Pastor Nicolas scheduled to visit Egitee falls sometime around mid-year. This time isn't a good time for Solomon and for a holy crusade event. During this time of the year in Egitee, people make sacrifices to their ancestors/gods for giving them good health and wealth. It's part of their tradition. It's an important festival. It happens once annually. Mostly the rich celebrate this festival while the poor are just there to watch. Most of the rich are among the government so it's a festival the country takes serious. It's a very spiritual day. It's also held on the Independence Day. Solomon had to clarify this to Pastor Nicolas. He begged Pastor Nicolas for a huge favour to try to come earlier before the festival. He discussed his plan with Pastor Nicolas.

Pastor Nicolas believes the people in Egitee really need to get closer to God. *"It's the problem of the country. People shouldn't just listen to the word of God but also practice it,"* Pastor Nicolas says to Solomon about his people. Pastor Nicolas is also highly concerned about the state the country is in. He knows exactly how Solomon feels. He knows Solomon alone can't make it happen. *"But what can a man of God do? The only thing I can do is to continue preaching the good gospel of God and hope people listen,"* Pastor Nicolas thought to himself.

Solomon strongly believes the problem in Egitee is due to bad leadership. He believes the leaders are the ones that really need to get closer to God. *"If the leaders are good, the people will follow,"* Solomon suggest to Pastor Nicolas. Pastor Nicolas thoughts of Solomon's plan then promised to visit Egitee as soon as possible.

Solomon and Pastor Nicolas eventually came to an agreement of when to visit Egitee. Pastor Nicolas then requested for an urgent change in his schedule as this is a situation of an urgent call of God in Egitee. But first, he will be visiting Australia before coming down to Egitee as his second country to visit for the holy crusade.

As Solomon has come to an agreement of when Pastor Nicolas will be coming to Egitee, he then announce to the country of the special holy crusade visit by world famous Pastor Nicolas. He makes it look and sound exciting. Things are going according to his plan. *"Get blessed this year, a new year, and a new beginning. The Holy Crusade by world famous Pastor*

Nicolas! LIVE ON TV! FREE TO ATTEND! WATCH OUT!," words on posters, radios and TVs.

Solomon has made this exciting for the people. People can't wait. It's going to be a big and memorable event. Apart from the event being shown on TV, people have always wanted to be present at Pastor Nicolas' holy preaching. Also, this is Pastor Nicolas' very first holy crusade; it's called - Message from God. Not only are the people from Egitee excited about Pastor Nicolas holy visit, but so are the people from other countries Pastor Nicolas will be visiting.

Pastor Nicolas has a vision for the world, most especially Egitee. On his last night in Australia, Pastor Nicolas had a 'terrible dream' about Egitee and Solomon. He saw BLOODSHED everywhere in Egitee and on Solomon's hands. Pastor Nicolas doesn't often have terrible dreams like that but when he does, something bad might happen. He really didn't understand or get the message of the dream but all he knows is that, *"Solomon needs to be extremely careful,"* he thinks.

However, people are getting prepared for this big holy event while Solomon is getting ready for the talk show with Pastor Nicolas. To him, it's the most important part of the whole event. Part of his plan is; *"After Pastor Nicolas' intensive holy preaching to the nation, I will then have my own intensive personal discussion with Pastor Nicolas live on TV. Hmm...,"* Solomon thought through his plan.

Solomon named the talk show 'Good4Good Bad4Good.' No one really knows or have an idea of the contents of the talk show. But the talk show is presented to be - 'Getting to know Pastor Nicolas and getting closer to God'.

Solomon invites most of the leaders including Gen. Fahruk to feel free to attend his talk show.

Chapter Three

The Holy Crusade

There are two days remaining before Pastor Nicolas will be visiting Egitee for the holy crusade. The news had spread everywhere around the country. People that live far away or outside the capital are already leaving their homes to travel far to the city/capital to see Pastor Nicolas. These people have to leave their various homes two days before because, most are poor and can't afford to own a motor or even afford to pay for the transport fee to the capital. They have no other choice than to walk if they really want to be present at Pastor Nicolas' holy preaching.

However, there's something common and confusing about the people in Egitee. People really will go anywhere to find God. They will go anywhere and do anything that involves worshiping, praying, sacrificing, and rituals to God to get better in life. Most of these people still claim to be Christians and strongly believe in Jesus. They believe with Jesus they will find peace. They also believe Jesus can provide everything and anything they ask for, just as they were told in church. But at the same time, most of these people still practice Voodoo. Several times pastors like Pastor Nicolas, priest, bishops, and other preachers of God that have come to Egitee to prophesise the word of God, have preached to the people, *"Never a man worship or make sacrifices to any other gods. Jesus is the only way. When you have Jesus, you will have peace. When you have Christ, you will have no crisis. Christianity rejects indigenous beliefs."*

Ever since the introduction of Christianity in Africa,

different African Christian groups separated themselves from European missionaries. They established their own Christian churches and blended African cultural traditions with Christianity.

Nevertheless, the majority of the people in Egitee are still trying not to believe in other gods but trying only to have strong faith and belief in Jesus, and Allah for those trying to be Muslims. But, voodoo practice (spirituality that cannot be explained by natural laws, relating to the mind) performed in public by some indigenous believers and witnessed by some people, makes it hard to ignore voodoo. And some of the indigenous believers that perform voodoo or consult these other gods to obtain power, find this route a quicker and easier way to get what they want. So they depend solely on it, and mostly use it against their fellow citizen. Using power claimed to be obtained from the gods for evil and paybacks also spells trouble within the country. Consequently, the problem in Egitee seems to be 'the misuse of power by the government', and 'the misuse of power claimed to be obtained from the gods.'

However, Solomon still got his plan going. A day before Pastor Nicolas' visit, Solomon decided to step down and handed in his retirement notice as a minister. He doesn't want to be part of Gen. Fahruk's government anymore. He wants to start an 'anti-corruption, pro-justice, and pro-peace campaign against Gen. Fahruk's government after Pastor Nicolas' holy visit. Gen. Fahruk being in power for almost fourteen years and his father ex-dictator of the country (apparently still alive and still suffering from spiritual illness), seems to have the whole country locked down. So this could be a very difficult challenge for Solomon to deal with. But Solomon being a strong believer, believes, *"Everyday is for the thieves, one day is for the owner."* He surely believes one day things will get better in Egitee.

The retirement of Solomon came as a shock to Gen. Fahruk. He wondered what Solomon could be up to. He warned Solomon not to try anything silly. *"Don't be like your late father. Don't carry the problem that isn't yours. Your family needs you,"* Gen. Fahruk warned Solomon.

Solomon replies, *"Really! You should be the one worrying not to end up like your sick father. He's halfway dead going through spiritual pain. You wouldn't want that for your end, would you? And for your information, I'm yet to accomplish what my father didn't finish... PEACE and JUSTICE. The Lord is my Sheppard."*

Evidently, Gen. Fahruk's father was the one that arranged to kill Solomon's dad during his time as the leader of Egitee. Solomon's dad was a top politician fighting for peace and justice against Gen. Fahruk's father's government those days before he finally got killed. Gen. Fahruk then, being his father's head security was ordered to organise soldiers to kill Solomon's dad. Solomon knows exactly who killed his dad but at that time, there was nothing he could do. He was scared of getting killed. But at this time, Solomon isn't scared anymore. He's ready to fight! He's had enough. He wants justice! He wants peace! Solomon is ready to do anything to win this combat.

Finally, the day everyone has been waiting for - the holy crusade by world famous Pastor Nicolas - as come. It's going to be an all night vigil event. People from all parts of the country and some people from close-by countries like Togo and Benin where Pastor Nicolas won't be visiting also came for the event. A lot of people have come out for this special holy event.

On the morning of the holy crusade, Gen. Fahruk, his father, and his son - Musiah (a name given to a son believed to be a blessing from the gods) are having a serious conversation about this holy event. Musiah and his grandfather were never Christians; they believe-in and worship other gods, but mostly consult a god known as EJA - their favourite. They both wonder why Gen. Fahruk allowed this holy event to take place. Part of Gen. Fahruk's belief laid in these other gods, and some in Jesus. Musiah and his grandfather also know about Jesus but have sold their souls to the goddess. *"They give us power, they give us wealth, they give us long life, they give us protection, and they give us freedom. They our gods,"* Musiah says, trying to convince his father (Gen. Fahruk) to give his full attention to their gods.

Anyway, nothing now can stop the holy crusade from taking place. People are already at the location because travelling around late at night anywhere in Egitee is not advisable, anything can happen. There aren't a lot of police out to support this event, only a few to guard the VIP guests. Gen. Fahruk instead has ordered most of the police and armies in the city to guard his latest new 'hot' girlfriend's birthday party which is on the same night as the holy crusade.

However, on this day, around 1:00 p.m., Pastor Nicolas finally arrived. He was welcomed by Solomon and other top bishops and pastors around the country. A few hours later after Pastor Nicolas' arrival, Pastor Nicolas got a welcome phone call from Gen. Fahruk. And at this time, Solomon is also present with Pastor Nicolas, discussing on how the event will take place.

"Hello Pastor? It's good to have you back, welcome. It must be a long journey coming all the way

from Australia down here to Egitee. I'm sure it going to worth all the effort by the time you start preaching the good gospel to the people. I wish I could join you guys tonight but as you know Pastor, I'm a very busy man, you see. But that shouldn't be an excuse. God should come first in everything that we do. I still remember that, Pastor. I will definitely tune-in since its going to be live on TV. And yeah, Pastor, before I forget, I will also like you to meet someone... someone special for me...you know Pastor...someone really special. But anyway Pastor, I'll see you sooner. Don't forget to pray for me. Bye bye pastor," Gen. Fahruk speaks to Pastor Nicolas on the phone.

"Bye. God bless you," Pastor Nicolas replies and then hangs-up.

"He sounds like a gentleman," Pastor Nicolas says to Solomon.

"No he's not. He's a pretender. He knows when to act good and when to act bad. For some reason, he likes to act good whenever you're around. That's more of the reason why I thought you should be the one to talk to him," Solomon says.

"And how will I do that?" Pastor Nicolas asks.

"Don't worry pastor, I have a plan," Solomon replies.

"Don't forget about my dream. You really need to be careful with this plan of yours," Pastor Nicolas warns Solomon.

"I've also got a dream too, Pastor. Peace and justice in my country. God is on my side," Solomon replies.

(A few hours later)

The altar is set. The choir are on stand-by. The lights are full. The translator is also on stand-by. Top bishops

25

and pastors are present. People are out. People are watching live on TV. Solomon is present at the VIP with his family. It's the biggest holy crusade event ever in Egitee. People are excited. Pastor Nicolas is ready to give the big **Message from God.** He reads from the Bible;

*"Be **strong in the Lord** and in his **mighty power**. Put on the full armour of God so that you can take your stand against the **devil's schemes**. For our struggle is not against **flesh** and **blood**, but against the **authorities**, against the **rulers**, against the **powers** of this **dark world** and against the **spiritual forces of evil** in the heavenly kingdoms. Therefore put on the full armour of God, so that when the **day of evil** comes, you may be able to **stand your ground**, and after you have done everything to stand, stand firm. Then with the **belt of truth** buckled around your waist, with the breastplate of **righteousness** in place, and with your feet fitter with the readiness that comes from the gospel of **peace**, take up the **shield of faith**, with which you can extinguish all the flaming arrows of the **evil one**. Take the helmet of salvation and the sword of the spirit on all occasions with all kinds of prayer and requests. With this in mind, be alert and always keep on praying for all the saints. Pray also for me, that whenever I open my mouth, words may be given me so that I will fearlessly make known the mystery of the gospel, for which I am an ambassador in chains. Pray that I may declare it fearlessly, as I should."* (Ephesians 6:10-19).

As the holy crusade goes on and Pastor Nicolas passes on his big message from God, Gen. Fahruk, his newly 'hot' girlfriend, family and friends are celebrating, rejoicing and enjoying the biggest birthday party in the city. It's all fun with lot of foods and drinks to be served round, and more cultural dances for entertainment. But for Gen. Fahruk, he still has a post to keep. He keeps going back to his room to see Pastor Nicolas live on TV to listen to his message. He needs to know what's going on. And at the same time, his attention is incredibly needed by his new 'hot' girlfriend. *"It's my birthday today darling, you need to stop locking yourself up in the bedroom and stay outside to party with me,"* 'hot' girlfriend moaning to Gen. Fahruk after lots of mixed Tropicana drinks in her system. But Gen. Fahruk is more interested with the event on TV than the usual event outside. *"Make sure she doesn't come in here, I'm busy!,"* Gen. Fahruk orders one of his guards.

Meanwhile at the holy crusade, many are being touched by the message from Pastor Nicolas. Solomon is impressed with the message Pastor Nicolas is giving. Pastor Nicolas continues to read from the Bible;

*"If you have any **encouragement** from **being united with God**, if any comfort from his **love,** if any **fellowship with the spirit**, if any tenderness and compassion, then make my joy complete by being like-minded, **having the same love**, being **one in spirit** and purpose. Do nothing out of **selfish ambition** or **vain conceit**, but in **humility** consider others better than you. Each of you should look not to your own interests, but also to the interests of others. **Your attitude should be the same as that of Christ Jesus:** Who, being in very nature - God, did not consider equality with God, but made himself nothing, taking the very nature of a servant, being made in human likeness. And being found in appearance as a man, he humbled himself and became obedient to death- even death on a cross! **Therefore God exalted him to the highest place and gave him the name that is above every name**, that at the name of Jesus every knee should bow, in heaven and on earth and under the earth, and every tongue confesses that Jesus Christ is Lord, to the glory of **God***

the Father. *Therefore, my dear friends, as you have always* **obeyed** *– not only in my presence, but now much more in my absence – continue to work out your* **salvation with fear** *and trembling, for* **it is God who works in you** *to will and to act according to his* **good purpose.** **Do everything without complaining or arguing,** *so that you may become* **blameless and pure,** *children of God* **without fault** *in a crooked and depraved generation, in which you* **shine like stars** *in the universe as you hold out the* **word of life**..."*
(Philippians 2:1-16)

Pastor Nicolas went-on for hours. He preached for almost four hours before calling it a night.

It was a successful night. People feel blessed and touched, but something horrific happened early hours that morning after the holy crusade came to an end. On a three-corner edge street not too far away from the crusade venue, there're some hefty (heavily built) men, about seven of them on the street performing spiritual rituals. And according to the tradition or belief of this spiritual ritual act, no woman should be out to see these men with their naked eyes. It's forbidden. It's a normal thing that happens around the country. People know about these things but because of the holy crusade, no one gets to hear about this men coming out that morning to perform this spiritual act. If they did, women would have avoided trespassing.

Early hours that morning, as soon as the holy event came to an end, many try to find their way home. People walked towards the north, south, east, and west directions, but unfortunately for some, they may have walked towards the wrong direction or been at the wrong place at the wrong time. About fourteen to twenty people going the same way, both men and women, boys and girls, in front of them they saw these hefty men holding big sharp long cutlasses performing rituals at the three-corner edge of the street. Immediately, they stopped; *"It's the IDIJU MEN!,"* a man shouted.

"Oh my God we're not meant to see them!," a pregnant woman screamed.

"Run! Run! Run!," another man shouted.

The Idiju Men have already seen these people and they could see women among them. As these people run for their life, the Idiju Men ran after them. Unluckily, the Idiju Men got hold of five among these people. It's a sad and horrific moment.

"Please! Please! Please!," these people beg for their lives.

Among the five people caught by the Idiju Men are; a pregnant woman and a twenty-one year old lady. They're family; a man, his pregnant wife, daughter, and two sons. The Idiju Men took away the women for rituals to console their god, and told the man to leave with his two boys. It was a bad thing to happen on a good day.

"It's sad, very sad," Solomon felt humiliated.

Meanwhile at Gen. Fahruk's, he isn't really thrilled with the preaching Pastor Nicolas gave, but it looks like he got the message. *"These boys are up to something,"* thought Gen. Fahruk, suspecting Solomon and Pastor Nicolas. For some reasons, Gen. Fahruk thinks part of the messages read from the bible by Pastor Nicolas was indirectly speaking to him. Parts like:

*"...my dear friends, as you have always **obeyed** – not only in my presence, but now much more in my absence – continue to work out your **salvation with fear** and trembling, for it is God who works in you to will and to act according to his **good purpose...**"*

*"...Do nothing out of **selfish ambition** or **vain conceit**, but in **humility** consider others better than you. Each of you should look not to your own interests,*

but also to the interests of others... "

However, there's still more to come - 'The Talk Show by Solomon'. Gen. Fahruk is desperately interested to see this one. He's losing patient. He can't wait to sum-up the plan these boys have for him.

Chapter Four

The Talk Show

(The following day)

"Get me my cigar... It's on the table in the bedroom. And pour us my favourite gin... The show is about to start," Gen. Fahruk says to his newly 'hot' girlfriend while he lay relaxed in his presidential suite Jacuzzi in the bathroom. He then picks up a TV remote control placed on a table close-by to the Jacuzzi, and then switches on the TV.

On TV, Solomon and Pastor Nicolas are already sited getting ready to start the show. On a big poster behind Solomon and Pastor Nicolas, in capital letters, it's written - GOD LOVES YOU.

"Good afternoon, and welcome to the Good4Good Bad4good Talk Show. My name is Solomon Gondi. For those of you that missed out on last night holy message, there's still chance for you to get the message. Here with me today is our favourite pastor... Pastor Nicolas James, ladies and gentlemen," Solomon starts-off the live show.

The live studio audience applauds.

A few minutes into the show, Solomon and Pastor Nicolas have been talking about how blessed the holy crusade was and the fatal incident that happened after the event.

"It was a fantastic night. I was really touched. Thank you for the good message, Pastor," Solomon shows some appreciation to Pastor Nicolas.

"Thank God," Pastor Nicolas replies.

"But it's very sad news to what happened to the innocent family, "Pastor Nicolas remarks to Solomon.

"It's sad. Very sad indeed," Solomon replies.

Solomon and Pastor Nicolas pay their condolences to the victimised family. The show continues;

"Now..., Pastor, my first question. God, who is He?" Solomon asks.

*"God... **God is good**. This is the most important questions we can ever ask. It is one thing to believe that God exists. Indeed many people feel sure that there must be a Supreme Being behind a universe that clearly shows evidence of order and design. But it is another matter altogether to say that we can actually know God personally. Look...God has told us in the Bible, when you go to Isaiah 55:6, it says 'seek the Lord while He may be found; call upon Him while He is near'. The Bible tells us that **God has revealed Himself to every one of us in various ways**,"* Pastor Nicolas explains.

"God has revealed Himself to us in various ways... Right," Solomon repeatedly says after Pastor Nicolas, nodding his head. He asks a second question; *"so what stops us from knowing God?"*

"What stop us from knowing God? The Bible... The Bible is the inspired word of God. From the beginning to the end, it reveals God to us. It also tells us why He seems so far off and remote from us. God is holy and righteous. He always does what is right. By contrast we are sinful and cannot obey God's commandments..."

"God's commandments," Solomon repeats.

"Yes God's commandments. Because of this we are separated from Him. In Isaiah 59:2, it says 'But your iniquities have separated you from your God; your sins have hidden his face from you, so that He will not hear. Sin creates a barrier between mankind and God. Until this is dealt with, we can never enjoy peace," Pastor

Nicolas explains.

"Right… Until this is dealt with, we can never enjoy peace," Solomon repeats.

"Yes! That's what the Bible says," Pastor Nicolas says.

"Right… Okay… sorry pastor, I know I just asked what's stopping us from knowing God but, is it really possible to know God?" Solomon asks.

"Oh yes of course! God loves us very much and he has provided a way for sinners to be brought back to Him. Even though we don't deserve it, God sent His Son, Jesus Christ…"

"God sent His son Jesus Christ?" Solomon repeats.

"Oh yes, God sent His son Jesus Christ into this world to die for sinners on the cross at Calvary. First Peter 3: 18 also says 'for Christ died for sins once for all, the just for the unjust, to bring you to God,'" Pastor Nicolas explains.

"The just for the unjust… You mean the righteous for the unrighteous?" Solomon says.

"Yes! Because Jesus died as a payment for sins," Pastor Nicolas says.

"Jesus died as a payment for sins?" Solomon repeats.

Yes! Because of that, God can now offer forgiveness and reconciliation to all those who come to Him," Pastor Nicolas says.

"Okay now Pastor, how can I, or people watching at home know God personally? Or what's our attempt to reach God personally?" Solomon asks.

"People have to bridge the gap between themselves and God. Proverbs 14:12 says 'There's a way that seems right to a man, but in the end it leads to death.' You must turn away from your sin and seek God's mercy and forgiveness, in Isaiah 55:7, it says 'Let the wicked forsake his way and the evil man his thoughts,'"

Pastor Nicolas explains.

"Let the wicked forsake his way and the evil man his thoughts," Solomon again repeats after Pastor Nicolas.

Yes! Let him return to the Lord, and He will have mercy on him, and to our God, for He will abundantly pardon'. Ask God to forgive your sins. Then put your faith and trust in the Lord Jesus Christ as your personal Saviour. Through him you can come to know God and become a member of His family...

"Sorry pastor, do you mean only through Jesus Christ we can get to know God personally?" Solomon asks.

"Yes! In the book of John, it says 'As many as receive Him, to them gave he the right to become children of God, even to those who believe in His name.' Also, like I mentioned earlier, Isaiah 59:2 says 'Your iniquities have separated you from your God; your sins have hidden his face from you, so that he will not hear.' **God has provided a way. Each person must make a choice.** *We must trust Jesus Christ as Lord and Saviour and receive him by personal invitation,"* Pastor Nicolas answered.

"Okay. Another question... What can you say to my people about God's purpose for Life and Peace?" Solomon asks.

"God loves you and wants you to experience Peace and Life: abundant and eternal. In the book of Bible story, Romans 5: 1, it says 'we have peace with God through our lord Jesus Christ.' Also in John 10:10, it says 'I have come that they may have life in abundance.' And, John 3: 16, it says 'For God so loved the world that he gave his only begotten SON, that whoever believes in him should not perish but have everlasting life.'" Pastor Nicolas replies.

"But why don't most people have this peace and abundant life that God panned for us to have?"

Solomon asks.

*"The problem is our separation from God. **God created us in his own image** to have an abundant life. He did not make us as robots to automatically love and obey him. God gave us a will and a freedom of choice. We chose to disobey God and go our own wilful way. We still make these choices today. This results in separation from God. In Romans 3:23 it says 'For all have sinned and fall short of the glory of God.' And also, Romans 6:23, it says 'for the wages of sin is death, but the gift of God is eternal life in Christ Jesus, our lord.'"* Pastor Nicolas explains.

"Final question Pastor... What have you got to say to the people and our leaders about doing what's GOOD?" Solomon asks his last question.

*"Well, according to the Bible, 'remind the people to be subject to rulers and authorities, to be obedient, to be ready to do whatever is good, to slander no one, to be peaceable and considerate, and to show true humility toward all men. Do not be foolish, disobedient, deceived and enslaved by all kinds of passion and pleasures. **Don't live in malice and envy, being hated and hating one another.** But let the kindness and love of God our Saviour appeared; he will save you, not because of his righteous things you had done, but because of his mercy. He will save you through the washing of rebirth and renewal by the Holy Spirit, whom he poured out on us generously through Jesus Christ our Saviour, so that, having been justified by his grace, we might become heirs having the hope of eternal life. Avoid foolish controversies and genealogies and arguments and quarrels about the law, because these are unprofitable and useless. Warn a divisive person once, and then warn him a second time. After that, have nothing to do with him'. (Titus 3:1-10),"* Pastor Nicolas explains.

"Have nothing to do with him?" Solomon asks.

"Yes! You may be sure that such a man is warped and sinful; he is self-condemned," Pastor Nicolas answered.

"Right..., but in the real world, we can always show such a man what's GOOD. Anyway, thank you once again Pastor for joining us. It has been a blessed moment having you with us. Thank you," Solomon says.

"You're welcome," Pastor Nicolas replies.

The TV went off. The show is over. Gen. Fahruk switches off his TV not looking very impressed. He picked up his mobile then called, *"Musiah!"* over the phone.

Meanwhile, at the studio where the live TV Show 'Good4Good Bad4Good' by Solomon just ended a few minutes ago, Pastor Nicolas is about to leave Egitee to carry-on preaching the big message from God he has for the world;

"May the Lord of peace give you peace at all times and in every way," Pastor Nicolas says his last prayers to Solomon before he starts to leave.

"Amen Pastor. Hope to speak to you again soon," Solomon replies.

As Pastor Nicolas was heading off to his convoyed to meet his Crusade Team, Gen. Fahruk, his new hot girlfriend, and Musiah followed by a full Presidential Armed Soldier Escort arrives at the TV studio. Pastor Nicolas looked back at Solomon with an expression on his face saying, *"ARE WE SAFE?"*

Gen. Fahruk gently got off his black-tinted limousine, wearing all black attire with dark shades; he gently walks up to Pastor Nicolas.

"Hey Pastor! Remember the person I told you on the phone I would like you to meet? My new girlfriend, she's hot isn't she? Her name is ALORA. It means beautiful," Gen. Fahruk first introduces his new girlfriend - Alora to Pastor Nicolas.

"Before you start getting anything wrong Pastor, she looks like the girl I'm going to marry. So Pastor, I will like you to bless us together before you continue with the big message you got from God. By the way Pastor... I got the message. Thank you," Gen. Fahruk says to Pastor Nicolas.

"You're welcome. May the Lord be with you and your new...hot...girl, oh sorry, Alora. I'm very sorry I wouldn't be able to talk to you much, General. I've got a flight to meet," Pastor Nicolas replied Gen. Fahruk, and then says to Alora, *"It nice meeting you young lady. You're blessed."*

"Thank you Pastor," Alora shows some appreciation.

"Thank Jesus. Stay blessed," Pastor Nicolas added.

He then walked up to his convoy while Gen. Fahruk and Alora walks-up to meet Solomon where he stood. Meanwhile, Musiah in dark shade, muscular, wearing a black harmless top on a camouflage army trouser with a black boot, carrying his favourite steel chrome plated gun - AK 47, standing next to his all black tinted Range Rover that leads the full Presidential Armed Soldier Escort that came with his father, is watching.

"Solomon, Solomon, sorry am late. Saw your invitation. You know I'm a very busy man. I'm not like you; you got time to run shows. Anyway, I'm here now with my beautiful hot young lady... 'Hi,' Alora says smiling, gently waves her hand standing behind Gen. Fahruk.

What a great show you put on today, I watched it on TV. I got the message. But there's something I will want you to know since you think you know how to run shows. This is one you need to look forward to since you're against me the leader, or should I say the king of Egitee Land, the great monster lying among the streams. You say, 'The Nile is mine; I made it for you.' But I will put hooks in your jaws and make the fish of the streams stick to your scales. I will pull you out from the streams, with all the fish sticking to your scales. I will leave you in the desert, you and all the fish from the stream. You will fall on the open field and not be gathered or picked up. I will give you as food to the beast of earth and the birds of the air. Then all who live in Egitee Land will know that, I am a god," Gen. Fahruk speaks his dark mind to Solomon.

Solomon keep silent, didn't say a word.

Gen. Fahruk continues;

"And also before I forget, I heard about the campaign tomorrow, ha-ha, good luck with that. Like I always tell you; you do not want to see the dark side of me, but since you think you're the man that can run a show and fight in the dark without a light, then, I must wish you good luck. It will be a good show. Have a nice day Solomon... See you in the dark. Ha-ha-ha-ha-ha!!!"

After Gen. Fahruk finished expressing his dark mind to Solomon, Gen. Fahruk with Alora and Musiah drove away with the escorts, leaving Solomon alone looking terrified, worried, and thinking *"...and may the dark be brought to light".*

Solomon eventually came back to his normal sense; remembered his family must have been waiting for him. He then quickly went off to his car to meet his family that has been waiting for him since the end of the talk show.

"Darling, we have been sitting and waiting in this car for quite a while, we're hungry," Solomon's wife

says.

"I'm very sorry. Why don't we all go to the restaurant? You know… me. You, the kids, lets go have our favourite," Solomon excitedly says to his family.

"Yeaaaaaa!," the kids shouted, excited going to have their favourite meal at their favourite restaurant.

"Ok kids, let's go have something good to eat," Solomon excitedly says, and then drives away with his family.

Chapter Five

At The Restaurant

Solomon in the car with his family driving to their favourite restaurant;

"How was the show?" Solomon asks his wife.

"You did pull it off. I'm sure the man you're trying to pass the message to, got the message. He wasn't looking that amazed by the whole show, was he? We could see his reaction towards you from the car. Are you sure everything is alright? You know...," Solomon's wife replies.

"Yeah, yeah, he's only trying it. There's nothing he's going to do darling. I've got my plan going. Don't worry darling, it's all going to be good. God is on our side," Solomon says.

"Look! Look, daddy!" Solomon's first daughter ANGEL shouted, pointing at a crowd gathered round dead bodies lying on the street.

Apparently, the gathering was over another deadly and horrible armed robbery incident that happened to some innocent people travelling by bus from their villages for the very first time to the capital to search for a better life. Although life isn't really enjoyable for the poor anywhere in Egitee but little opportunities could still be found in the capital or city compared to the villages, which is what brought these people to the capital. But unluckily and unfortunately for them, they were attacked by armed robbers.

Armed robbers attacking people travelling in and out of the city is common in Egitee. Most of the time people get robbed on the motor way by armed robbers.

It's either armed robbers' double-cross another vehicle with their vehicle with a gun pointing at the driver, or they jump out of the forest to stop vehicles on gun point. People are always careful and watching out for robbers when driving along the motorways to the city or villages. Sometimes there're soldiers patrolling and army checkpoints along the motorways to prevent or stop armed-robbery on motorways but most times, these soldiers are there for their own reasons - bribery.

The innocent victims that got killed on this day didn't get attacked on the motorway but got attacked when they got to the city. It was unfortunate for the first timer in the city. According to the news 'the armed robbers tried to double cross the bus with their jeep, pointing a gun at the bus driver to stop the bus on the motor way but the bus driver wouldn't give them the chance to. So the armed robbers' followed the bus all the way to it destination. And as soon as the bus arrived at it destination, outside the bus garage, the armed robbers double crossed the bus. They came out of their jeep; about 5 to 6 of them all carrying heavy machine guns, went straight to the bus driver. One of them then said, *"You don't f**k with us like that!"* before he then blew off the bus driver's head with bullets. According to an eye witness on the bus, the same robber then said, *"Stay where you are or am gonna have to blow-off some more skulls!,"* after killing the bus driver. The robbers then went ahead to rob the passengers. Some passengers had money to give but some didn't. Those that didn't have money or any valuable stuff to give to the robbers were forced-off the bus, and told to lay-down in the middle of the road. Then with a machine gun, they were all sprayed bullets by the robbers'. It was a horrific moment. No one was around to stop the robbers. Neither the police nor the army were anywhere to be found. And people around always run when incident like this happens; no one wants to die. After the robbers went is when people came out and gathered round the dead bodies. Few minutes later is when Solomon and his family were driving past.

"You see! Did you just see that! How many of this are we going to let our children experience, enh? How many...?" Solomon says to his wife, feeling very angry.

"I don't know darling. I just don't know. So what are we going to do? This is getting too scary. What is this country turning into? Darling, honestly, I'm sick and tired. I'm sick and tired," Solomon's wife says and then started crying.

"Don't worry darling, it's all going to be alright. Don't worry," Solomon says trying to console his wife.

Statistic shows that over 900 people die every year in Egitee at the hands of armed robbers over the past decades. Armed robbery has become so common in Egitee that it has become deeply infused into the national psyche. There are daily reports of bank bullion vans been ambushed, police escorts been killed, banks and home invasions by armed robbers. There are also several instances when robbers have calmly invaded neighbourhoods to carry out house-to-house operations lasting several hours. Armed robbers in Egitee really are not scared of any.

However, Solomon and his family eventually got to the restaurant. The restaurant owner is a good friend of Solomon.

"Welcome Mr Solomon, it's good to see you," the restaurant owner welcomes Solomon and his family.

"Hurry! Get a table ready for Mr Solomon and his family," the restaurant owner says to one of his

workers.

"Come this way sir, while my boy gets the table ready for you," the restaurant owner says to Solomon and then takes them to the lobby to sit while they wait for their table to be ready.

"What a fantastic show it was. I got the message. It's good. Hope our people will learn from it because, the way this country is going is scary. May the almighty God help us? And I pray we get to have the right person to lead us. Anyway, you must be feeling very hungry by now. You deserve a good meal. After-all, you did put-on a good show. Your favourite meal is on it way, excuse me," the restaurant owner says to Solomon and then went to the kitchen to prepare Solomon and his family's favourite meal.

While Solomon and his family wait at the lobby for their table to be ready, a black tinted bus is parking outside the restaurant behind Solomon's car.

"Darling... darling," Solomon's wife – TINA - says tapping Solomon on his knee to see the black tinted bus parking behind his car.

Solomon and his wife -Tina- starts to get nervous. It could be anyone. The way things are now for Solomon is cautious. He needs to be extra careful and vigilant. Since he stepped-down from his minister's post, he's lost his Government Security Protection (GSP). He can now be easily be attacked.

"Your table is ready sir," one of the restaurant workers says to Solomon.

Solomon quickly holds-on to both of his daughters' hands and with Tina went-in to their table. Solomon and Tina still nervously continue looking back at the black tinted bus as they walk-in to their table.

"Is anything the matter sir?" restaurant worker asks.

"No, no, no, we're just looking out for our car, you

know...," Tina replies.

In the restaurant, there're also other customers present. It's quite busy. All eyes were on Solomon and his family as they walk-in to their table. Solomon is now more recognised by the people being the man that organised the holy crusade and the talk show. A happy couple that just finish having their meals walks up to Solomon's table to thank him for his efforts and encouragement in trying to bring good and change to Egitee.

"We did enjoy the talk show sir, it was fun. We watched it here. And just seeing you now after the show and a beautiful meal...," the man says.

"Obviously...," his wife added sincerely, smiling.

"...yeah, have really made our day. Hope our people and our leaders will learn from it?" The couple says to Solomon.

"Thank you, I hope so too," Solomon says to the couple while himself and Tina still continue looking out for the black tinted bus.

While this couple were showing their appreciation to Solomon, the restaurant owner came out of the kitchen holding a knife in his hand. He walked towards the cash desk and then places the knife close to the cash-till. He then went to see if Solomon and his family are okay.

"Is everything alright?" The restaurant owner asks Solomon.

"Yes MR. THOMAS, everything is alright. Thank you," Solomon says to the restaurant owner – Mr Thomas - and fretfully still looking out for the black tinted bus.

The way Solomon and his wife – Tina keep nervously looking outside; the restaurant worker, the Couple, and Mr. Thomas all by Solomon's table and everyone else in the restaurant looking towards

Solomon's table turn around to see what Solomon and his wife keep looking at.

By the black tinted bus; four men and a woman all dressed corporately in black, wearing dark shades, came out of the black tinted bus, then walk-up gently towards the restaurant.

All eyes on them;

Immediately, Mr. Thomas leaves Solomon's table and walk-up quickly to meet them by the entrance door. *"How can I help you gentlemen? Oh sorry, there is a lady, I didn't really notice you, sorry,"* Mr. Thomas says to the four men and the lady.

"Who are you?," one of the men asks Mr. Thomas.

"I am Mr. Thomas, the restaurant owner," Mr. Thomas replied.

"Take me to your cash desk," the man says to Mr. Thomas.

"What?" Mr. Thomas shouts-out.

"I say take me to your cash desk!," the man shouted back and then brings out an automatic gun then, *"Ggrrrrrrrrrrrrrrrrr,"* he sprays the ceiling with bullets.

"Everybody lie down!," the armed man shouts at everyone in the restaurant.

"Oh my God, darling, hope they're not here for us?" Tina says to Solomon, shivering.

"Come over here," Solomon quietly says to his daughters.

Everyone in the restaurant immediately takes cover.

"Baby we're in for it," the man (couple) at Solomon's table says to his wife. *"Oh my God, armed robbers! Oh my God! Oh my God,"* his wife cries holding-on-to him, looking terrified, hoping for good.

"Sir, are we safe?," the restaurant worker serving Solomon and his family asks Solomon.

The armed man that sprayed the ceiling with bullets

from an automatic gun points it at Mr. Thomas; *"Move it! Move it!,"* he shouts at Mr. Thomas and at the same time pushing Mr. Thomas towards the cash desk.

At this time; the rest of the armed men and the lady also bring out full loaded automatic guns. They spread out to reach everyone in the restaurant. The lady happens to be the one to harass Solomon, his family, and those next to his table. One of the armed men went to the kitchen; another man went to harass the rest of the customers, while one man remains standing at the door watching out.

"Stay down low or I blow your skulls off your heads!," the armed robber lady shouts at Solomon and his family, the restaurant worker, and the couple.

"Move it! Move it! You don't wanna see blood all over your restaurant, you're a dead man!," the armed man with Mr. Thomas keeps shouting at Mr. Thomas while pushing Mr. Thomas on his back towards the cash desk.

"Move it! Move it... lie down here! Over here! Lie down!" The armed robber that went to the kitchen shouting at the kitchen workers while they come out of the kitchen to lay in front of the counter.

However, the armed robber with Mr. Thomas got to the cash desk.

"Open it! Take this and put it all in there. Hurry up! Put them there! Everything! I want everything! Do it! Do it now! Is this all the money you have? Is it? Is it?," the armed robber screams at Mr. Thomas while he gives him a big black bag to put all the money in the cash-till in it.

"You need to be easy on me. I've got customers in here. Please, please, be easy," Mr. Thomas begs.

"Shut-up!," the armed-robber shouts and at the same time gives Mr. Thomas a hard slap on his face. He then says, *"Customers... You really care about your*

customers, don't you? Ok... MARY!" He calls the lady/female robber by her name.

"Yes GAGMAN," Mary the lady robber answered.

"Bring me a customer and let me show this man what we're all about," Gagman the armed-robber with Mr. Thomas gives an order.

"Hey you, stand-up!," the lady robber - Mary - says to Solomon.

Solomon looks up; *"Mary!,"* he yells, shocked.

"Brother!" Mary the lady robber also yells, shocked.

"What are you doing here?" Mary asks Solomon.

Actually, Mary the lady robber is Solomon's younger sister.

"I don't know actually, I shouldn't have come here. It must have been a wrong movement for me. Is this what you turn out to be?" Solomon says to Mary, regretting and disappointed being present at this horrific scene with his family.

"Oh! Solomon is that you?" Gagman says while still pointing the gun at Mr. Thomas.

"Hurry up you!" Gagman hurries Mr. Thomas to put all the money in the big black bag.

Mr. Thomas isn't looking happy with the whole incident happening. He gently puts the money in the big black bag Gagman gave to him, and at the same time looking at the knife he placed close to the cash-till earlier before the robbers came-in.

"Bring him over here!" Gagman orders Mary to bring Solomon to the centre.

"Move it...to the centre...stay there!" Mary says to Solomon.

"Ha-ha-ha-ha-ha! It's good to see you, Mr. Solomon the good man. I finally get to meet you. Oh, you also came to have a good meal with wife and kids, I see. Look... you also have your younger sister here to

join you. What a good timing for you, huh. But I can always change your good timing into bad timing. Isn't that so Mr. Thomas? Isn't that so? Ha-ha-ha-ha! Too bad, too bad. Now, Mary! It looks like this man here likes his customers more than his money. He wants me to take it easy. Now we're going to make it very easy and simple," Gagman says.

Everyone in the restaurant starts to get really nervous. Anything can happen.

"Hey you, take me to where you keep the rest of your money, now! Take me! Or you lose one of your customers. I'm sure you wouldn't like to lose a good one. Give me that and take me to where you keep the rest," Gagman says to Mr. Thomas and tries to take the big black bag full of money off Mr. Thomas's hand.

"I'm not letting this one off easily this time. I worked hard for it, very hard. And I believe it should be hard to take it off me. It's been over fifty years I've been working hard and now you call yourself... Bad Man...? Gagman...? Or whatever you call yourself. It is going be hard and bad for you this time. It's not going to come easy for you this time, Mr. Bad man," Mr. Thomas with frustration gently speaks to Gagman while he gently goes for the knife he placed close to the cash-till earlier. And in a blink sec, Mr. Thomas stabs Gagman straight through his neck.

"Ye! Ye! Ye! Ye...!" Gagman screams, fell down, and instantly, he died.

And immediately; *"Ggrrrrrrrrrrrrrrrrr,"* gun shoots.

Mary - Solomon's younger sister - shoots Mr. Thomas the restaurant owner.

"No! No! No!
...Oh my goodness!
Oh my God...!
...Mummy!

48

Daddy...!," Solomon's wife-Tina, the kids, and others present at this terrible scene screams.

"BRUNO!!! KOMO!!! TANKO!!!," Mary shouts out to the rest of the robbers. She takes the leads as Gagman is now dead.

"Be alert! Kill anyone that tries anything silly!" Mary gives an order.

"Yes madam!!!" Bruno, Komo, and Tanko shout out.

"You all stay where you are! Or else, I'm gonna have to blow off some skulls! Stay where you are!" Mary warns everyone.

Solomon ignores what she says, he immediately run up to Mr. Thomas where he laid. But by the time he got to Mr. Thomas; he's already dead. Solomon looks-up at Mary and then says, *"You just killed a man right in the presence of God and man."*

Mary took-off her dark shade and says, *"Yes I just killed a man right in the present of God and man. It was a man that kidnapped me, raped me, got me pregnant at the age of fourteen, and then took my son away from me! Where was Gods' presence when I was going through hell? Where...where! I mean... I wanted to live a good life and be happy but the way man have made things for us have made me gone bad! I'm sorry to have turn-out to be bad for you but... I didn't have a choice; I was caught-up in it. Keep doing what you do. The gods might be on your side. Bruno! Pick-up the bag and lets move!"* Mary express herself to her brother- Solomon, then commands one of the gang member to pick-up the big black bag full of money.

Bruno picks-up the big black bag full of money, and with Mary and the rest of the gang, quickly run-out of the restaurant back to the black tinted bus they packed outside the restaurant, and drove away.

Apparently, Mary got caught-up into this business

49

ever since;

Gen. Fahruk (thirty-two years old then and also the Head Security of the Army) and his father (The Chief Commander of the Army and the leader of Egitee) then, tried to discipline Solomon's dad because of the anti-democracy, anti-corruption protests Solomon's dad had against them. They really wanted to get bad at Solomon's dad back in those days before they eventually killed him. Gen. Fahruk (then a Lt Colonel) was ordered by his father to kidnap Mary. He kidnapped Mary, and on the same night, he raped her. The rape incident got her pregnant. She gave birth to a baby boy. They took the baby away from her and named the baby boy Musiah (A name given to a baby boy believed to be a blessing from the gods), who's now twenty eight, a Major in the Army, and also the Head Security for his father - Gen. Fahruk. Gen. Fahruk was actually going to kill Mary but Mary was saved and rescued by Gagman. Gagman was also in the Army at that time. He was a Colonel. He was supposed to be the Head Security but instead, Gen. Fahruk's father put his son as his Head Security. Gagman wasn't happy with it. He dislikes Gen. Fahruk. He hated how he's been controlled by Gen. Fahruk who is one rank below him. So on the day he was going to leave the Army, he decided to rescue Mary from where she was hidden. He fancied her.

"Don't worry; I'm going to help you. These people will kill you. I can help you. You need to come with me if you want to be rescued," Gagman said to Mary then.

She had no choice than to run for her life. Both Mary and Gagman safely escaped out of the country. They ran away far to the Northern part of Nigeria. They both got into robbery through a close pal of Gagman who is also an Ex-Army veteran in the Nigerian Military Force. He introduces them into the business.

The ex-Nigerian army with Mary and Gagman participate in; bank robbery, motto hijacking, home raiding etc.

After eighteen years moving violently around Nigeria trying to make it, Mary and Gagman got married and decided to go back to Egitee where they both believe they could carry-out more of their criminal expertise. When they came back to Egitee, they formed their own gang and decided to go hard on the people. They robbed; banks, shops, schools, even churches. Anywhere they could simply get money, they robbed.

Mr. Thomas restaurant was their next target. Mr. Thomas restaurant is like a four star restaurant. A lot of people do go there to buy or eat food. Mr. Thomas has been robbed before but never in his restaurant. Most of the time top people in the government come there to eat. And when they're there, they have armed security guards over them. But unfortunately for Mr. Thomas, Solomon who is meant to be the top government body present have resigned and has no more Government Security Protection (GSP) over him.

(Back at the restaurant)

Solomon is on his knee holding-on to Mr. Thomas's dead body. He's just experience and saw his younger sister kill someone and ran away with armed robbers. He didn't believe what he's just seen or happened. He looks-up and says, *"God why? What have we done wrong to deserve this? All this killing is getting out of hand. We want peace. We want justice. God, only you can save us."*

Everyone in the restaurant - Tina and the kids, the couple, the restaurant workers, and the rest of the customer present at this horrific scene - gathered round Solomon while he speaks in sorrow over Mr. Thomas death.

Few minutes later, an ambulance arrives to collect Mr. Thomas and Gagman bodies. Solomon then leaves the restaurant with his family before anymore horrific scenes to be seen by his two little girls.

(In the car, Solomon driving)

"Darling, you don't understand, that was shocking and a taboo. Mary! I can't just believe it! Mary! Kills! In a gang...," Solomon takes a deep breath, he continues; *"This is serious, very serious! I'm out of words...out of words. Mary! I know that devil kidnapped her but then she escaped. So she says anyway. I remember she sent us a latter saying she's in Nigeria that she's doing fine. Mary! No! No! This can't be true,"* Solomon keep saying and at the same time feeling very angry.

Meanwhile, Tina is exhausted and hungry. She keeps silent. She's got nothing to say about the whole incident. She just wants to get home and feed her kids. They must be very hungry too. They had nothing since the end of the talk show.

"Are you not going to say anything, are you not? Didn't you see what happen, didn't you?" Solomon continues to moan.

"Darling! The kids! They must be really exhausted by now. Don't you think they've had enough? This is not the time to moan! You need to take it easy," Tina says with annoyance. She's tired and not happy.

"Yeah? Alright then," Solomon says and then takes another deep breath.

Half an hour later, Solomon and his family eventually got home safely.

Chapter Six

Move to Yemojaja

After the horrific incident that happened at the restaurant, Solomon and his family are exhausted and very hungry. They haven't eaten since the end of the talk show. Tina quickly went to prepare some food.

Few minutes later, food is ready. Solomon and his family at last are at the dining table finally having something to eat.

"Darling you need to eat. You haven't eaten anything today, you need to eat," Tina says to Solomon.

"Daddy, who is that lady? Do you know her?" Angel - first daughter - asks.

"Not really. Maybe I use to but not anymore," Solomon replied Angel.

"Darling! Ok I think it's now time for you two to go to bed, it's late," Tina says to the kids.

"Oh mummy why? We want to spend more time with daddy," Angel says.

"No my darling, it's late. It's now your bed time. You have tomorrow and many more days and time to spend with daddy," Tina says to Angel.

"Ok mummy, if you say so," Angel replies.

"Goodnight daddy...

...goodnight mummy," both girls says.

"Goodnight," Tina and Solomon replies and gave both kisses on their forehead.

Angel and ANGELINA (the second daughter) both went to bed.

"What is really wrong with you? The poor girl needs help. Our leaders have given some no other

choice than to get involve in...you know...pray for her," Tina says.

"May God put her in right direction? You don't understand. This is tough for me. She was a innocent little girl not until that beast that call himself a king, kidnapped her, and apparently raped her, got her pregnant, and took her son away from her! And don't tell me that demonic son of his, is my nephew! No-no-no, this can't be right, this can't just be right," Solomon says. Not happy, feeling very angry.

"Darling you really need to calm down. Maybe we should leave the country to a better place where we can find peace and forget the past," Tina makes a suggestion.

"Forget the past? He killed my dad, raped my sister, and put the whole country into mess. No-no-no, there's nothing to forget about that!" Solomon angrily says.

*"So what are you going to do now? Pastor Nicolas has passed the message and I'm sure the people you want to get the message across to, got the message. So what now? Start a rebellious campaign over him, and then what? You know this entire plan of yours isn't going to change anything. You know that darling, you know that. I'm only saying this because we don't want to lose you. You're all we got. Please. Think about the girls and me. We love you dearly. There's still a brighter future for us. I think we should do what your uncle did, leave. Or run away. Move away from here, far away. Your Uncle left to avoid problems and conflict one faces every single day in this bloody country. He's now in the western world living in peace. You know darling, think. It's something you can arrange. Instead of you fighting this man, leave him in God's hands, let God deal with him. **Let go, let God.** You need to stop this plan of yours and let us move-on*

with our life. Darling please," Tina says.

"No darling. No! Stop begging me!," Solomon says and with annoyance he got off the dining table and walk towards the window to look outside.

Outside; a heavy thunder strikes and heavy rain start to pour. The electricity went off as usual. Everywhere is looking dark.

Solomon and Tina in the dark; Tina lights-up a candle and walks-up to meet Solomon standing by the window; *"am sorry,"* she says.

"No you're not! You're not sorry. You're not helping," Solomon says.

"I said am sorry. I was only making a suggestion," Tina says.

"You're only making a suggestion... At least give a man a chance to do what he has to do. There's no point running away. A man should be able to face any challenges that come his way. That's why he's a man. And as a man, I'm ready to face any challenges that come my way," Solomon says.

"I know darling, I know. I'm sorry," Tina says.

"At least let me finish the plan I started. Talking about the west, some people representing the west are also going to be present at tomorrow's campaign. I've arranged and invited big TV world news broadcasters to tape the live courage of the whole campaign. And let me assure you; I will bring him the dark to light. Like my favourite writer Ade Tokunbo will always say: **'GOOD should never fear BAD'.** *And I think is now time for us not to. We are good people. God is on our side. The world watching will make him harmless. There will be nothing he will be able to do than to, with shame step down and allow the right person to lead,"* Solomon says. He then looks straight into Tina eyes and says; *"You see darling, I understand what you're trying to say but...you know...sometimes someone*

needs to fight for his right. I love you and the kids so much. I wouldn't want anything bad happen to anyone of you. I really hope we get this through together. It's all going to be good, don't worry. It's all going to be good. Give me a chance let me do this, okay?"

Tina takes a deep breath, "*okay. If you say so darling, I'm with you. You know…I care. I didn't know you had this entire plan. I'm sorry,*" she says.

"*It alright darling, don't be sorry. I'm also sorry for raising my voice at you,*" Solomon says and then gave Tina a huge. "*I love you,*" he says.

"*I love you too,*" Tina replies holding-on tight to Solomon. "*It's late. And I think we should go to bed. It's dark. It's raining. You got a lot to do tomorrow. Come on darling, you need some rest,*" Tina sympathetically says to Solomon.

Solomon smiles, look into Tina eyes, and then gave her a kiss on her forehead. "*I love you and the kids dearly,*" he says.

"*We love you too,*" she replied.

They both eventually went to bed.

A few hours later into the night:

"*Run!!! Run!!!....*

…Help!!! Help!!!

Fire!!! Fire!!!...

…Boom!!! Boom!!! Boom!!!," gunshots, bomb explosion, people outside screaming running for their life.

Solomon quickly jumps off the bed. His house is on fire, so as outside.

"*Tina! Tina! Tina! Tina! Wake-up! Wake-up! Wake-up! Fire! Fire! Fire! Wake-up!,*" Solomon screams, shaking-up Tina, trying to wake her up.

Tina wakes-up;

"*Oh my God! Oh my God! Oh my God! The Kids!,*"

she screams.

Solomon and Tina quickly went to get the kids from their room and then try to find their way out to escape the fire in the house. On their front door a man was banging the door screaming,

"Help! Help! Help!" before he got sprayed bullets.

"Oh my God darling, they're after us," Tina says, panicking.

"Ok, ok, let's go through the back door," Solomon says, also panicking.

The kids started crying.

Solomon with his family quickly went through the back door to run away from whatever that is after them, or before the house gets burnt down. They manage to escape outside through the back door.

Outside it still heavily raining, thunder striking, fire, gunshots, and people running all over the place. Solomon is so confuse, he doesn't know what to do. A bomb shell exploded, *"BOOOOOM!!!"*

Solomon and his family got really scared. Immediately they run for their lives. As they run running crossing the road, right at the middle of the road, suddenly from nowhere a big army lorry full of soldiers with full lights-on is speeding towards them. There's nothing they can do at this point in time. The big lorry is already too close to them to make any attempt of escaping. Solomon screams, *"NOOOOOOOOO!,"* holding-on tight to his family.

"Darling! Darling! What it is?" Tina jumps off sleep.

"I think... I just... had a bad dream," Solomon says looking and sounding terrify.

"Darling what is it again?" Tina says, anxious.

"Nothing... I was only having a dream, it just a dream," Solomon says and then got-off the bed. He walks to the cupboard were he keeps important

documents.

Tina looks at the wall clock in the bedroom. *"It's just 4 o'clock darling. It's still early. You got a big day ahead of you. You need to have some rest,"* she says.

"Yes it's a big day today. It's the first day of the campaign and I need to get myself ready for the day. I've got a lot to do you know," Solomon says while he goes through the cupboard looking for something that seems important.

"Yeah but it's just few minutes past four. Don't you think is too early for you to be going through all this papers? I'm sure you already have people in charge of the day. It's what you do. Getting messages out there being the former Minister of Information and communications shouldn't be this stressful for you," Tina says.

Solomon turns round to look at Tina and says, *"This isn't the support I need from you."*

"Yeah I know darling, I'm only trying to help. The way you screamed and jump out of sleep...you know...is scary. I know you can't wait to put him to justice but all I'm saying is; you need to calm down...you know...relax." Tina says.

"Relax! You want me to relax? How long have we relaxed for? I should relax. Is that all you can say, relax. If you haven't got any thing contributing to say please count yourself out. I'm a grown man and I can handle my bad dreams and my bad days and keep going. So please stay out of my way if you're not ready to support. By the way, I've arranged a place for you and the kids to stay during this campaign," Solomon says.

"Arranged a place for us to stay?" Tina says, surprised.

"Yes. I have arranged a place for you and the kids to stay during the campaign," Solomon repeats.

"Where? Where this time have you arranged for us to stay? Noooo, I don't think myself and the kids will be leaving you to stay by ourselves. No. Not this time. We are staying together. Staying with you throughout this campaign," Tina says. Not having it.

"You and the kids are not staying by yourselves. I will be coming home every night, I promise. Here isn't safe for you and the kids, you know that," Solomon says.

"Yeah but where?," Tina asks.

"Somewhere secretive. Somewhere hidden. You know, somewhere safer. Don't worry everything you will need will be there. I've also hired private security guards to protect you and the kids," Solomon says and then walk-up to Tina.

"You need to bear with me. Me, you, and the kids will see this through together. Please bear with me, please," Solomon says.

"Okay, so when should we start getting ready?" Tina asks.

Solomon looks at the time, it's 4:30am. *"Now,"* he says.

"Now?" Tina asked again.

"Yes now. You need to get the kids ready so that we can start moving," Solomon replied.

Tina with Solomon then quickly went to pack together one or two travelling boxes of their belongings, get the kids, and then in a rush, heads up straight to the new place.

On their way in the car; the kids are in the back seat still sleeping.

"Darling, hope this will end good for you?" Tina says.

"Oh yes it will. Like my favourite writer Ade tokunbo always says; **'No matter what circumstances**

the good and the bad gets-in, the good will always ends good and the bad will always end bad.' Which is true, I believe. I believe in good. The good should always win. That's why they're good. The bad ones might think they're bad enough to escape the judgement that should be pass-on against them for their wrongdoing. Or believe they can hide the truth linking-out for them to be judged upon. But the truth is, from the very day or moment the truth comes out about them being bad, that day will be the end for the bad. You can call that the judgement day. And what the bad don't know is that, the truth will always come out no matter how long they might try to hide the truth. It will eventually link-out some day to come. So my dear, all I need is to continue doing good. And if any truth is going to come out of it, it will be nothing but the good truth. So I got nothing to worry about. Unlike the bad ones, they have so much to worry about because, they know the bad they've done in the past will one day catch up on them. But for those that have been doing good in the past, all that could or can catch-up on them will be nothing but pure goodness, if you know what I mean. And I can also say, or I should in-fact say, if you're good and you believe you have God's protection over you, or you believe God is always by your side, then you should have the believe that it will end good for you no matter what circumstances you're in. **Good people, God's people will always end good.** That's the belief,"* Solomon honestly speaks.

"Well if you say so. May the good God be with you," Tina prayed.

"Amen! And you too and the kids," Solomon answered excitedly, smiling. He then puts his right hand on Tina's laps, looking at Tina, trying to get her attention to look at him in the eye but Tina instead concentrate-on looking forward. She's more at alert

looking out for armed robbers that might want to over take them or jump out of the forest to attack them because, driving on the motor-way can be dangerous. Anything can happen.

"Darling! Darling! Look! Look! Look! Soldiers! Checkpoint! They will recognise you, look!" Tina nervously says.

"Noooo… not this time. Okay, just relax. Don't worry, I will talk to them," Solomon calmly says.

Solomon with his family have travelled 10miles away from the city and still got about 10 more miles to reach their destination. Solomon hasn't got that much time on his hand and now he's been stopped by a soldier by the army checkpoint.

"Stoooooop! Park! Park! Park over here," one of the soldiers at the checkpoint stopped Solomon.

As Solomon parks to the side of the road, another soldier takes a stand in front of the car pointing a machine gun at the car in case Solomon tries to make a run move. The soldier that stopped Solomon then walks-up to the car, also carrying a machine gun.

Solomon wanes down; the soldier, wearing a dark shade, puts his head down to see the people in the car.

"Hi," Solomon greets.

"Show me your license and particulars," soldier asks Solomon.

"Here is my license," Solomon shows his ID.

The soldier collected the license, takes a look at it carefully, looked back at Solomon and his family, and then walked away with the license.

"Where is he going with your license?" Tina quietly asks.

"I don't know; just let him do his job. Let see," Solomon whispers and keep his eyes on the side mirror

to see where the soldier is going with his ID.

On the side mirror; Solomon could see the soldier that got his license showing it to his boss. The boss takes a look at the license, looked at Solomon's car then went on his radio.

"What's going on? What's going on?" Tina asks, worried.

"I don't know. He's on the radio and I wonder why," Solomon says.

"Do you think they recognise you?" Tina asks.

"I'm sure they do but... here he comes. He's coming, stay calm," Solomon says while he watches the soldier walk back with his license from the side mirror.

The soldier gave Solomon back his license. Then one more time, he takes a deep look in the car before he then says, *"You can now go."*

"Thank you," Solomon immediately replies.

While Solomon was driving away; Tina keeps steering at the soldier in front pointing gun at them. She could sense something dodgy about these soldiers.

"Are you sure everything is okay? Because the way this people are looking seems they're up to something," Tina says, suspecting the soldiers.

"Well I don't know," Solomon says. Not sure of what's going-on. He continues to watch the soldiers but now through the inner mirror, to notice anything strange about these soldiers.

Looking through the inner mirror, Solomon could still see the head of the soldier at the check-point still on his radio, and still looking towards them.

On the army radio;

"What way are they heading to?" voice from the army radio.

"Towards the east," the head of the soldiers at the checkpoint replies.

"Make sure you find out where exactly they're going," voice from the army radio.

"Yes sir! No problem," the head of the soldiers at the checkpoint replies and then makes a follow up signal to one of his colleague.

Back in Solomon's car;

"He's still on the radio. I wonder who is on the radio to him," Solomon says to Tina.

After driving 10 more miles away from the army checkpoint, Solomon and his family eventually reach the village they will be staying throughout the campaign. It looks very quiet, not that much people on road, and not that many buildings can be seen except forest.

"This is more or less a jungle, darling," Tina says.

"No is not. It's a very quiet village, people do live here. It's also peaceful. People don't cause trouble. It hardly anyone can find you here. Besides, I've arranged private security men, don't worry, everything will be fine. And for food, this village got the best in fresh vegetables and bush meat. It's good for you and the kids. You can always pick that up at the market, it's close by," Solomon says trying to make Tina feels comfortable.

Solomon drives through a motor pathway along the forest; they arrive at the new house.

"Beep! Beep!," Solomon beeps.

Two old men, each carrying a long hunter's gun opens the gate for Solomon to drive-in.

"Welcome sir!," they welcomed Solomon and his family.

The two old men are members of a vigilante group formed many years ago by KING YEMOJAJA also known as Samuel Yemojaja (the first leader of Egitee).

The creation of this group is to protect the integrity of the Egite people. After the British handed over authority power to Yemojaja, for assisting them to win the war against the Germans during World War II, he then form a group called THE IBAKARI BOYS. The fundamental objective of the Ibakari Boys is to fight crime and make sure there's peace throughout the country. They were more or less the police in those days. They have both physical and mental power to fight and stop crime. Samuel Yemojaja many years ago during the slavery apparently was also given a special power by the gods of the land, which is what he uses to form the group. Back then during the early 1940s while the British were still at war with the Germans, Yemojaja try to assure the British a "black magical wristband" he created with the special/magical power he had can help defeat the undefeated Wehrmacht (Garman soldiers).

"This black wristband can protect your men. It protects any man from getting harm by any physical weapon made by man. It protects man from knife stab, bullets, and any form of weapon man can physically use to harm the other man. With this magical wristband, you will have armies still standing to fight your battles. Trust me," Yemojaja says to top British Army Commanders back then during the war.

"But first, we have to test it on you, Samuel, if you don't mind?" Army commander suggest to Yemojaja.

"If it works, will you hand over the authority power to me to rule my people?" Yemojaja replied.

They shoot at Yemojaja but bullets wouldn't penetrate into his body. This magical act by Yemojaja baffles the British and got their interest of wanting to use the same conjure tactics at war. The British promise to hand over the authority to Yemojaja if they win the war.

"But you must keep this agreement SECRETIVE," the Army Commanders makes a deal with Yemojaja.

The British truly didn't lose many of their armies and also won the war. A year after the war as they promised, the British handed over the authority to Samuel Yemojaja (later called king Yemojaja). And ever since then, during his time as the leader of Egitee, he's uses both his magical and authorized powers positively. Up till recent, he's been a better leader than the Agaja's. In 1948, he formed the Ibakari Boys to work alongside with the police force. Not just ordinary or any kind of man could join the group. The Ibakari Boys vigilante roles are well-established and always maintain an active presence, patrolling the streets and ostensibly maintaining security in the local communities. They were doing alright to stop, reduce, and fight crime not until Gen. Fahruk's father came alongside to take out King Yemojaja. King Yemojaja was ruling for twenty-one years before Gen. Fahruk's father came to take over. Gen. Fahruk's father took over the authority and formed his own group – The Cult Boyz – still presently working alongside with the police force.

Back in those days, Gen. Fahruk's father was a young man in the military. He was a Colonel in the army. Yemojaja wasn't in the military, he didn't have that much control over the military, but because of his spiritual/magical power, people feared him. Gen. Fahruk's father also claims he's been given a special power by the gods of the land. And with this special power he claimed he had and being in the military, he organise men from the army to fight the Ibakari Boys. They were five times more than the Ibakari Boys. There wasn't that much the Ibakari boys could do. And also, Gen. Fahruk's fathers' somehow knows the weakness and secret to defeat the Ibakari Boys. During this battle, King Yemojaja got killed. And after the Ibakari Boys lost their leader, they had no choice than to give-up the fight and then went back to the land/territory they believe the source of the power of their leader originated from, which is the same place Solomon came to hide his family – YEMOJAJA VILLAGE – named after King Yemojaja.

"Darling, this is Yemojaja village, the land of peace," Solomon says to Tina, while they pack their belongings, making an entrance into the new house with the kids.

"Really?," Tina replies.

"Yes! I know there have been so many troubles, fights, conflict, and crisis, or whatever you want to call it all around this country but, when it comes to that, count this village out. Don't you know the story of the first leader?" Solomon says and asks.

"Of course I do, everyone was taught that at school, but to be honest, I didn't really pay attention. All I know is that, a stronger power was found and then King Yemojaja got killed. And I think his men lost the fight and... that it really, that's all I know," Tina says.

"Yeah that's true. They lost the fight to... this same man... his father. He killed the first leader and took over the authority. And ever since then, the country has been upside down. And were you also taught at school that, before King Yemojaja died, he spells a curse on Fahruk's father that, 'as long as any of his relation rule this land, there will be no peace in the country, and that the people of the nation will never see a way forward'. This is what we're facing today. The fight isn't over yet, is still on. The Ibakari Boys have become stronger ever since the last fight. They have rectified their weakness and now it will be difficult for the Court Boyz to fight them, not on their land. They're not trouble makers.

They are easy going. They've to come with to agreement with the government to still allow them carry on their vigilante role in some communities. The Ibakari Boys haven't got many men because they're trying to keep it tradition. Only certain men are qualified to join the group. Is not like Cults Boys, they're all criminals, nothing but pure hooligans. So don't worry my dear, you have two Ibakari Boys to protect you. You're in safe hands," Solomon says.

"Oh don't tell me these are the Ibakari Boys? These two old men you're calling boys, huh? Darling," Tina says looking at Solomon with a face impression that says, *"Are you sure we're safe."*

"Come on darling, don't give me that look. They're not just ordinary old men. They're strong men with strong mind. Don't worry, everything is under control. I really need to be on my way back to the city. People must be waiting for me," Solomon says and then his phone rings - *Ring! Ring!* - *"Hello,"* he picks up.

"Sir! Sir! Where are you? Everything is set and ready. The international broadcasters are now here. We all are waiting for you," the Head Campaign Supervisor on the phone to Solomon.

"I'm on my way. I'm on my way. Give me an hour, I will be there," Solomon says, hangs-up, and then looks at his hand watch. *"It's 10am!,"* he unconsciously says.

"I need to start going. Being the leader of the campaign, I need to be there early," Solomon says to Tina. He then picks up his briefcase and then gave Tina a kiss on her forehead. *"I love you,"* he says. He then bends down to Angel and Angelina (his daughters), gave both kisses on their foreheads too and says, *"Daddy loves you so much. Daddy will be coming back home very soon. Make sure you're goods girls to mummy, okay?"* *"Okay,"* the girls replies and gave him a hug.

Solomon show some love to his dearest family before heading back straight to the capital – FREELAND - for the campaign.

Before the campaign, next chapter tells the history and economy background of Egitee.

Chapter Seven

The History of Egitee

Egitee is a small land demarcated round by a river crossing Togo, Benin, and Nigeria. It's on the south coast of West Africa bordering on Togo to the northwest, Benin to the centre north, and Nigeria to the northeast. Egitee is a small land extending along over 100miles on the south coast West Africa border. It extends along the south of Togo and Benin to the west of Nigeria. Its official name is Egitee Land (the land popularly known as the land of the Dark-gods). There is no road leading to this land. If not by air, then the only way to get to Egitee Land is by crossing the popularly known river – River Ijogun – named after a Nigerian informant that tries to swim his way to the land to spy on the real truth behind the power of the land but didn't made it through or back. He was never found. Several attempts on trying to build a bridge over River Ijogun for people to be able to travel by road always lead to disaster. Even the famous known expert in building bridges in West Africa – Julius Berger - couldn't successfully build a bridge over River Ijogun without the bridge collapsing after it full completion. People instead travel by canoe. Another way to get to the land is through the Atlantic.

Back in the early 18th century, Egitee was an empty piece of land on the south coast along the West Africa border with no humans living on it but flourish with forest and mountains, beautiful birds, lagoon and stream, crops such as yam, beans, cassava, corn, palm oil, peanut and cashews, founded by a British abolitionist - Granville Sheep, to use for a practical experiment for humanity. As many as 50,000 slaves were brought in British vessels to the land. The first year of the humanity experiment starts off to be disastrous. Many of the people (slaves, including British troops) brought to the land died of an unknown disease. No one knows the cause and cure of this disease not until a boy, one of the slaves named Samuel Yemojaja, on one night in his dream came across a spirit/ghost/holy spirit claiming to be a descendant of the land;

"Yemojaja! Yemojaja! Yemojaja! Do not be afraid. I have been sent by the Almighty to appear to you because you are a chosen one to rescue your people and bring them together as one. You have been given a special power. It's a blessing from the Almighty. You can use it to cure and rescue your people. How you use it is entirely up to you. So use it wisely. Go! Go now and rescue your fellow people," spirit/ghost/holy spirit says to Yemojaja in his dream.

The next morning, Samuel Yemojaja confronts the British sailors to explain his mysterious dream. The British sailors didn't believe their eyes until they actually could see that Samuel Yemojaja truly has the cue to stop the deadly disease that has also spread on some of their senior sailors. Yemojaja did not just have the cure to stop the deadly disease but also could perform magical tricks like; make himself disappear or invisible, make non-living things move or disappear, and all sort of other magic tricks. Samuel Yemojaja in his teenage age performs magic to entertain the British sailors. The British never came across such magic before. They named it "Black Magic"

Soon after the outbreak of the World War I in August 1914, the British brought in more slaves to work on the land to draw a border round the land, built roads and railroads, and established administrative, legal, military, economic, educational, and other institutions. The British then start to use the land as one of a refuge for slaves freed by naval action in the South Atlantic. Many of these slaves brought to the land have no language in common. The Anglican and Methodist missionaries came to provide the slaves a shared culture in the form of the English language and Christianity. Most slaves where given Christian names. Also, as the reconstruction and development of the land take place, natural resources like coal, gas, and crud oil was found.

By 1918, Granville Sheep - the British abolitionist, the founder of the land, was given an honour to name the land. He named the land after a young beautiful black woman (one of the slaves) he fell in love with but died of the deadly disease, her name- Egiete Egitete - which is where he got the word/name "Egitee." The centre of Egitee was made the capital, named Freeland.

At this time, Samuel Yemojaja has grown older and stronger in his magical power. He was appointed to be a Head Supervisor of a small part in the eastern part of the land named after his name – Yemojaja village – the part of the land believed Yemojaja found his special/magical power. Thereafter, Yemojaja continue to petition the British for full control over his people. He wants to bring his people together as one to accomplish what the spirit/ghost/holy spirit he saw in his dream sent him to do. Also, ever since the interaction of the spirit/ghost/holy spirit with Yemojaja in his dream, Yemojaja with some other people of his kind both young and old have been thereafter consulting or communicating and making sacrifices to this spirit. Such behaviour isn't something new to some of this people because, before the British came to collect them as slaves from their formal villages or town where they originally came from, they've been doing the same, worshiping and making sacrifices to their ancestors. The Anglican and Methodist missionaries are the ones that try to introduce them to God of Christian as the creator and the one and only to worship. Some try to follow the Christianity way but for most, it already a habit.

On May 8^{th,,} 1946, exactly a year after the end of WW II, Samuel Yemojaja gained independence for his people which became history as the first West Africa country to be awarded independence. The British handed over authority as they promised to Yemojaja to take full control over his people and the country. Egitee then became a sovereign nation with Samuel Yemojaja as president.

Full name: Egitee Land
Capital: Freeland
Major language: English (official), Egite
Ethnic group: one – Egite people
Major religions: Christianity, indigenous beliefs
Monetary unit: K100 Kudus = 100 cents (U.S$1)
Main exports: agricultural product, fuel

Samuel Yemojaja didn't want to be called the president and also didn't like the name "Samuel" given to him by the Anglican and Methodist missionaries. He rather wants to be called the King of Egitee - King Yemojaja. In 1947, he eventually starts his own religion called The Eeyemojaja Followers. And in 1948, he set up or formed a vigilante group called The Ibakari Boys. He also had a deal going-on with some of the British sailors. He exchanges slaves for natural recourses. He was given more slaves in the exchange of natural recourses to enlarge his force men in the military and to have more people to rule and control.

By 1950, his religion as spread throughout the country and to some part of the West Africa countries. Same year, May 8th, the Independence Day, Yemojaja made it official to have a big festival for the gods because, he believes is with the help of the gods/spirits/ancestors they gain independence. Since thereafter, there's always been a big celebration to the gods/spirits/ancestors on the Independence Day.

King Yemojaja was ruling for twenty-one years before he got assassinated by a military insurgent – Major (Maj.) General (Gen) Grunitzky Agaja – Gen. Fahruk's father - on May 8th, 1967 - the Independence Day - on the night after a big festivity to the gods. Grunitzky Agaja claimed he also was given a special power by the gods of the land to rule the nation better, claiming Yemojaja is not using the power appropriately. He creates his own cult traits – The Cult Boyz - joined with some group of army to assassinate Yemojaja. He believed the power he had is stronger, and also knows the weakness to the one of King Yemojaja's, which in that advantage, he uses to conquer and overthrown King Yemojaja and his boys (the Ibakari Boys). And at the insurgents' behest, Maj. Gen. Grunitzky Agaja made himself the exiled leader of the Egite Party for Progress (started and form by King Yemojaja) and formed a provisional government. He abrogated the constitution, and dissolved all democratic political institutions. Agaja choose new member National Assembly, replace governors with military officers, and new constitution was approved by the national referendum. By June, 1967, Maj. Gen. Grunitzky Agaja officially became the new president of Egitee.

Gen Grunitzky carried on ruling for another 18years until a man – a top politician - Ezekiel Gondi – Solomon's dad eventually comes up to protest against his regime. Ezekiel Gondi starts an anti-democracy protest against Gen Grunitzky in 1985. He raised a presidential election against Gen Grunitzky. A new political institution and union was promulgated, which set national election for 1986 but Grunitzky annulled the results of that presidential election, claming fraud. Since then, unrest led to Gen Grunitzky' resignation. There was a big riot and turmoil on Grunitzky must go. Ezekiel Gondi got assassinated by a group of military men led by Lt Col Fahruk Agaja (Maj. Gen. Grunitzky's son). By 1988, Maj. Gen. Grunitzky got spiritually ill then stepped down and handed power over to Dr ERNEST GONDI, Ezekiel Gondi younger half brother, a civilian appointed as the interim leader, who later was forced out after just three months by Grunitzky Agaja's son who only just became a General in the army. Gen. Fahruk Agaja then became the president and banned all political institution and unions. In 1990, Gen. Fahruk extended military rule for at least three more years while proposing a program for a return to civilian rule after that period. In 1993, Fahruk decided to mix up the government body, gave few major governmental post to civilians. Part of the civilians given major governmental post was Solomon Gondi - son of Ezekiel Gondi - as the Minister of Information. Solomon was given the post as a form of compensation for his father's lost.

Egitee oil and economy review since the take over of the military regime.

Egitee is one of Africa most populous countries. The only Africa country with one ethnic, thanks to King Yemojaja that makes sure he unite his people as one. Egitee being an oil-rich country, the world's twelfth biggest oil exporter, and one of Africa largest oil producer, has been a member of the Organization of the Petroleum Exporting Countries (OPEC) since 1961. The Egitee oil-industry generated about $200 billion rents for Egitee economy. Since the first oil price stock in 1974, oil has annually produced 90% of the country's export income. Egitee in year 1990 received 92.6% of it export income from oil, making it the world's most oil-dependant country.

The oil business plays a big role in the country's economy. It has influenced economic and political life. The country's real GDP grew approximately 4.5% in 1998 and it was expected to grow by 6.2% in 2000. Egitee economy is heavily dependent on the oil sector which accounts for 95% of government revenues. Even with the strong oil wealth, Egitee is rank as one of the poorest countries in the world with a $1,000 per annum income and more than 80% of the population living in poverty.

One of the problems Egitee is facing today is corruption. One persistent "award" given to Egitee is; 'the most corrupt countries in the world'. The succession of dictatorial regimes, disregard of human rights, political instability and economic mismanagement have all contributed to cast Egitee in a bad light internationally. Oil has been a blessing and also a curse to Egitee. The oil wealth provided Egitee with an easy entry into international capital markets and also allowed the country to embark on large scale public and private sector projects. However, the oil wealth has also introduced opportunities for corruption in both private and public sectors of the economy. The government-spending process has become the gateway to fortune. Also the big issue affecting the oil industry today in Egitee is that, there is always continuous pipeline vandalism in the north-western part of Egitee which has lead to the deaths of many people. Various big oil companies in the country have experienced vandalism, kidnapping, and killings of some of their employees. Companies like the RDS1 in January 1994 have had four foreign employees kidnapped and then held for 19 days before being released on "humanitarian grounds."

As people get kidnapped over oil in Egitee, Gen. Fahruk Agaja remains as the President and The Chief Commander of the Army up to this present.

Solomon Gondi is from a Christian family. His grandfather also called "Solomon" started his own Christian church and blended it with African cultural tradition named - The Africa Christian Church of God (ACCG). The Gondi's family is quite a famous family in Egitee. Solomon as been the Minister of Information for almost nine years before he resign and decided to start an 'anti-corruption, pro-justice, and pro-peace campaign' against Gen. Fahruk's government. And now today, 28th March, 2002, Solomon is on his way back to the city/capital – Freeland - coming from Yemojaja village where he kept his loving family safe from any trouble that might happen during the campaign.

Chapter Eight

The Campaign

Solomon is running late for the campaign. He's been held down by traffic jam on the motor way due to a fatal car accident. A drunkard officer driving a government official car is reported to have crashed underneath an oil tanker.

Solomon on the phone;

"Hello....hello, ANDREW (the Campaign Head Supervisor)*! I'm sorry am running late. I'm tight-up in traffic jam. There must have been a big motor accident. This lane is not moving at all. How is everything going? Everyone is waiting for me? You're about to go live on air in ten minute? I'll be there as soon as the road is clear. What! Sorry! I can't hear you...! What! Radio...? Ok, ok, I will."* The phone reception was disrupted. Solomon couldn't hear Mr Andrew properly before the line disengages. He quickly puts on the car radio.

Air (Radio);

"ROAD TRAFFIC NEWS: There's a huge motor accident on the highway heading to the capital coming from the east. Early this morning a government official car crashes underneath an oil tanker. The driver is report to be drunk, in an officer uniform, mid thirties, and accompanied with three females. No one knows where they were coming from but an eye witness who was also on road said 'he saw the government official black car from his side mirror coming fast from behind with full headlight trying to over take him and the oil tanker ahead of him. He tries to warn the driver about his dangerous driving when the car got to his side but,

all he could see in the government official car is an officer in dark shade, acting so drunk, singing along to the loud music playing in the car, accompanied with three drunk females.' The eye witness also said 'one of the female, he believed must be drunk, brought out her head out of the car window to blow kisses at him, but by the time he was going to blow his back at her, the car as already blown fast away ahead of him next to the oil tanker. He wished them luck.' But unluckily for them, they couldn't make it fast enough to beat the oil tanker. The car was moving too fast that the drunk driver must have lost control and went straight underneath the oil tanker. The oil tanker tumbles. The officer and all the three ladies died instantly. It could have been worst but the oil tanker wasn't carrying any fuel. MR KELU KELO, the eye witness, thanks his God. Road traffic wardens are now trying to move the big oil tanker off the road to clear the traffic. Stay with us while we take a short commercial break. More updates on road traffic and weather yet to come. Stay tune." Radio went on commercial break.

"Oh, what's going on here," Solomon morns.

Back on air;

"TODAY'S WEATHER: is going to be cloudy with possible heavy rain and heavy winds. Temperature will drop down to 20-21C (52-53F). So people, don't forget to go out without your umbrellas at hand. And for those coming out today in the Capital to support the campaign to stop corruption, and for peace and justice, don't forget to wear your t-shirt with your voice written on it. Mine says 'Peace'," radio presenter broadcasting.

"Oh, I don't think I got any umbrellas in this car. I hope Andrew is giving out the t-shirts," Solomon speaking to himself.

Radio; *"It's few seconds to noon and it is now time to hand over to our RADIO 1 entertainment news correspondent - TEEMII MAH. She's live in the Capital to give us news and updates on today's campaign. I'm ADELE OMOGA and I'll be here with you live from our studio join with Teemii Mah live in the Capital, to take you through all that's going on live at the campaign. Now, I'm about to speak to Teemii Mah... Hello Teemii? Can you here me? Hello...,"* Adele speaking.

"Yeah, yeah, yeah, Adele, I can here you loud and clear," Teemii responding.

"Oh you can? Great! I can here you too loud and clear, and I'm sure our lovely listener can also hear us loud and clear too. You know, how is it out there? Are there a lot of people out to support the campaign? What's really happening out there?" Adele asks Teemii.

"Well first of all, I'll like to say good afternoon to our good and lovely listeners. Emmh... the weather isn't really saying much. It looks cloudy and it a bit windy. Hope it won't start to pour soon," Teemii reporting.

"Yeah I know. I hope so too," Adele says.

"But the campaign is really saying much. People are out here already with their banners, umbrellas, raincoats with rain boots, ready for the bad weather to come. And more people are making their way here outside the City Hall where the campaign will take place...."

"Yes! People are coming out, good!," Solomon says.

Radio; *....and most excitedly, we have international TV broadcasters to take live courage of the whole campaign. This is so exciting! Egitee will be known to people all around the world! You know, big international TV stations like BBTV and CNW are present here with us today live in Freeland for the very* *first time! And I am so proud to be joined by these people!"* Teemii reporting and at the same time excited

"Yeah I know. That's the fun part of it. Let's go to the serious part, Teemii," Adele says.

Meanwhile, Solomon is still stuck-up in traffic, anxious, listening to Adele and Teemii on radio, waiting for the road traffic wardens to clear the road.

Radio; *"Yeah, everything and everyone is kind of ready for today's... hold on a second, I think I just saw the head supervisor, the President of the Committee for the Defence of Human Rights. Let me run after him... Hello, hello sir! Hi,"* Teemii greets.

"Hi," he replies.

"I'm Teemii Mah representing Radio 1. Can I ask you one or two questions sir?"

"Sure," Mr Andrew says.

"How important is today to you sir?," Teemii asks.

"Emmh... today is surely a big day for the people. It's the beginning of us trying to face the right direction. Is a very important day," Mr Andrew, head supervisor answered.

"How long will this go for, sir?" Teemii asks.

"How long...? Emmh... until our voice is heard and our right is given back to us," Mr Andrew answered.

"Okay sir, thank you," Teemii says.

"You're welcome," Mr Andrew replies.

After couple of hours went-by, finally, the road got cleared and Solomon gets to get back on road to the city. Few minutes later, Solomon eventually makes it to the city. People, world press are already been waiting for Solomon's arrival.

Live on radio, international and local TVs (World News);

"There're hundreds of people out here today as you

can see here in the capital of Egitee – Freeland - outside the City Hall...," BBTV reporter reporting.

"....to supports the campaign for peace, justice, and how to put an end to corruption," CNW reporter reporting.

"It's definitely a big one," Teemii reporting.

"...and I think the leader of today's campaign as just arrived," BBTV reporter reporting.

"Oh no, here comes Mr Solomon, the man we all have been waiting for," Teemii reporting.

Solomon took the stand with Mr Andrew standing behind. Behind the stand is a big notice board saying-CAMPAIGN FOR PEACE AND JUCTICE. The world is watching. The people are shouting: *Solomon! Solomon! Solomon!*

"Thank you. Thank you," Solomon says to the crowd. He then started;

"My fellow citizens, I stand here today humbled and honoured to start and raise the fight for peace, to stop corruption, and injustice! Egitee till today has been going through agony ever since the army took over. There is no peace. Injustice is been rubbed on our faces and fed to us on a daily bases. Everywhere is full of corruption right from the top to the bottom. And poverty we suffer. Our economy is badly weakened due to greed and irresponsibility of our leaders. Most of you here today have no homes and jobless. Our health care and schools are too costly for the poor and badly operated. Electricity is never constant. The government shows no care which have forced and made some citizens go bad, believing if the government could get away with it, why can't they. Teenage boys are out on the street carrying guns. Killing, kidnapping, gang rape, and armed-robbery are everyday experiences we suffer. These are signs of bad living from a country that is blessed with natural resources. Today I stand here

81

right in front of the world to challenge the government; to give us peace! We want justice! We want them to lead us right and serve the people and not just themselves. Today I say to you that the challenges we face are real, they are serious, and they are many. They will not be met easily or in short span of time. But know this today my good people of Egitee: They will be met as we stand here today to start the fight!

APPLAUSE – crowd

Today we gather because we have chosen hope over fear and unity of purpose over conflict. We remain as one nation, but in the time of scripture, the time has come to set aside childish things. The time has come to reaffirm our enduring spirit; to carry forward the precious gift, the noble idea, passed on from generation to generation: the God-given promise that all are one, all are free, and all deserve a chance to pursue their full measure of happiness.

APPLAUSE – crowd

We have suffered and fall-out for too long. We are off track. We have no direction. It's like we taking five steps forward ten steps backwards. But starting from today, my fellow good people, we should try and pick ourselves up, dust our shoulders, and begin the work of remaking Egitee. Show the good people that we are. Show the world watching us today the great nation that we are. Show that we as one can live in peace. There is no need to kill each other or do harm to one another. No one has the right to. Instead of doing bad to one another, you have the right to challenge the government! Right to protest and fight for your right, which seems the only way forward if the government are not ready to lead us right. The government are the reason we all are in this terrible situation. They are the ones in charge. They are the ones to make sure there is; peace, security, jobs, good hospitality, good schools, good roads, and constant electricity. They are the ones you hold responsible not your fellow citizen. So my fellow citizen, it about time we pull up our shoulders and stand for what's ours because, for everywhere we look, there is work to be done. We as one must do this together!"

APPLAUSE – crowd.

Meanwhile, as Solomon gives his campaign's speech, Gen. Fahruk and his son - Musiah are in the office - The State House (the president office) - watching Solomon live on TV.

"He surely does not like his family," Gen. Fahruk says, fuming.

"Why are you giving him chance to do this? He's exposing us to the world," Musiah says, also fuming.

"Good. Let him do, because very soon, his time will be up. Go. Go now. Go get the boys ready," Gen. Fahruk commands Musiah. *"Yes sir!"* Musiah obeys.

Solomon carries on;

"I know I used to be part of this irresponsible government. I have several times sincerely spoken to the president about change, about peace making, and the impact of corruption. But I never got any positive reply, instead, he replies; 'Enjoy your post and stop crying. You do not want to see the dark side of me.' That shows no sign of care in this man. Such person can't be the leader. It's the same way his father ruled. We do not need a father and his son running us down. We need to fight both physically and spiritually! We

want justice! We want peace!
APPLAUSE – crowd.

It took me a long while to realise that; they that leads us can also be brought to justice. No one should be above the law. And may the good God we serve do that for us, if one believes no one can reach them. I will like to use this opportunity to call for the West to extend their hands to unclench our fist because, our leaders cling to power through corruption and dishonesty and silencing of dissent, if only they know they are on the wrong side of history.

*However, my good fellow citizens, I've arranged this campaign to educate you and make you all realize or put to your notice on what's going-on and what step to make to start the fight for peace and justice. Life without peace is no life, and Corruption is not the way forward - Books that I have written to educate you more on peace, justice, and corruption. Make sure you pick each one for yourself. It's written both in English and Egite language for those of you that don't speak English. This is the time to move forward. We have suffered enough. Enough is enough. We can't take this no more. It's time to leave our bad behaviour behind and start the good move. **So my dearest brothers and sisters, lets us for the sake of one love and for goodness sake, put bad to dark, and bring good to light.** May the good God we serve be with us all. God bless Egitee. Thank you,"* Solomon ends his campaign speech.

APPLAUSE – crowd

Meanwhile, back in Yemojaja village, Solomon's family – Tina with her two beautiful daughters- Angel and Angelina are in the house, lights-out, locked-in, and all cuddled-up on a sofa in the front-room in front of the TV watching the campaign live. They're panicking, scared, missing and hoping for good to end the fight of their loving father and husband. All they've got protecting them all alone in the middle of a dark forest is two old vigilante men (the Ibakari boys) outside, and their God. *"Don't worry girls. Daddy will be coming home soon, it's okay. Daddy is coming home. God is with us,"* Tina says trying to cheer-up the kids but she herself seems worried.

Back in the city, after a great speech to the people from the man himself - Solomon, it's now time for him to face the world Press.

"Mr Solomon...!

...Mr Solomon!

Mr Solomon...!" The Press gathered round Solomon as he stepped down the pulpit.

"Mr Solomon! Mr Solomon! How far does the culture of corruption go in Egitee?" first question from the Press.

"Emmh... Corruption is chronic here in this part of the world, you see. The breeding grounds for corruption in this part of the would lie in a culture where there seems to be very little or almost no punishment for it and where the rewards for being corrupt seem much greater than the risk of being caught. Egitee or should I rather say Africa, is a place where gift culture exists, in which it's a tradition that a small reward is paid for services rendered. Such a gratuity or tip becomes part of the cultural environment, and that's how far corruption has gone in this part of the world," Solomon calmly answered the first question.

"Mr Solomon! Is it only perpetuated by big businesses, government officials or does it start with you?" Press

"Good question. Emmh... corruption is practice everywhere in this country not only by big businesses or government officials. It takes place in many forums, like being favoured at the expense of a more qualified and experienced colleague, nepotism, or giving favours to females in exchange for sex, if you know what I mean. But emmh, corruption in this country is mostly practised by the government officials. Civil servants believe they are in privileged positions so they demand bribes before they render service to the public. But on the other hand, this is all due to poverty, you see. With very low salaries, the typical civil servant would need much more money to cater for their immediate family, extend a helping hand to ageing parent, pay school fees, high rent and so on and so forth. Corruption is often attributed to low salaries. It may be true that it is more difficult to stay honest, hardworking and trustworthy on a low salary, but it is also true that most people with high salaries are still able to do so and many corrupt officials actually are people in high, responsible positions, earning good salaries. However, low salaries are not a valid reason for and do not justify corruption. There are still some honest, hardworking, sincere and committed Egite people or should I say Africans around the world. When such people are in power, you will see the change," Solomon answered.

"But Mr Solomon, how would you explain poverty and corruption?" Press

"Poverty and corruption...? Emmh... Corruption is the major cause of poverty and conflicts, which wouldn't bring a peaceful environment. Many of our people today live below the poverty line because of the evil of corruption. The day when corruption is stopped in this country or in Africa, will be the very day that we shall wave goodbye to poverty, war, crime and so on.

Poverty also leads to corruption. The only way to eliminate corruption is to eliminate poverty," Solomon answered.

"And how will you do that? I mean, if you were to have or given the POWER to stop corruption and poverty, how will you tackle or eliminate this shameful behaviour – corruption, and this deadly disease - poverty?" Press

"Good question. First of all, I will tackle the government. Corruption has become the main branch on which the government is sitting and any attempt to fight it will signal the end of the regime. The government really should be the ones held accountable for this. Public leaders should be accountable to the people. The absence of accountability causes corruption. Good leaders should provide logical and acceptable explanations for their actions and decisions to the people. However, accountability is dependant on the enforcement of rules, regulations and policies. If there is a lack of effective institutional mechanisms, civil servants cannot be held accountable and corrupt practices will flourish. If I have the POWER, I will create a WATCHDOG institution, an overseer. If there are no internal or external institutions or bodies that investigate cases of corruption, people may take advantage of the fact that the chance of being caught, the consequences would probably be minimal if the system has no institute like watchdog functioning. Crime of corruption should be combated proactively from the highest rank of government, private enterprise, and society. Corruption must be exposed and criminals must realise that they will be caught and held accountable for their actions. This campaign is to raise the awareness of corruption and injustice. At least for now is what my power can do. May God be with us? And also, I have written books - Life without peace is

no life, and Corruption is not the way forward – to give out free to the people that came out today to support this campaign. And I would like to use this opportunity also to say a very big thank you to the people that came out today. It's what we need in this country. We need to start to support and push forward positive things. It is essential that all citizens are informed of what corruption is and what their roles in combating corruption are. People in the community need to be educated about these things. In my books they will find all these things; how to combat corruption, fight for justice, and how to live in peace. I mean; a culture of peace will be achieved when citizens understand their problems, have the skills or knowledge to resolve conflict constructively, know and live by international standards of human rights, gender and racial equality, appreciate cultural diversity, and respect the integrity of the Earth. Such leaning can not be achieved without campaigns like this," Solomon answers.

"Mr Solomon, so what can civil servant or the present government do to prevent corruption?" Press

"What can they do? I believe they know what to do but emmh..., if they want to hear my opinion, no problem. First I will start with the civil servant. As a civil servant you should ensure that, one; your top priority is to act in the public interest. Two; you observe the principles of the codes of conduct that apply to civil servants. And three; you stick strictly to the rules and regulations of the public service. And for those in the government, they must set an example of the highest integrity and honesty. The government must create a policy framework that has effective regulations and measures against corruption. That's all I have to say. It's time for me to go. Thank you," Solomon says and then tries to walk away from the bunch of Press.

"Mr Solomon...

...Mr Solomon

Mr Solomon..., " the Press still trying to bombard more questions at Solomon but Solomon wouldn't wait; *"That's enough from me for today, I need to go speak to my team. I will be back shortly. Thank you all. Thank you, "* Solomon says while he tries to squeeze himself through the bunch of world press/journalists standing outside the City Hall, to get in to the City Hall to go have meetings on the progress of the campaign with the campaign head organisers in a private room in the City Hall.

But meanwhile, back in the State House, Gen. Fahruk is joined with his girlfriend Alora. The phone rings. Gen. Fahruk puts the phone on speaker; *"Hello, "* he says

"Father, I had one of the boys followed him and his family early this morning. They head to Y V, the town of the other boys. Sir, I'm just waiting for your final order, " Musiah on the phone.

"Kill them all, " Gen. Fahruk gives his final order, locks-off the phone, and then looks straight into Alora's eyes. She felt terrified. She didn't know what to say or what to do. The phone conversation was horrifying and too much for her. Gen. Fahruk could tell by the look on her face but she tries to fake it and pretend like she didn't hear any of the conversations.

"So honey... when are we going to the beach? You know... go away for a romantic holiday. Remember you promise to take me abroad for a romantic holiday, " Alora girlishly says and then fake smile.

"Don't worry sweetie, very soon we're going to go. There's something I really need to sort-out first, " Gen. Fahruk replies Alora then picks-up the TV remote control to increase it volume.

On TV: WORLD NEWS;

"That was a beautiful speech by the man himself Mr

Solomon Gondi. And now I'm joined by one of the campaign organisers, LINDA. Hello Linda and how are you today?, " BBTV reporter reporting live.

"I'm very fine thank you. Its feel good to be part of this, " Linda joyfully says.

"You should. It's been a remarkable day so far today. Everyone feels happy. I mean; that was a great speech given by the man himself Mr Solomon. What do you think of him? " BBTV reporter asks.

"I think he's such a great man. He's the man to take us forward. He's the man to bring us peace and justice. He's such a wonderful man. You know, he's trying to do his best to make sure there is peace. You know, trying to make people see the good side of life. He's such a great man, " Linda honestly answered.

"Oh yeah he's such a great man indeed. So now that he's given the speech, what's yet to come? I can see you've been giving out free t-shirts like the one you're wearing which says 'No to corruption', some says 'working for peace', and also free giveaway books written by the man himself. Anymore free giveaways to make the people feel thrilled? " BBTV reporter asks.

"Oh yes! There are lot of free foods and drinks for everyone. We're just waiting for the canopy to be set and ready. You know, the weather isn't looking very much pleasant. And we are not going to make it ruin today, the day we face our journey forward. There's also going to be music by local artist to entertain us. You know, it's really going to be fun tonight, " Linda says, feeling excited.

"Well that sounds like much fun and pleasant to me. Thank you and I wish you all the best, " BBTV reporter.

"Thank you, " Linda excitedly says.

"Well, as you all can hear from Linda one of the campaign organiser, there is still more to come. As for me, I guess its time to go and enjoy the good foods and

music with the good people of Egitee. I'm ANDRE MORGAN, reporting live in Freeland, the capital of Egitee. Goodnight," BBTV reporter reports live.

The TV went off;

"May our lord Jesus Christ be with him," Pastor Nicolas says while he turns-off the TV in South Africa, still touring round the world for his Holly Crusade (a preaching and praying mission for God).

Meanwhile back in Egitee, heavy rain starts to pour along with heavy wind and heavy thunders striking, not a pleasant weather. But the people out for the campaign wouldn't give-up, they're still partying and rejoicing underneath the canopy, enjoying the free food & drinks and music. Apart from the yearly festival, such fun might not come again in the next decade. Also the main purpose of the party is to wave goodbye to poverty and hope for better life to come.

While the weather gets worse and the campaign still goes-on outside the City Hall, inside the City Hall in a private room, Solomon just finish having meeting with the head campaign organisers.

"It has been such a great day. Thank you. We all are really proud of you. May the good God we serve see us through and be with you and your family. Thank you," Mr Andrew shows some appreciation to Solomon for all his good effort he's made to try and make a change.

Solomon's mobile rings, *"RINGGGGSSS"* *"Hello?"* Solomon picks up.

"Hello, hello, hello, is that Mr Solomon?" Alora on the phone sounding frighten.

"Yes, speaking. How can I help you? And who are you?" Solomon replies while he tries to figure-out who's on the line.

"Your family... Your family.... Your wife and kids... Your wife and kids," Alora quietly and nervously says.

"Yes! Yes! What about my wife and kids? What about them!" Solomon shouts out, panicking.

"Is anything the matter sir?" Mr Andrew kindly asks.

"Trouble... They are in danger. You have to leave now. You need to leave now. Sorry I have to go now. Bye," Alora quickly and quietly says and then hangs-up.

"Hello! Hello! Hello! Who are you? Hello!" Solomon repeatedly says while the call line disengages.

"Sir, anything the matter sir?," Mr Andrew asks again.

"No. No. My family is in danger. My family! You know what? Stay here and make sure everything is going on well. I will be back shortly. I need to go now. Do not say anything to anyone. I will be back," Solomon says to Mr Andrew and then in a rush quickly makes his way out. He was going to past through the front door but he realise people outside will see him leaving which he didn't want people to see him leaving. So he then sneaky went through the back doors of the City Hall. He quietly got into his car, start it, and quietly drove away, heading straight back to the village to rescue his loving family from the expected danger he try to hide them away from.

"Oh my God! Oh God. It's all in your hands now," Solomon says while he drives fast to rescue his family in danger.

On the motor way while the rain falls heavily are Musiah and his boys (The Cult Boyz) packed in about five to seven buses full of weapons, heading to Yemojaja Village to cause massacre.

Half hour gone past, Solomon is still on his way to rescue his family, driving so fast trying to make it on time. On the motor way ahead of him is yet another traffic block.

"Oh God. Oh God. Not again," Solomon says, fuming. He then puts on the car radio.

On radio: *"Yes! Yes! Yes! It's been a wonderful day today here at the City Hall apart from this horrible weather coming through like something bad is about to happen. But the people here actually believe the heavy rain is to wash away all the bad things and leave them nothing but good life ahead. What a good believe. It's a good way to start. Anyway, Adele, it's been a joyful and touching day today. Credit to the man himself, Mr Solomon,"* Teemii reporting live on radio.

"Yeah credit to the man himself. Where is he now? I mean, Mr Solomon, is he still there? Is he still around? Let's talk to him," Adele suggested.

"Emmh, Mr Solomon? I think they say he's still inside having meeting with the Head Campaign Organisers. I'm sure when he finishes, he will come out here to talk to us. I could still see some of the head organisers around. Anyway, apart from the good speech from Mr Solomon, it's touching to see happiness again on these people's faces. You know, this doesn't usually happen. As you can here from the back ground, loud music and voices of the people rejoicing, enjoying the music, free foods and drinks. This is beautiful," Teemii reports.

"What's really making this people happy? Is it because of the free foods and drinks? Or they're happy that a change it about to happen? Or what is it really?" Adele asks.

"Emm, it's everything really. I think they're happy to see that there's someone that cares and wants to make a change. And for once, the people actually believe in change. They actually start to believe Mr Solomon Gondi is the man to take us forward. May God be with him? He's doing well at the moment," Teemii says, reporting.

Meanwhile at this moment, Solomon is less concerned about the people. His family is in danger. He needs to find a way to beat the traffic and as soon as possible reach to his family.

"Oh God! Oh God. What am I going to do now?" Solomon says while he looks for an umbrella in his car whilst stuck in traffic.

Suddenly, Solomon saw bunch of people running towards him. It looks like these people are running away for their lives. Solomon wonder what could make these people leave their cars and run carelessly in the rain. He starts to fear. This doesn't look good. Ahead is where his family is kept and seeing people running away from there really worries Solomon. He immediately opens the car door; *"Hello! Hello? What's going on here? What's going on here?"* Solomon asks a man running.

"Is the evil boys again! The Cult Boys and the Ibakari Boys! Trouble! Trouble! They're fighting! Killing! Run! Run!" The man shouts-out while he keeps running.

"Wait! Wait!" Solomon shouts-out trying to stop the man to find out more. But the man wouldn't stop to hear any of what Solomon have to say. Solomon looks around him, he saw people running, cars reversing, and ahead he could see fire smoke gathering up to the sky. It's dark and it's heavily raining. Immediately, Solomon starts to run ahead towards the smoke. He knows his family is in big danger. He needs to get to them quickly before any horror happens.

But meanwhile, horror has already happened at the State House.

"You don't play games like that with me young lady," Gen. Fahruk says to Alora's dead body laying on the bathroom floor in the president office, after shooting her on her forehead for calling Solomon. She

94

died instantly.

"May her soul rest in perfect peace," Solomon says to a dead woman's body cover with blood laying on the edge of the road. He accidentally fell on the dead body while he was running, trying to find his way to his family. Solomon put his head-up while he's still on the dead woman's body, exhausted, to see where he is and what's going-on around him. Ahead of him is Yemojaja village and the Cult Boyz in front of the main entrance where they park their buses, shooting and throwing fire bombs. And around him, it's dark, heavily raining, thunder striking, foggy, fire, gunshots, and dead bodies laying on the floor *"Oh my God. Oh my God. Oh my God,"* Solomon says, worried.

A flash back of the terrible dream he had before bringing his family to the village came to is head.

"No! Not this time! Not this time! This must be another dream. This can't be real," he aggressively says while he struggles to get-up to continue running to safe his family that's in danger. He's soaking wet and stain with blood. Solomon decided to go through the back forest of the village to jump over the back fence into the house since the main entrance to the village is blocked by the Cult Boyz. Solomon makes his way. As he finds his way to rescue his family, quick thought of the situation he had put the nation and his family in at this moment went through his head, '*the Cult Boys and the Ibakari Boys are in big fight outside and inside the village, causing commotion in the neighbourhood where my loving family is met to be kept safe. And back in the City is a big campaign after party organised by me. It's like half of the country is going through agony and half is rejoicing, hoping to wave goodbye to agony. All I want to do is bring peace to my people. God please help*'.

Solomon felts all this is his fault. He felt he's

deceived his people and his family, making them hope for a better future while he knows or could see something like this happening. He feels he's a let-down to his loving family and his fellow people. *"But what can a man really do? God, this is now all in your hands, help,"* Solomon says to himself, hoping for the worse not to happen and leaving the rest to God while he struggles to jump over the back fence into the compound of the house he kept his loving family.

"Oh... my... God!," Solomon shouts-out. The house he kept his family is on FIRE.

"ZZZRAAAA!!!," heavy thunder strikes.

Solomon immediately, staggering, runs towards the house to put his wife and two beautiful daughters to safety. *"Oh my God. Oh my God. How am I going to get in,"* Solomon says while he tries to get into the house. The house is seriously on fire. No way can he get into the house through the back. He runs round to the front. *"Oh my God!,"* Solomon shouts-out again, he just saw the heads of the two old vigilante men (Ibakari Boys) both hung on the edge of both sides of the entrance gate to the house. Solomon starts to intensively get panic. He starts to shout, *"Tina! Tina! Tina!"* There's no way he can also get into the house through the front. Right in front of his eyes he watches the house he kept his loving family burns down. All he can do is shout out their names. *"Angel! Angelina! Tina!!!,"* he keeps shouting until two of the Cult Boyz over heard him; *"I can hear him. I can hear him. Lets go get him,"* two of the Cult Boyz hidden in the forest whisper to one another. They went for Solomon. Meanwhile, Solomon also can sense people coming for him. He hid himself. *"Where is he? Where is he?,"* the two Cult Boyz aggressively ask each other. As they look around and look round for Solomon, Solomon came out from nowhere and hit one of the Cult Boyz on his forehead with a big stick he finds somewhere in the bush. The Cult Boy instantly collapsed. Solomon instantly starts to run deep down into the dark rain forest. The other Cult Boy followed him and radio the rest. They came out from nowhere. Eleven to twelve of the Cult Boyz after Solomon, chasing him down the forest where it dark, raining, fire, thunder striking, and dangerous for man. *"Beware of the gods,"* a sign written in white on an enormous tree Solomon ran past. And as Solomon ran past this enormous tree, a final heavy thunder strikes *"ZZZRAAAA!!!"* Everywhere went silence.

Chapter Nine

Solomon gone missing

"It as been another tragedy end to what's meant to be 'hope for good' to the people of Egitee. Yesterday as the people in the city campaign for peace, justice, and putting a stop to corruption, terror was taking place at one of the small villages in the country. The Ibakari Boys vs. The Cult Boyz. The leader of the campaign also an ex-minister - Mr Solomon Gondi has been pronounced missing. He could be DEAD or ALIVE. The last person that spoke to him before he went missing, Mr Andrew the Campaign head supervisor also the President of the Committee for the Defence of Human Rights (CDHR) said 'as he was congratulating Mr Solomon Gondi for his good effort towards the country, Mr Solomon Gondi picks-up an anonymous call on his mobile'. He also said 'it must have been a bad call because Mr Solomon Gondi wasn't looking happy and sounding very anxious from the tone on his voice when speaking on his mobile'. Mr Andrew also said 'Mr Solomon Gondi told him not to mention his absent to the people at the campaign that he will be coming back soon before he left'. His wife Tina age 32, and two daughters Angel - 7 and Angelina -5 are pronounced DEAD. Their bodies were found in one of the houses in the village, burned down by the Cult Boyz, a villager says. We also found out Mr Solomon Gondi secretly move his family to this house here behind me, now burns down to ashes, to hid his family

away from any trouble his enemies might bring during the campaign...," BBTV reporter reporting live.

"Yesterday was a day to try and stop terror but it looks like it just the beginning of horror, because yesterday many lost their lives just sitting by their homes or going by their businesses. An eye witness whose brother was a victim of yesterday's horror said...," CNW reporter reporting live.

'My brother is a shoemaker. He was killed in the crisis. I was sitting outside our house with my brother underneath the tent he makes his shoes at about seven in the evening while the rain was pouring. There was no light inside so we decided to stay outside for a bit. We heard the Cult Boyz's were around but we didn't know what was happening so we went to see. As we got to the main road, we see burning vehicles and people running and shouting 'Cult Boyz! Cult Boyz!' we said 'there are no Cult Boyz here.' Then we saw them with guns, machetes, and daggers. Some were wearing charms. They were all wearing black rain coats and boots with "CB" written in red in front and back of the coat. They were shooting in the air, not at people at first but I guess looking for attention as they always do if they want to start trouble, but it [h]as been a while [since] they came around. They wouldn't answer when we ask what was happening. We were told that one of the Ibakari Boys had stolen an iron from them and ran into the village. Because my brother was wearing a black wristband on his left arm which normally is what the Ibakari Boys wear to represent themselves, they said to my brother; 'are you one of them?' Before he replies, they stab my brother in the neck which is a secretive place to kill the Ibakari boys. In front of my eye my brother fell down and died.'

"...What a sad story," Teemii Mah reporting for radio 1.

"Andre, what kind of power do these cult groups claim to have?," question from the BBTV studio live in the UK.

"Emmh both groups have especially drawn support from the less-educated sectors of the population by surrounding themselves with myths, which have a strong appeal. The beliefs that these groups or gangs have charms to protect themselves against gunfire and that they can overpower their opponents through secret, magical means has a powerful aspect of their public image and has increased the fear which some members of the public fell towards them. These people actually believe that these groups or gangs, most especially the Cult Boyz members can not be harmed by bullets or ammunition; that the canes they carry have magical powers; that if they touch a vehicle, it will not work; that if they throw a raw egg towards a house, the house will catch fire; that if they spray water over a house, it will be protected; or that if they wave a red handkerchief, no harm will be done," Andre Morgan explains, reporting for BBTV.

"That's a lot of power, isn't it? Ha-ha-ha-ha-ha!," people in the BBTV studio laugh out load.

"Yes indeed it is. Emm but if you ask me, a readiness on the population to believe in these special powers and in the use of fetishes and charms has provided the Cult Boyz with an easy way to mobilize people and to give new recruits a sense of courage and confidence, however artificial, with which to fight their cause. These groups are mainly joined by the mass of young and unemployed men, which have simply taken advantage of the organisation as a channel for venting their general frustration...," Andre reporting.

"Yeah but who are the ones that have given them this power or make them believe they can do such magical things you just mention earlier that they do

with this power?" question from BBTV studio.

"The gods of the land I presume. According to the history of this country, it's believed that the first leader had this magical powers giving to him by the gods of the land to help stop crime. So he created a vigilante group called the Ibakari Boys to help support the police with their spiritual charm or power to fight crime. But when the power gets out of hand, it causes chaos. The Ibakari Boys were hailed as heroes by many residents in the east and credited with dramatically reducing the rate of violent crime in their areas of operation. But since the creation of the Cult Boys created by an ex-dictator also the father of the present leader, who also 'apparently' is believed to have the same magical powers by the gods and knows the secret to the power of the Ibakari Boys which he uses to kill their leader-the first president of the country, then overthrow, claiming the Ibakari Boys were misusing the power given to them, which for that reason was given a stronger power by the gods of the land to rule the nation better. Since then, uproar has been the pattern of both groups. However, the police have been operating along with these cult groups for many years now and still there's still huge crime going-on around and everywhere in the country. It like this power isn't helping but making things worse. The man that wants to put all these to a stop and make a change for the better is apparently gone missing. His loving family is dead and the man himself - Mr Solomon Gondi could be dead or alive. No one knows where he could or can be. An eye witness, a farmer at yesterday's terror said 'he was in the forest hunting, as time like this when it's raining is a good time to hunt for buffalos. He heard voices of people screaming for help and gunshots from the village so he decided to stay in the forest longer and at the same time very scared'. He also said 'he saw

about up-to eleven to twelve men he believe are the Cult Boys, chasing after a man that looks like Mr Solomon Gondi in the forest. He didn't really see the face of the man but he could remember seeing the out fit Mr Solomon Gondi worn on TV for the campaign, it looks similar to the one of the man being chased. But then again, he believes Mr Solomon Gondi should be at the campaign'. He also said it was obvious the man is really what the Boyz are after because he could hear the Cult Boyz shouting, 'It's him! It's him! Get him! Get him!' He felt sorry for the man and pray to the gods to seek help for the man. As soon as he realise the Cult Boyz are in the forest and more making their way into the forest, he decided to quickly make his way out of the forest. And as soon as he ran out of the forest to the centre of the village, a heavy thunder strikes. He fell on the floor and everywhere went silent. He laid on the floor unconscious until half an hour later when his son - the brother of the shoe maker - came to get him from where he laid'. Everyone in the forest at the time the final thunder strikes all died. Mr Solomon Gondi's body isn't among the dead bodies found. His personal car was found a mile away burn down at the motor way that leads to the village.

Could Mr Solomon Gondi be the man being chased by this bunch of men in the forest? Or could it just be he's been kidnapped or killed by his enemies? No one knows and the police aren't saying anything. I'm sorry but this is where I stop for now. I will be bringing you more news updates as soon as we get updated on the missing of Mr Solomon Gondi. Stay tune. I'm Andre Morgan reporting live in Yemojaja Village, Egitee. Have a good day," BBTV reporter reporting live on International TV.

The TV went off.

"I hope he's gone dead," Gen. Fahruk says.

Chapter Ten

The Festival

It's been forty days and forty nights and yet Solomon hasn't been found. Killing, kidnapping, gang rape, and armed-robbery are still everyday experiences the good citizen suffers. The country still remains a lawless country. People in government still take advantage and misuse the power. No one says anything even though it seems obvious to point out who might have been behind the missing of Solomon. Certain people get paid or get killed and everything dies down. The country runs upside down. The richer gets richer and the poorer gets poorer. But when would it ever get better for the innocent and poor who are still hoping for when the day will come for them to live the happy, peaceful, and good life? It's all still a struggle for the good poor people while the bad rich enjoys.

Today is another day of big celebration, not only for the bad and rich this time, but assume for everyone to celebrate. It's the biggest festival in West Africa. It's the day and time for the gods of the land. The day people of Egitee make sacrifices to their ancestors/gods for giving them good health, wealth, and keeping them alive. It's part of their tradition. It's an important festival, and also very SPIRITUAL. It also marks the birth of the country – The Independence day – May 8th, 2002. Egitee is 56 and the country is still classified as an undeveloped country even though it's among the twelve biggest oil exporters in the world and the oldest Western African country. This really isn't a concern to the leaders. What really matter is they got money to show off to the people and today is a day to show it off.

It's a way of life in Egitee. It doesn't really matter how and where one gets the money. All that matter is MONEY. And to be the leader of the nation or a leader of an organisation or any form of congregation, one should have the most money. Money is what that really talks in Egitee. If one doesn't have money, one can't have a say. Someone can be bad and still be praised and credited for doing nothing. As long as one has money, one really is the boss. The more money one has, the more respect one gets. This is the mentality of the people. It's not really about whom you are but how much money you have. That's why most in the government gets away with the dodgy things they do. They make sure they take as much as they could to meet up with the riches around the world. And today marks the day to show it all off, "obviously not only to the people" but to the gods that has also been providing for them according to their belief. This is the only time the government really spends money to the country. Whatever that will make this day the very best is what they will do.

"Let's all raise our glasses and make a toast to our blessed and great land, the land of the gods. May we all live long to enjoy it all. To Egitee!," Gen. Fahruk starts-off the day raising a toast with his committee in the State House.

(On air – Radio 1)

Adele Omoga: *"Good morning ladies and gentlemen. Today is another day of festive. A day we Egite believe to pay respect to the gods of the land that obtain us not only freedom but gives us good health and wealth. Although I'm a Christian and I'm not meant to believe in these other gods, but according to history of Africa they were our ancestors. Several Africa countries use the end of the calendar year as a time of annual reunion, but we the Egite believes the day we gain independence should be the day we also celebrate and pay tribute to our ancestors. In 1950, the powerful king Yemojaja made it official to have a big festival for the gods of the land because he believes is with the help of the gods we gain independence. He's the one that spoke to the gods; he's the one that knows. Anyway, it is now time for me to hand over to our favourite one and only party girl - Teemii Mah, who is always on time, no Africa time. And always present at all event happening in the country. She right about now in the city, let's join her... What's up girl? How is it going out there and how are you?"*

"I'm very well, thank you. It's another day of celebration here in the city and I will be bringing all the excitement here today live to our wonderful listeners that for some reasons wouldn't be able to make it to the city to see the beautiful parades and performances by the masquerades. It's a big one as usual. It's always getting bigger every year. Emm... many people are out here today, coming from far and wide across the country and other parts of the world. It's a sort of carnival and a gathering of thanks giving and display of all sorts of cultural masquerade and related dances. Also a time or day for interaction and meeting of old and new friends if you know what I mean? Ha-ha-ha-ha-ha, am so excited!," Teemii says, excited for the day ahead.

"Yeah, yeah, yeah Teemii, we all know when its party time, you're number one on the list," Adele says.

"Of course Adele, I love social gathering. Party time is my time. And let me tell you, when its party time anywhere in the country, radio 1 is the number one radio station to bring it to you live and direct. Anyway, the party will kick off around noon and lasts into the

night. For those of you that aren't here, don't worry, am here for you, representing radio 1 to bring to you live and direct the whole gist of the festival. Just make sure you're tuned-in with us. Firstly, I will be speaking to a very special person - the Head Planer and Organiser of the Masquerade parade – PROFESSOR KETE OGUNDE from Nigeria. So people, don't go nowhere. We're going to talk about so many things. It will be fun. So don't go nowhere, just stay tuned-in with us. Back to you Adele," Teemii reports.

"Oh yes it will be fun. Thank you, Teemii. So people, you just heard it from our party girl, we'll be bringing you live and direct the whole gist of today's festival. So don't go anywhere. It's now time for us to take a short break. This is radio 1, and I'm Adele Omoga. Stay tune."

Its noon and many people around the country and from other parts of the world including African leaders have come to Freeland city to join celebrate the Independence Day. Truly there is nothing to celebrate on the progress the country has made since they gained independence, but the government still makes it worthwhile for the people that comes out to celebrate. It's not everyone that comes out to celebrate today. Some people think it a pointless celebration because to them, *"why celebrate when the country isn't in good shape, it pointless! I don't believe in the gods, am a Christian, I am a Muslim,"* thoughts and words from people that don't celebrate the festival/independence day.

However, there's a lot of food, music from big name artists around the world, different African masquerade dances, and lot & lot of drinks including the country's favourite - Palm Wine - to celebrate the day.

"At least we're still strong and alive. I'll make sure

I continue doing my very best to get the country to it very best. I, General Fahruk Agaja, promise to make sure from now on, things will get better. Now isn't the time for us to get political but time to raise our glasses to thank our ancestors, the gods, that has been protecting, providing, and making sure we don't stumble right in front of our enemies. We Africans need to come together as one. Today is Egitee Independence Day and also a day we egite pay tribute to our ancestors. Not only Egitee is a great and blessed land, but so as we all, the great people of Africa! So I therefore, raise a toast to a better and greater nation and continent. To Africa!," Gen. Fahruk gives his open speech to begin the festival.

As Gen. Fahruk gives the open speech, Teemii Mah is joined with Professor Kete Ogunde along the high street in front of the State House where the parades will be taking place.

"Hello sir? How are you and how are you doing?" Teemii says, excited.

"I'm doing very well. All thanks to the gods," Professor Kete replies calmly.

"Emm, Mr Kete... Sorry... professor Kete... Ha-ha-ha... Sorry I understand professors don't like to be called Mr, am very sorry," Teemii apologizes.

"Oh that's fine, you don't have to apologize, am fine with it. Mr..., Professor... It's not an issue," Professor Kete replies.

"Ok, but I would like to call you professor, if you don't mind," Teemii says.

"That's fine by me," Professor Kete replies.

"Ok. Now, professor, you are live on radio 1. Today we want you as a professor in African Mythology Gods, to enlighten or educate us on all of these...scary...looking masquerades...ha-ha-ha-ha... Am only joking, don't mind me," Teemii says smiling.

"That's ok. Some of these masquerades are scaring looking, most especially to kids," Professor Kete says.

"Ha-ha, very funny professor. Are you now saying am a kid?" Teemii says.

"Emmh...not exactly. But if you're scared of masquerades, then I must put you in that category," Professor Kete says.

"Well, am not! But anyway, you're going to enlighten us on the masquerades that will be parading here on this road today. So at least people at home listening that couldn't make it here to see for themselves, can have a visual and understanding impression of the meaning of this parade or today should I rather say. It will be also great and nice of you to as well enlighten us more about the gods, the reason we all are gathered hear today. You know; tell us more we don't know because, if you ask me, I know jack-all. I don't really believe in it, and I don't care. Sorry professor, I was brought-up in a Christian family," Teemii says and then put on a sad face.

"That's alright. What you believe-in should be your choice. You're no more a kid," Professor Kete calmly says.

"Yeah I know professor but, sometimes I think I should know at least a little bit of my tradition. My history! My root! I know nothing. I feel like am not being myself enough. But thank God you're here with us today to give us a little bit of lecture. I was only joking when I said I don't care. Emmh... first thing first professor... Do you think am lost for knowing jack-all about Africa tradition and I claim to be true African?" Teemii sincerely asks.

"Absolutely, yes! If you ask me. First of all to start with; there are no people without traditions, and traditions are the lifeblood of a people," Professor Kete answered.

"That's right professor, I see what you're saying but first, before we go deep into all of that, I know there're so many but, I will like you to first tell us about your favourite's gods," Teemii asks.

"My favourite gods?" Professor Kete repeats.

"Yes your favourite gods," Teemii repeats.

"Okay. But first, let me explain something to you, Teemii. African mythology covers a large area. There are so many countries, regions, languages, tribes, cultures, and imperialist crossovers that the complete mixture of existing gods would seem irresistible if there weren't a few handy shortcuts...," Professor Kete explaining.

"I didn't get that, professor," Teemii says, confuse.

"Wait let me finish. Traditional African belief is overwhelmingly monotheistic."

"Mono...fiat... Wot...?" Teemii says, again confuse.

"Monotheistic - it means believing in only one God," Professor Kete explains.

"Believing in only one God? But...," Teemii says.

"Wait, let me finish before you start talking," Professor Kate says.

"Ok. Sorry. Am listening professor," Teemii calmly says.

"You should... if you want to learn something. Anyway, there may be spirits and ancestors floating around but there's only one God. Early missionaries made a complete pig's ear of their research in this respect. Let us not go into that for now. What am trying to say is that, there is a remarkable innocence about the gods of Africa. They seem naïve and unworldly, believing the best of everyone and optimistically giving the benefit of the doubt to all. I believe the gods must found it rudely disappointing when it turns out their badly chosen favourite are up to no good or has

abandon them," Professor Kete explains.

"You mean the ones given the power?" Teemii whispers to Professor Kete.

"Emmh... not exactly. But anyway, let us put that story aside and talk more of the story that brought us here today. I've got this book here with me today, it tells short stories about African gods. It's called - The Gods of Africa. This story book only talks about ten."

"Ten?" Teemii says.

"Yes, only ten. Which are;

Shango – god of Thunder

Bumba – the African God of Vomit..."

"Vomit?," Teemii says, interrupting.

"Yes, vomit. I will soon read out the short stories but first let me just mention the ten listed in this book. The third one is Eshu – Very popular Con Artist god, also known as the devil..."

"The devil! I hate him," Teemii says, again interrupting.

"But God says don't hate," Professor Kate says.

"I don't care, I hate him. He's evil," Teemii angrily says.

"God also says don't judge," Professor Kate says.

"I don't care, I will judge him. He's done lot of evil to me, my friends, and my family," Teemii says, looking unhappy.

"Well, if you're definitely sure about that and can prove that, then you can say that," Professor Kate says.

"Am very sure about it and I can prove it. He's evil. Everybody knows that!" Teemii loudly says.

"Well, you can say what you want but at the end of life, God will be the only one to judge us all. And I hope you wouldn't be blaming the devil for your wrong and evil doings on that day, would you?" Professor Kate says.

"Of course not... But sometimes to be honest,

professor, I get so scared when I think of the judgement day. I don't know what God will think of me. But I think am a good girl. What do you think professor? What do you think?" Teemii anxiously says.

"It's a good thing to see yourself as a good human being. That's what God wants us to see ourselves as. Always think positive," Professor Kate says.

"Yeah but professor, you know, sometimes I get to, you know, party a lot. Do you think God will see this as bad?" Teemii sincerely asks.

"No, not at all. Party, social gathering, get-together, festivity or whatever you want to call it, is a good thing. Having party or going to party is fun. Just like today, we're having a party, a festive, a celebration to honour the gods and God. Party brings people together and makes us happy. So why not party," Professor Kate replies.

"Professor, are you now saying God and the gods likes to party?" Teemii asks.

"Of course, I believe there is always a celebration going-on up there," Professor Kate says pointing to the sky.

"Really! I will so like to be up there to join them to celebrate, but not any time soon," Teemii says

"Why not any time soon?" Professor Kate asks.

"Because I still want to party more down here for now before I die to go up there to party. And also, the one up there might be a bit boring for me," Teemii answered.

"Ha-ha-ha! You mean heaven will be boring for you?" Professor Kate asks laughing.

"Yeah because, if is really what the Bible portraits on how to live life is what heaven will be like, then I think is going to be boring for me," Teemii replies.

"No one apart from God knows what or how heaven will be like, even the gods including the devil don't

know. It meant to be the next stage of life. Everyone has to pass through life to get to heaven. And to get-in, everyone and even the gods will first go through judgement by God. Only He knows who is qualified to be in heaven, that's what I believe," Professor Kate explains.

"Yeah but professor, what do you think or believe we need to do to qualify?" Teemii sincerely asks.

*"What do I think you need to do to qualify? Emmh... to **be good at all times and always have good intension towards everything you do. Always follow the good part of your mind. And always be your self,** its very important. I believe doing that will save you anywhere you go in this life and the next to come. God is good. By doing good, you're automatically doing God's will, I believe. And sometimes when I sincerely think it through about the whole issue about heaven, I personally think or believe, and this is just my own saying, that; **one mans' heaven is another mans' hell. And one mans' hell is another mans' heaven.** Just like some will say; one mans' food is another mans' poison. Or some will say 'one mans' happiness is another mans' sadness, which is true. For example; you like to party..."*

"That's right professor, that's right!" Teemii boldly says.

"So your kind of heaven will be a place where you can freely party and party all-day and all-night long without people pointing fingers at you or judging you for being a party girl..."

"That's right professor, that's right. That's exactly what I will like to imagine or see as heaven, or should I instead say 'my kind of heaven'," Teemii girlishly says.

"You're getting my point. But some don't like to party you see, they like it quiet and calm. These kinds of people I assume will like to end-up in a place that's

quiet and calm, that they can call heaven or see as heaven," Professor Kate explains.

"Definitely not my kind of place," Teemii honestly says.

"Oh well, is not everybody that likes to party. So that's just my own thinking or should I just say 'theory'. And to also include, I believe there're many ways to heaven, you just need to find yours, if you know what I mean," Professor Kate says.

"Yep, I know what you mean. It makes sense. I feel so much better now. Thank you," Teemii sincerely says.

"You're welcome. So, can I continue with the list of the ten gods I was mentioning?" Professor Kate asks.

"Oh yeah professor, I forgot about them. Sorry, continue," Teemii says.

"You're busy thinking about yourself, huh?" Professor Kate says.

"Wot do you expect professor, I love myself," Teemii girlishly says.

"Just make sure you love your neighbours too," Professor Kate says.

"Oh yeah, sure," Teemii says.

"Good! Anyway, where was I?" Professor Kate asks.

"The devil!," Teemii shouts-out, screwed face.

"Oh yes, Eshu the devil was number four. Now number five;

Obatala – one of the gods that was giving the honour to create

Olorun - Top Sky King of Yoruba mythology in Nigeria. He's the God of peace, justice and the Yoruba way. He is the Almighty!

"Wow! He is big!" Teemii shouts-out.

"Oh yes, He is the almighty God," Professor Kate says.

"The almighty God that create heaven and earth?," Teemii asks.

"Yes, according to the belief of the Yoruba people of Nigeria. I will read out the short stories soon. But first let me quickly finish mentioning the ten gods because time is not on our side. There is: Yemaya, Abassi, Elegua, Anansi, and the last mention is, the Orishas," Professor Kate quickly mentions the names of the other gods listed in the book.

"Is that it? What about Eeyemojaja - The God of Yemojaja? Is He not among the ten? At least if I don't know any of the ones you've just mention, I at least know about Eeyemojaja," Teemii implies.

"Well, not in this book, but we can make it eleven since we're in Egitee. So the 11th one will are going to talk about is Eeyemojaja – The God of Yemojaja. Or you can say JAJA. Jaja means God in your language and Eeyemojaja means 'The God of Yemojaja'. Yemojaja means 'God has blessed me'," Professor Kate explains.

"Oh yeah that's true, Jaja means God in egite. And Eja means devil. I hate him. Hope he's not going to be in my kind of heaven?" Teemii says.

"Ha-ha-ha! I don't know about that young lady, but I think the devil also likes to party," Professor Kate says and carried-on laughing, *"ha-ha-ha-ha."*

"No-no-no professor, such a person is not invited to my party, my kind of party. He gets kicked out," Teemii girlishly says.

"Ok. If you say so, am only just saying," Professor Kate says smiling.

"As long as he knows so... Well, I was gonna asks, are these gods listed according to how stronger and powerful they are?" Teemii asks.

"Good question. No. I don't think so. If it has to be judge on that, then Olorun, meaning the owner of

heaven in my language Yoruba, should be number one because, He is the king sky God and the God of the universe. He is the greatest and the most merciful. The other small gods are His Orishas, as in, his descendant. Olorun also is the most powerful and wisest among all. He's also got other names like; Eledumare, Olodumare, Oluwa, Eledaa and some other ones I can't remember. He is the God people emphasize or express with capital G, " Professor Kate explains.

"So Jaja should be number one for me then?" Teemii asks.

"Oh yes, you can say that, since you're from Egitee and Jaja means God in your language. The name for God in Africa is as many as there are words and dialects, but the concept of one supreme spirit is set. You see, **God has revealed Himself to us in various languages, ways, and in various forms**, *I believe. That's why we have various stories about God and how earth was form or created. For example; Jaja which also means God in your language, is believed to be the Creator or God of Egitee land, that sent a Holy Spirit to appear in Yemojaja's dream to give Yemojaja a power to rescue his people, "* Professor Kate explains.

"Ok... yeah that's true. I remember we were taught that in school, " Teemii says.

"Were you? That's good. But were you also taught about these other gods I have mentioned?" Professor Kete sincerely asks.

"No I don't think so, " Teemii replies.

"Ok then. But before I start, I will like to say some of these stories might sound a bit silly and make no sense but, so as some of the stories in the Bible, " Professor Kate says.

"No problem professor, take your time. But before you start, we're going to take a short break. So listeners at home, stay tune with us. We'll be right

116

back! I'm Teemii Mah, representing radio 1 live at the
festival. Stay tune."

While Teemii and Professor Kete go for a short break,
Gen. Fahruk is on the high table of the festival set in
front of the State House, joined with his fellow African
leaders, and being entertained by the Army - matching
and parading, saluting and paying respect to their Chief
Army in Command - before the masquerade dances
will then take place.

"This is a beautiful day. Am loving it. Are you?"
Gen. Fahruk says to a close pal (one of the African
leaders).

"Oh yes, this is great. The weather is sunny and
bright. The people are in good spirit. You know,
everyone is happy. Well done," close pal says.

"Oh yes, thanks to the gods. Without them, I don't
think I will be able to pull this off. That's why I have to
make sure everything goes on right, at least for today.
Even to the extent that I make sure there isn't going to
be any drop of rain to disturb the day," Gen. Fahruk
says.

"Any drop of rain to disturb the day? Do you now
control the weather?" Close pal asks looking confuse.
"Ha-ha-ha-ha-ha-ha!," Gen. Fahruks laughs out load.
He then says, *"You know nothing my friend. Don't you*
know anything and everything is possible with our
gods? I guess you've been drawn away by the western
God, too bad. Come closer let me whisper to your
hears; I have consult my spiritual adviser and he
promise me a good and sunny day ahead. Anyone that
dares to disrupt this day will be stroked by thunder. He
also said if I see any form of dark clouds gathering up
in the sky, I should assume something bad is about to
happen, and I should immediately put myself to safety.
It's not something for me to worry about, but something

for me to be aware of. So pal, you've been warned."

"Dark clouds gathering up in the sky? You mean it is going to rain later-on in the day?" Close pal asks, wondering. *"Ha-ha-ha-ha-ha! Honestly, I don't think that will be happening. I have given the gods everything they wanted, to make sure there will be no such dark clouds, not to talk of it raining. Come on pal, drink up, it a celebration, you have nothing to worry about,"* Gen. Fahruk says and then makes a big smile on his face while he waves to the people cheering at him.

"Oh yeah, I almost forgot. What about your in-law. Have you heard anything from him? Or is he still gone missing in the dark forest? He must be suffering anywhere that he may be by now. His body wasn't found among the dead bodies found in the dark forest. And he was the one your boys were definitely after. Where on this land could he then be? Doesn't that borders' you?" Close pal asks.

"Borders' me? That boy is not coming back. Like I said, anything and everything is possible with my gods. I don't just deal with one god, I deal with many. And they all got my back because I pay my dues. They must have taken him away completely that he will be nowhere to be found. That boy is vanished off this planet. Forget about him. No one, and I mean it, no one messes with the Agaja's. We run this land. The gods has given us the power to. I warned him never to mess with me or he will see the dark side of me. But he wouldn't listen. He wanted to play it his way, not realizing he's only a jellyfish trying to fight a killer whale. Forget about that boy, he's been dealt with," Gen. Fahruk confidently says.

"Hmm… the General, also a small god himself, I trust you. I really envy you, you know. I know you would have seriously dealt with him. Don't you think

that one day, when you have become very old and gone, people will see you as their god? You've really shown them power," Close pal says. *"I know. I am the next god to be,"* Gen. Fahruk says and then laughs out loud along with his pal, *"Ha-ha-ha-ha-ha!"*

As Gen. Fahruk laughs along with his close pal thinking of him being the next god, Teemii and Professor Kete are back on air to tell stories about some African Gods and gods.

"Welcome back. We're still live at the festival in Freeland. Am Teemii Mah and I'm still joined with Professor Kete Ogunde from Nigeria. Professor, you where about to read out the short stories of the African gods you mentioned earlier," Teemii says.

"Oh yes I was. I don't think we have got the time to read out the whole of the ten gods mentioned in this book because very soon the masquerades will start their dancing parade. Emmh let me quickly start reading. First, let me start with;

Shango*: god of thunder, drums and dance, having been well-known from being a famous warrior and the fourth King of the Yoruba, also known as Chango or Xango. He's one of the Orishas...*

"O...RI...shas, who are those?" Teemii asks.

"Orishas are spirits or deities that reflect on the manifestation of Olorun Olodumare (God) in the Yoruba spiritual or religious system," Professor Kete answered.

"Okay, I see," Teemii says nodding her head.

As I was saying, also Shango special number is six...

"Six? Oh that's my special number too," Teemii says.

Really? Good. He also likes colour red and white...

"Oh colour red and white? That's not really my favourite colour but I look good in red and white. I look hot and sexy," Teemii girlishly says, interrupting.

Really? Good for you. He also likes to party...

"Oh you said the gods do party. Oh I love to party. I'm a party freak," Teemii says.

"Really?" Professor Kete says.

"Oh yes professor, I love partying. I told you," Teemii says.

"You did said you love to party but I didn't know you're a freak when it comes to it. But anyway, has long as you don't abuse it and you know what you're doing and you got your mind set on the good side, then you're good to go," Professor Kete says.

"Oh yes professor. I'm a bright girl and I hundred percent know what I'm doing. I'm a good and loving person that just love to party, that's all," Teemii sincerely says.

"That's no problem, I understand you my dear. But anyway, as I was reading about Shango, when thunder is heard you should salute Shango by shouting-out 'Cabio Sile Shango' or words to that effect," Professor Kate reading out about Shango.

"Oh my God, so every time a thunder is heard means Shango the god of thunder is striking?" Teemii asks.

"Emm... yes! To the Yoruba's," Professor Kete answered.

"Wow! That's great," Teemii says, amazed.

He also has a dog...

"Oh I love dogs," Teemii says.

Apart from his dog, he also prefers roosters and turtles, and if you invite him to a feast you will need to stock up on bananas, apples, cornmeal, okra, red wine and rum. His special Feast Day is 4th of December and he also has a piper employed to play all the latest hits...

"*Really!*" Teemii says.

Yes! That's what is written about him in this book. And apart from partying and partying just like you, Shango leads a full red-blooded life. He has a relationship with a woman called OYA which can at times be very tempestuous as Shango is very much a ladies man, and a great demand as a dancer and for playing the drums...

"*Oh he sounds like my kind of man,*" Teemii says.

Ha-ha-ha! Really? That's good for you young lady. ...He does not get on well with his brother, OGUN...

"*Ogun! Who is he again?*" Teemii asks.

"*The god of Iron. He was said to be the first of the Orishas to descend to the land of the earth to find suitable habitation for future human life,*" Professor Kete answered.

"*Really?*" Teemii says, curious.

"*Yes, that's the story. It also says here that Shango is definitely a good god to have on your side as he can be very loyal and protective,*" Professor Kete reads.

"*Oh yeah, that's the way I like him to be; loyal and protective. Wow, I think I'm in love now,*" Teemii says while she twinkle her eyelashes.

"*That's what I like to hear, LOVE,*" Professor Kete says.

"*No! No! No! No! No! I'm not in love with Shango. I'm only just having a thought in my head of a man like Shango, you know - strong, powerful, loyal, protective, and also a great dancer. What else can a lady like me want, huh? And I'm very sure he has money. Wow! Sexy!*" Teemii says.

"*Emmh back in those days there's no such as money,*" Professor Kete says.

"*No money! I'm sure he must be strong and powerful enough to get me anything and everything I*

121

wanted," Teemii says while she twinkle her eyelashes.

"Oh yes, he's a powerful one. Let's move to the others gods before you get carried away," Professor Kete says.

"Ok! I'm enjoying this. Hope you guys listening are," Teemii cheerfully says.

Bumba: *from the Bushongo in the Congo comes Bumba, the African God creator of vomit. In the beginning, all was dark. Then out of the darkness came Bumba, a giant pale-skinned figure. He was not feeling well. He had not been feeling well for millions of years. He was lonely, and the unbearable isolation was making him ill. Troubled by a bellyache, he staggered, moaned and vomited up the sun...*

"Yak!" Teemii says.

Yes. Light breaks open out into the world and he choked out the moon. The stars came next and then, with an incredible effort, he threw up the planet Earth...

"We do live in a very sick world you know," Professor Kete says.

"Yeah I know. This one is very messy and sick, not my type," Teemii says moving her head left and right.

"Ha-ha-ha! You're very funny. But anyway, let us continue," Professor Kete says.

His revolting behaviour was brought to a successful ending when, as an encore; he vomited forward nine animals, different type of humans, and a pile of diced carrots. Tired from his labours, he sat and watched as the nine creatures multiplied. After a while, the creatures developed into every living thing on Earth - Which shows that Creationism and Evolution are both right. His entire creature was friendly and respectful. His loneliness abated and finally he was happy. His three sons then appeared – NYONYE–NGANA, CHONGANDA and CHEDI-BUMBA came and added the finishing touches and thus the world was made.

Bumba spoke kindly to his creations before ascending to heaven, never to been seen again. So far since then, his stomach has never troubled him.

"*Good! His stomach shouldn't trouble him anymore because we don't want any vomit on our heads,*" Teemii says.

"*Ha-ha-ha! I'm sure you don't. Anyway, let's move on. Ha, now is time for your very good friend - Eshu – the devil,*" Professor Kete says.

"*The devil! I hate him,*" Teemii says.

"*I know you do. You've mention this many times today. Am sure the devil by now should know where he stands with you,*" Professor Kete says.

"*He better do,*" Teemii says looking very serious.

Eshu*; he directs traffic along the road of life from his home at the crossroads of destiny. He's also one of the Orishas. Eshu can offer advice to help swing things your way if you're faced with an important choice or a powerful opportunity…*

"*Haa! That's why this people go to him, I see,*" Teemii says.

"*Well, maybe,*" Professor Kete says and carrying-on reading.

He can also carry compliant to the gods, questions to the spirit world, and messages to any living things. With his connections, he can be a powerful supporter. He's also a god with a sense of humour and will often throw a spanner in the works to keep life interesting. This could explain why we don't always get what we want…

"*Really? Now you see the reason why I hate him,*" Teemii says.

Be careful, it is also written here that, this god of crossroad is also a master of cross-purposes…

"*Master of cross-purposes?*" Teemii repeats.

"*Yeah, cross-purposes – as in – misunderstanding*

each other," Professor Kete explains.

"Now you see. May God Almighty be with us?" Teemii prayed.

"I will say amen to that. Let's move-on. Next," Professor Kete says.

Obatala *- he was issued with the task of building the Earth by the Sky God – OLORUN, who gave him, blueprints, a handful of sand, a chain, a five-toed chicken, and detailed instructions...*

"Hold-on a second, if Bumba was the one that vomited the Earth, why is he given the task to build the Earth?" Teemii asks.

"Bumba vomiting the Earth is the belief of the Bushongo people of the Congo. Obatala and many of these gods mentioned in this book is the belief of the Yoruba people of Nigeria and Benin," Professor Kete explains.

"Oh I see. So Obatala is also one of the Orishas?" Teemii asks.

"Yes he is. Now you're getting it. Let's move-on," Professor Kete replies and carried on reading.

Unfortunately for Obatala, on his way to perform this important task, he accidentally gate-crash a god-party and spent the rest of the evening roaring drunk on palm wine...

"Roaring drunk on palm wine? Why are these gods always drinking and partying? They all just sound like they're here to party. No wonder some wouldn't take them serious," Teemii says.

"Is there anything wrong in drinking and partying?" Professor Kete asks.

"No, not at all. Come on professor, am a party freak. But as a god, don't you think they should be more serious than that. Jesus wasn't drinking and partying," Teemii says.

"Yes you're right. Obatala did learn from his

124

mistakes and promises never to drink again. But Jesus did also turn water into wine," Professor Kete says.

"Oh yeah that's true," Teemii says.

"So there is nothing wrong in drinking then," Professor Kete says.

"Oh yeah sure," Teemii says.

"But make sure you don't abuse it," Professor Kete says.

"That right professor, abuse is what's bad," Teemii says.

"That right. Let's move-on Teemii, we've got no time. Where was I? Okay, drunk on palm wine... As Obatala was roaring drunk on palm wine, ODUDUWA..."

"Who is he again?" Teemii asks.

Obatala's younger brother - He sees this as an opportunity for fame and glory so he took the holy building materials and attempted to build the Earth himself, advised by AGEMO - a chameleon – also Olorun's messenger. He lowered the chain over the edge of the heaven, climbed down, and poured sand into the ancient sea. He then releases the chicken to jump onto the mud and began scratching it in all directions. And then a little while later there was a decent size landscape and thus was the Earth born. Olorun the King Sky God was so pleased with Oduduwa that he promoted him to be god of the Earth, while the disgraced and boozy Obatala was put to work making mankind as punishment. So if you ever wondered why humans aren't quite as perfect as they should be, there's the answer: he was drunk at the time while making humans.

"Ha-ha-ha-ha-ha! Useless! He's a joker!" Teemii says laughing.

Hold-on... Obatala later-on eventually learned the error of his ways and became the great white god of mankind, specialising in white wine, laundry and refrigerators. That's the short story of Obatala.

"Before I start with the sixth god, I will also like to say that there is another story on how the earth was created by Obatala," Professor Kete explains.

"Another story?" Teemii asks.

"Yes there is another story because the people of Africa did not use written language until modern times. Instead, they pass the mythology, legends, and history from generation to generation through word of mouth. Written account of African mythology began to appear in the early 1800s. So some people might have misinterpreted the story. When we get to Olorun, I will explain it to you better," Professor Kete explains.

"Okay," Teemii says.

*Now, **Abassi** - Believed to be the creator and lord of the sky according to the belief of the Ekif people of Nigeria. On suggestion of his wife- ATAI, he created the first humans and to some extent fearfully introduces them into the wild. As he feared, the first couple he created somehow discovered sex...*

"Discovered Sex?," Teemii asks.

Yes, sex. And not so soon, they were doing their own creating...

"Naughty," Teemii says.

This created a terrible over-population problem, and made Abassi feel rather insecure. His wife then gave humanity two gifts – Argument and Death - to keep the human numbers under control...

"Ha! She's such a b***h, but sorry, what's her own," Teemii says with a screwed face.

"Her own? I don't know, you tell me. But anyway, let's move to the next," Professor Kete says.

Olorun/Oluwa *- The Owner of Heaven - The top Sky King of Yoruba Mythology in Nigeria - God Almighty in the Yoruba spiritual or religious system.*

He's the God of Peace, Justice and the Yoruba way. Most Yoruba's are named after Him. For example; Oluwadamilare, which means; God has bless me. His wonderful blueprints for planet Earth were so amazingly ambitious, He wisely decided to hand over the job to someone else. So He called upon Obatala, handed over the chicken of creation and told him to get on with it...

"Then he went on drinking and partying. Useless," Teemii added.

"You know the story, don't you?" Professor Kete says.

"Yes I do. Ha-ha-ha," Teemii says laughing.

Yes he did go drinking and partying which led to all kinds of embarrassing complications before life as we know it was achieved. As top God, Olorun's fame has spread as far as the Caribbean. But rumours spread that he was secretly married. Some even claim that he leads a secret double life, which is what brings the other story that Olorun was one of two original creator Gods. The other was the goddess OLOKUN, which her story was that, in the beginning, the universe consisted of only the sky and a formless disorder of soggy water. Olorun rule the sky while Olokun rule the soggy water below. Olokun was content with her watery kingdom, then Obatala had ideas about improving her Kingdom. He went to Olorun and suggested the creation of solid land, with fields and forests, hills and valleys, and various living things to populate it. Olorun agree and gave Obatala permission to create. Obatala then went to ORUMILA, the eldest son of Olorun, to ask on how he can proceed. Orumila then gave Obatala the material he will need to create the land. Obatala then went on to create the land not Oduduwa. Obatala later became lonely and build clay figures. Olorun then made these figures into humans by breathing life into them. Many gods descended from the sky to live on earth, and Olorun told them to listen to the prayers of humans and protect them. Not so please by these acts of creation, the water goddess Olokun tried to flood the land to regain the area she had lost but Obatala use his powers to make the waters move away. She was angry so she challenges Olorun to a weaving contest to see who is more powerful. Every time she made a beautiful cloth, Agemo the chameleon (Olorun's messenger) change the colour of it skin to match her finest cloths. She accepted defeat and acknowledge Olorun as the supreme God.

"So that was the other side of the story," Professor Kete explains.

"But sorry professor, which story should we now believe?" Teemii sincerely asks.

"Very good question. You believe whichever story you want to believe my dear. But one thing you should understand is that, there is a God. And this God is good. This God also have portrait Himself to us in various languages, ways, and forms. All these stories let us know that there is a God. That's all I can say to you. But some of the Africans that have adopted Christianity...," professor Kete explaining.

"Like me," Teemii added.

"Yes like you. Or Islam, sometimes identifies the God of those faiths with the God of traditional African religion and mythology," Professor Kate explains.

"Yeah but professor as a Christian, I know I don't go to church that often but we believe Jesus is the only way to get to know God," Teemii says.

"Yes you're right, if you're from where Jesus is from, I expect you to believe that. People in China or India don't believe that," Professor Kete says.

"So what are you now saying professor? Are you now saying being African we should be worshiping and

praying to these gods? I mean, which one of them are we meant to pray to? You have only just mentioned ten. There are so many more," Teemii sincerely says.

"You see my dear; there is something you're getting wrong or you don't understand. Like I said earlier, God has revealed Himself to us in various forms, ways, and languages. **Africa theosophy has its own share of attempts to explain the nature of God.** *Like I also said earlier, the name for God in Africa is as many as there are words and dialects, but the idea of one supreme spirit is set. No matter how and where, the names for God convey the idea of one Supreme Being. Why it seem we have so many Gods is because, Africa is full of different ethnics and God has portrait Himself to these different ethnics in different languages, ways, and forms. Let me now tell you something you should know,"* Professor Kete explains.

"What is it professor, tell me," Teemii says.

"You see, people having different stories don't have to mean there are many Gods. Actually, all these different stories about God are to show and prove that the story about God isn't just a made-up story by one man from one place or region to control and rule over people. **These different stories about God are actually to prove that there is a God and it's not just a made-up story by one man from one place to control all.** *The people trying to make the story about God a one way story are the ones trying to control and rule over people. No soul should have the right to condemn any stories about God. Instead, people can use these different stories as references to prevail the story about God. You see,* **other nation might have different stories and names for God but in almost all the cases, the concept of one God endures.** *For instance, if we were both ask to share or tell a story on what God has done in our lives and how, we'll probably have*

129

different stories to share. For example; a man might have come from nowhere to rescue or save you from dieing in a car crash or accident which you might want to see or believe this man is God-sent to rescue or save your life. And it is also possible for a dog to rescue or save me from dieing in a car crash which I might also want to believe the dog is also a God-sent to save my life. Because it wasn't a man or you might want to say not 'a human being' that came to rescue me from the car crash doesn't mean the dog isn't a God-sent. My story different from your story doesn't have to mean I have no clue of what God is all about. The Jewish has their own story to share about God, the Arabs has their own story to share, the Greek also has their own story to share, and so as Africans. Like I said earlier, Africa theosophy has its own share of attempts to explain the nature of God," Professor Kete explains.

"Yeah I understand what you're trying to say professor but, what about someone like Shango? He's not God but why do people worship him?" Teemii sincerely asks.

"People that worship Shango believes Shango is one of God's descendants. And the story about Shango will take you back to the story about God. So in a way, the story about Shango is to prove or show to the people from that region that there is a God. And to some people, the belief is; one can always connect with Shango to connect to God. It's just the same way the Christians or I should say the people from where Jesus is from believe through Jesus one can connect to God, and some of these people also worship Jesus and see him as their God. It's not written anywhere that Jesus Christ created heaven & earth and human beings, is it?" Professor Kete explains and asks.

"Emmh am not sure, I don't think so," Teemii says.

"You're not sure. That's not good enough. But

*anyway, the story about Jesus and Satan is also to prove or show to the people from that region or from that side of the world that there is a God. And even though some might want to say the African gods are devil's advocate, the story will still prove that we know God because, the story of the devil comes from the story about God. So we must know God for us to know the devil. You can't talk about the devil without talking about God. And you can't talk about God without talking about the devil. You can't have heard about the devil and not have heard about God. Is not that God abandon the devil in Africa and then went to stay in the Middle East. We know God to exist, but **no one truly knows the true nature of God. All claims to the contrary are deep delusion.** People trying to make this a one way thing is what's causing problems all around the world today. Let me now answer your question about worshipping and praying, or who to pray to; I would say whichever way some have chose or believe to pray to God should be no man's business. When and how you pray to God should have nothing to do with nobody. Things between you and your God should be personal. Let me now tell you what Jesus said in the Bible about praying since you claim to be a Christian or a follower of the Bible. He says: 'when you pray, do not be like the hypocrites'. Do you know who are called hypocrites?"* Professor Kete explains and asks.

"Oh yes of course professor. People that pretends to be what they're not," Teemii answered.

"Very good. Jesus then continue saying, 'for they love to pray standing in the synagogues...'"

"What's that?" Teemii asks.

"Jewish place of worship and religious instruction," Professor Kete replies.

"Okay, like the church," Teemii says.

"You can say that. As I was saying, 'standing in the

synagogues and on the street corners to be seen by men. Jesus was very honest here. He then says, 'I tell you the truth, they have received their reward in full.'"

"What did Jesus mean by *receive their reward in full?*" Teemii asks.

"Let me leave that question for your pastor to answer for you. As I was saying, Jesus continue saying **'But when you pray, go into your room, close the door and pray to your Father**. Who is Jesus referring to as 'your Father'?" Professor Kete says and asks.

"*God,*" Teemii answered.

"*Very good. What do you call God in your language?*" Professor Kete asks.

"*Jaja,*" Teemii answered.

"*Very good. As I was saying, '**close the door and pray to your Father, who is unseen**. Then your Father, who sees what is done in secret, will reward you. And when you pray, do not keep on babbling like pagans, for they think they will be heard because of their many words. Do not be like them, for your Father knows what you need before you ask him'. Did you get any sense in what was been said by Jesus?*" Professor Kete asks.

"*Yeah I think so. I should go into my room, close the door and pray to my Father – as-in - God. And I shouldn't be like the hypocrite that likes to go to church on the street corners to be seen by men,*" Teemii replies.

"*Very good. So when you want to pray, go into your room, close your door, and pray to your Father - as-in – God or Jaja as you will say in your language. Whichever way you pray to Jaja your Father in your room as got nothing to do with nobody. And when you go out to people, do not go out babbling like Jesus said. Instead, when you go out to mix with people, this is what Jesus also said '**do to others what you would** *have them do to you, for this sums up the Law and the Prophets.'* Jesus also said **'Do not judge, or you too will be judged. For in the same way you judge others, you will be judged, and with the measures you use, it will be measured to you.'** *So when you finish praying to Jaja in your room, don't then go out to people and start judging them because they don't follow your religion. Because the same way you judge them, you will be judged too,"* Professor Kete explains.

"That right professor, I don't judge people," Teemii says.

*"I know you don't. That's very good. Keep it up. And let me tell you one thing, **do not let anybody tells you who your Father is.** You should be the one to tell them who your Father is. You should know your Father better than anyone else. He's your Father too. And if you think you don't really know Him that much to tell people about Him, its never too late, you can always still get to know Him personally, if you're willing. Your Father will always be there for you,"* Professor Kete gives Teemii a personal advice.

"That's right professor, that's right. Oh my God, professor, you know so much," Teemii says.

"Oh yes of course, that's why I'm a professor. I studied all the stories said and written about God and how life was formed. If one [someone] wants to really know about God, I personally think one needs to study all the stories said and written about God before one can fully get the full gist. And to be honest, even with all that I have read and learnt about God, I honestly think I still don't know enough. I think there's still so much more to learn about God. You can't just read on one book, or stick to one side of the story and believe you know it all. You will learn more when you look into other peoples' point of view or story they have to share about God. And even with all these different stories, no

one really still truly knows the true nature of God. The study about God is probably the biggest and widest subject anyone can ever study. I learnt from every story I've studied so far. It's normal. I even learnt something from the scientist point of view on how earth and human being came to existence. One should learn from every constructive story they read or hear. Whether a story is a true life story or a fiction, one will still learn at least one thing from it. And there is one thing I learnt from most of these stories; how God is good and being good is the moral of most of these stories. I put together all what I've learnt from every story to guide myself along as I follow my traditions or as I live my life. The story about God doesn't have to be a real or true life story. It could or can just be a story to try to show or prove to people that there is God. Which is true, I believe there is God. I don't need physical proves. I could and can feel God in me. And to also mention, stories are not usually told or written-down for one to believe it true, but for one to learn from it. But the thing is, you got to imagine the story is true for you to enjoy it and for you to be able to learn from it. And even if am going or meant to believe in any story, I honestly think is only right and appropriate for me to stick to the story and history of my root/origin about God, how earth was created and how life started, than to follow the story of another man's root. The story from my home-town should make more sense to me and more related to me. I would rather stick-to or follow the story of my own kind than follow the story of another mankind. I would rather stick-to and have faith in the tradition or ways my forefathers have set or created to get us through life, than to abandon it to follow another man's way. Instead of abandoning my way to follow another mans' way, I will instead learn from the other mans' way to improve my own way. I would rather not disown *the Father at home to adopt another. It will be better staying home with God than running away from home looking for God. God is here, at home. It will be better for me to stick to the home story about my Father than to accept the story of an outsider. Olorun, Oluwa is what I know He[God] to be. Why should I abandon the way God as appear or shown to me to follow another mans' way? God has given me a way and that's the only way am going to follow or sick to, no matter what anyone says. When a man abandon the way God has given or shown to him to follow another man's way, then you should know such a man will forever be a slave to the other man for the rest of his life. **A man who stands for nothing will fall for anything.** Never give-up your rightful way to follow another mans' way - is one thing I leant from the Arabs. They will never give-up Islam to follow any other religion, never. They will always stick to Allah, no matter what. So I don't understand why these people now want me to give-up mine to follow theirs. To me, this religion issue is like someone coming to your home telling you how bad or evil your father or forefathers are just to steal you away or get you adopted. You see, let me tell you something; the adoption of the Christian religion back in the slavery days, especially by the male adults, may be seen as a clear method of adjusting to the new colonial regime in which Christianity offered visible social advantages. Communities which embraced the new religion then believed that by associating with the Christian missionaries they would perhaps escape various forms of colonial over-rule. Later-on from there, it starts to become fashionable to be called a Christian,"* Professor Kete express.

"Really?," Teemii says.

"Oh yes! Colonialism brought Christianity to Africans which challenge and sought to change our

belief. Which I think is unfair and not right. How will they feel if we were the ones to come to their land to challenge and sought to change their belief? Or force them to follow our gods. How will they feel?" Professor Kete express.

"Yeah I know. I see what you're saying professor, I see what you're saying. But professor, what advice will you then give to someone like me to stick, follow, or try to understand the story of his or her own root?" Teemii sincerely asks.

Very good question. Emmh First of all, I will say; talk honestly to the elders, those who have not yet abandoned the story...

"Like someone like you?" Teemii includes.

*"Emmh maybe but it will be better for people to consult the priest. Learn from them to discover the source of the story. People must understand that when others extend their values, religion and institutions, they are penetrating into their traditions with the poison of alien power that teaches them to hate themselves and to love their oppressors. Meanwhile, they never follow the prescription they leave them. Our African history has been a recent orgy of absent-mindedness. We have often lost our memories and accepted the Gods of those who enslaved and colonized us. Sorry to have mention, but this is what the Chinese and Indians have fought hard to keep at home. I'm sorry to say, but those who speak to us of Christianity or Islamic ethical have often been the ones who had dishonoured our ancestors' memories. **Malcom X once said that 'the world pushes the African around because we give the impression that we are chumps, not champs, but chumps, weaklings, falling over ourselves to follow other people rather than our own traditions'.** Africans need to enhance the economic, political and military power of their countries because,*

a lack of such power creates self doubt, identity crisis, and a search for the material Gods of the west who seem to produce these things. But spirit is greater if we use it and we can only use it if we practice it."

"You mean practice more and believe in our traditions and not the west?" Teemii implies.

"You're getting my point. We need boldness from our leaders to accomplish this transformation. We can achieve our aims not so much by modernizing African traditions as Africanizing modernity itself. I personally believe we are the modern people. Our ecological values, relationships values, respect for others values are the keys to the future. We should also believe our names are as blessed as Arabic or European names," Professor Kete explains.

"Oh yeah, I love my name, Teemii Mah. It's so African, and it sound so sexy," Teemii enthusiastically says.

"Ha-ha-ha, definitely a good name. Anyway, as I was saying; create our African personality and identity in art, dance - like you will see performed by the masquerades, in education, science, medicine, and religion. I believe in the African gods and believe just as we have exported our cultural forms in music, art and science, the world needs a more rational and sensible ethnic..."

"Oh! Hold-on a second professor, it seems like the leaders are coming down off the high table. Where are they going? Or what are they up to now?" Teemii says pointing towards the high table.

"Oh yeah, it's time for the masquerades parade," Professor Kete says.

"Oh time for the masquerades to come out, exciting! Sorry guys, we have to put an end to the story about the gods. Sorry we couldn't finish reading the whole stories about the gods' professor mentioned to us today. We

*got carried away by other things. Hope you guys did
enjoy the ones we got time to talk about today. Anyway,
before we continue to the next agenda, we're quickly
going to take a short break. Am Teemii Mah,
representing radio 1 live at the festival, right here, the
centre of Egitee, Freeland. Stay tune."*

As the leaders come down off the high table with their
wives, to salute and show some appreciation to pay
respect to the gods, Musiah on dark shade as usual, is at
one corner standing next to his all black tinted Range
Rover, carrying his favourite steel chrome plated gun-
AK 47, surrounded by some of his men and three of his
girlfriends in his Range. All having rum, smoking
weed, listening to Teemii and Professor Kete on radio.
Musiah must have heard Teemii over the radio
mentioned the leaders leaving the high table,
immediately he went for his army radio.

"UMARU(Musiah right-hand man)! *Make sure
everyone is standing at alert. Cover all possible angles.
And make sure, I repeat, make sure no one tries
anything silly. If anyone does, you have my order.
They're leaving the high table now. Make sure they're
all covered,"* Musiah gives order for a tightened
security over the leaders while he does his own
celebration in his own way at one corner.

As Gen. Fahruk leads his fellow Africa leaders with
their wives, dancing, rejoicing and celebrating along
the high street in front of the State House, Teemii is
back on air with Professor Kete.

*"Welcome back guys. Oh I really like this music
playing by the Cultural Group Singers, you know… the
drums, the trumpets, it sounds really good,"* Teemii
says, happy.

*"It's a traditional music. Its music you have to play
at times like this. Its music they play only for the*

leaders. It's meant to boost up their ego," Professor Kete explains.

"Really? Mehn! This music is really boosting up my ego mehnnn. Maybe am also a leader too. You know... am feeling the music, am feeling the music mehnnn," Teemii joyfully says shaking her head.

"Ha- ha- ha! You might as well go join them," Professor Kete suggests.

"Really? Can I?" Teemii excitedly asks.

"Emmh not exactly, I don't think the security will allow you to," Professor Kete says.

"I know professor, there is too much security. Sometimes I wonder if our police and soldiers could ever keep peace. Today they surely are doing a great job," Teemii says.

"What do you expect? They've got their leaders to protect," Professor Kete says.

"Yeah I know. Anyway, what agenda are we on now?" Teemii asks.

"Emmh...this is the time where the leaders pay respect to the gods. This is the time they give sacrifices to the gods. Gold's, diamonds, animals, and human blood will be given to the gods," Professor Kete explains.

"Yeah I know, some are going to lose their lives for this," Teemii says.

"Yep! Seven prisoners with death sentences blood will be shed to the gods. I don't know why they do that, but I personally think is not right. They only do this in Egitee. The first leader, King Yemojaja thinks it a better way to executes those that have been pass-on death sentence by the Court on a day like this. He believes instead of wasting their life on a normal day, it will be better to waste it to the gods. Can you see where the stone images are kept on the other side of the high table?" Professor Kete says pointing.

"Yeah, yeah, yeah," Teemii nervously says.

"Are you okay?" Professor Kete asks.

"Not really professor. I find it dreadful when I think about people getting killed. I get scared," Teemii says.

"Don't worry, you will be fine," Professor Kete says.

"I hope so professor, I hope so. But anyway, let's continue please," Teemii says.

"Sure! The stone images represent men, woman, children and animals"

"Animals!" Teemii says, curious.

"Yes animals. The stone images are all of different sizes and shapes range in height from about 10 centimetres to a little over a meter. Stones weight varies from small fragment to the heaviest which is about 104 kilograms. Lots of the images are seated on stools, some are standing, and some have tribal marks on their faces. And you know, all is to reflect to the social status of the original people, you know – the gods, who were said to have been turned into images according to some believes," Professor Kete explains.

"Really? So that's where the leaders are going to drop their gifts – diamonds and gold's, next to the stones," Teemii says.

"Yes, next to the stone images of the gods. And after the leaders have all put down their various gifts, then the masquerades will come out to dance and give praises to the gods. In African societies, dance offers a complex diversity of social purposes. In a native traditional dance like this, each masquerade performance is to express or reflect the mutual values and social relationships of the people. Many of these beliefs, are based on relationship connection between the living and their dead ancestors, who they believe return as masquerade performers to guide and judge the living," Professor Kete explains.

140

"Return as masquerades?" Teemii asks.

"Yes as masquerade performers. The masquerade dancers are a feature of religious societies. They are identified by the roles they play. Material masquerades that perform as entertainer have emerged from the ritual societies. For example, the Egungun masquerades entertainers of the Oyo- Yoruba people most of the time are invited to perform for a fee as entertainers," Professor Kete explains.

"Are they going to be performing here today?" Teemii asks.

"Oh yes of course. They will first start with their popular acrobatic dances and then display their magic powers," Professor Kete says.

"Magic powers," Teemii says, excited.

"Oh yes. They will change into a series of animal and masked figures. They use a creative sort of imitate and dance to praise gods and heroes, and to ridicule wrongdoers. They're also accompanied by singers and led by drum ensemble," Professor Kete explains.

"Wow! That sounds interesting. I can't wait," Teemii says, excited.

"In all African cultures, dance, music, and song help define the role of the individual and the group within the community. Dance is also important as an educational tool. Repetitive dances teach children physical control and stress accepted standards of behaviour. Children may from their own dance and masquerade groups, join adults at the end of a dance line, or simply have a space allocated to them in a performing area at the time of a festival," Professor Kete explains.

"Oh no wonder all this kids are running up and down. They must be very excited to join the masquerade at the end of the dance line. Can I join them too? This really sounds exciting!" Teemii says sounding very excited.

"Sure you can. In-fact you should," Professor Kete gives Teemii more encouragement.

"Sorry professor, before we go quickly for another short break. There is something I would like to say," Teemii says.

"Go ahead. What is it?" Professor Kete asks.

"You see professor, Christians... sorry am going into all of this again," Teemii says.

"That's no problem, it okay. We're all learning," Professor Kete says.

"They say it is wrong for any man to bow down to any stone images of any sizes and shapes range in height. What do you have to say to this?" Teemii asks.

"Very good question. I'm happy you raise that question. Emmh... You see, let me tell you something. They say no man should bow down to any stone images but when you go to church, you will see a huge stone image of a woman they call 'Mary mother of Jesus' that people bow down to. Not only that, in churches they have a picture of a blue eyes white man with longhair to represent Jesus, people also bow down to this picture. This same white man is also carved nailed to a cross. People bow down to this too. You see, all this people that says don't do this while they do, is a typical example of hypocrisy," Professor Kete answered.

"That's right professor, you're absolutely right. They do all this things in my church. I go to a catholic church," Teemii says.

"I know. Let me tell you a short personal story of how I end up studying the stories about God, and how I end up sticking to my root," Professor Kete says.

"Oh yes professor, go ahead. But you have to be quick, we haven't got that much air time," Teemii says.

"Ok, I'll be quick. First of all, I will start by saying;

I'm from a Muslim and Christian family background. My dad is a Muslim and my mum is a Christian. My dad is from Lagos, Nigeria, while my mum is from Accra, Ghana but she lives all her life in Lagos. I'm the only child my parent had. In Africa, the religion your father follows is expected to be the religion one follows. So as a little boy, my dad always take me to the mosque. Going to the mosque, there was something that really bothers me; the language I had to speak. You see, to become a full proper Muslim, you must learn how to speak Arabic, you can't escape it. They might want to make you feel speaking Arabic is not important, or you don't have to speak Arabic to be a Muslim but, to be a full proper Muslim, or to be a leader in the religion, or to be a qualify Imam; one must be able to speak Arabic fluently, which for me makes the language important. I might one day want to be a qualify Imam. Also, when you want to pray to Allah which means God in Arabic, you must follow the method that is set to speak or pray to Allah, which is the crucial five times daily prayer. The language use in this method is only set in Arabic. Now, what I'm trying to say is; then as a little kid, I wonder why I can't use my home tongue to speak or pray to Allah. In my bed those days, as a little kid, I sometimes wonder why Allah/God didn't create me with the language He knows I would need to pray to Him or worship Him. I ask myself why Allah/God as created some with this crucial language and some without. I was worried. I didn't feel much love from Allah/God. So I decided to speak to my dad. When I ask my dad, my dad said to me the Imam at the mosque said to him 'the language set for these prayers is a holy language that can't be change. That changing it will misinterpret the meaning'. And being a kid that is interested in getting to know God, I thought to myself that, me not being able to speak this language they speak in mosque, means I won't be able to speak or pray to God. So I had no other choice than to learn this language if I really want God/Allah to hear or answer my prayers. But I would honestly prefer or rather use the language I can speak or understand to pray to God than use another language I don't understand or don't really want to speak. I believe praying to God in my language will make me feel closer to God. However, when I go to the mosque with my dad, after the praying times, we always stay behind to learn more of the language. As a kid, I didn't really find it interesting. I find it so hard to understand. I wish I never had to use this language to pray to God. One evening at the Arabic lesson, the man teaching was going to beat me for not picking-up fast on the language. I didn't want to get beaten so I ran away from the mosque. On this very day I ran away from the mosque, my dad had to leave me behind to go back to work and was going to pick me up on his way back from work. I think I was around the age six or seven at that time. I knew running away from the mosque to be on my own was dangerous. I was so scared of getting kidnap, or getting lost. So I prayed to God in my language to guide me as I find my way home. And luckily for me, one of my mum's friends saw me wandering about the street. She stopped me and took me to my mum's shop. I was so happy to see my mum. After that day was when I realise God can also answer my prayers in my language because, at the end of the day, I got home safe. I told my dad I never want to go back to the mosque again, that I would prefer to go to the church with my mum, which wasn't a problem for my dad. He wasn't against me trying to be a Christian, which is one thing I love about my parent. They never force a particular religion on me. They wanted that aspect of my life to be my own choice. But anyway, I started going to the church with my mum. I didn't have the language problem in church because one can use any language to speak to God in church. I'd prefer and enjoy going to church with my mum not until I became eighteen. On my 18th birthday, I lost both my mum and dad..."

"Awww.... Sorry professor. What happened?" Teemii sadly says.

"We had a vital car accident coming from a restaurant we went to have dinner to celebrate my birthday. A big heavy iron container full of goods fell on our car from a lorry. The container full of goods wasn't properly tightened up to the lorry; it loosens up and fell on our car..."

"Awww... that's so sad," Teemii says.

"Yes it was. It was unfortunate. Both my dad and my mum died instantly. I was the only survival. I was so distraught to lose both my mum and my dad at the same time."

"I can imagine. Awww... am so sorry to hear that professor," Teemii sadly says.

No that's ok. Such is life. What can we do? God knows best. And at 18 with no parent or brothers and sisters, God was the only one I could look-up to, or believe I can only have or use as a guardian. And for me to get close to God, I had to decide on what religion to follow, I believed then. I didn't want to condemn my father's belief and also didn't want to condemn my mother's belief, because both are good God fearing people. So I started to call myself half-Muslim half-Christian. But then again people say I can't call myself that. Why not? I always ask and wondered. I don't really understand nor get-it up till today why I can't and why people are so against me calling myself both. I have to choose one is what they always say. From the encouragement and advice these people try to tell or give to me, I notice that these people will say anything

145

*to try convincing me to condemn one for another,
which I really didn't want to do. It's like they're trying
to make me hate people I don't want to hate. Even
though I wasn't happy with the language they speak in
the mosque, in my mind, the same God I pray to in the
mosque is also the same God I pray to in the church. So
I find it hard to condemn any. If I had to condemn one
to follow the other, then I would rather prefer to ride
solo with God than condemn any. So I decided to stay
away from these people because, they were starting to
confuse me and wanting to turn me into something am
not or wants to be. All I want to be is a good human
being. I don't want to hate nobody. I don't want to have
to condemn any religion that preaches about good. I
don't want to judge nobody. All I just want to be is a
good human being; friendly, polite, honest, humble,
understanding, and accepting people for whom they
are. Not condemning and trying to separate people.
That's not me. Then I didn't really see my own religion
or tradition as another option to follow because, being
with or following these people, they already have
completely turn my back against it, just like they will
make you do to any other religion. But being a wise kid,
I decided to go solo to study more about God if I really
want to know Him. Which I believe was a good move
for me, I must say. Which is what then led me to
learning about all that is written and said so far about
God and how life was created or formed. During my
research was when I realise I can get to know God
personally, and that God is actually home. I don't need
to runaway from home to join or follow any group or
religion. Sixty-eight years of me living this life, I think
by now, I understood clearly what the story about God
is all about. Like I said earlier, I learnt from all the
stories. And from my leanings, I get to understand that,
it doesn't really matter what language you use to speak*

*to God, or what name you call God, or what religion you follow. Your loyalty and honesty is what that really matters. To me, the language I can't use to speak to my God, is useless. In other sense, I might as well condemn myself to follow another man's way. There is nothing wrong in using another mans' language to pray to God or practicing and following another man's way of worshiping God. But I personally would prefer to use my dialect and would prefer to follow my traditional way of worship. I appreciate and am proud of whom God has made me. And don't get me wrong, I don't mind speaking Arabic, or any other languages. I actually honestly think is a good thing to learn and to be able to speak other peoples' languages. I honestly think it will be a good thing if we all understand and can speak each others' languages. But when it time to speak to God, I just believe it's more appropriate to use my home tongue, my dialect. It connects me more. Thank God nowadays people are not force to follow one particular religion unlike the olden days where most of our fathers were force to follow one particular religion. I've got to a stage nobody tells me about God, I tell them. He's my God too. I am glad and proud to stick to my root and tradition. I personally believe everyone should stick to theirs too because, **God is everywhere**. People just need to be confident, believe more in themselves, and be able to stand-firm with God by themselves. There is no point running away from home looking for God. **God is home.** God is everywhere. **God is in us all. God looks after everybody. God helps everybody.** According to my research and studies about religion, I find out **every religion has a testimony**. Every religion has something great to say about God or whatever they see as God. **God loves and cares about everybody. Anything can happen to anybody.** One doesn't have to join or be part* of any group to get God's blessings. **God has blessed us all**. *That why we say, 'God is wonderful, God is good, He's the greatest, and the most merciful,'"* Professor Kete tells his personal story.

"Yep, I guess you're right professor. What a story. But anyway professor, thank you so much. I have really learnt a lot from you today. Hope our lovely listeners also have learnt one or two things from you today. But anyway, before we call it a day with you Professor Kete, what advice will you give to our lovely and beautiful listeners listening to you right now?" Teemii asks.

"Well, my advice will be; believe in yourself, hold-on to your tradition and culture if you can, and do what's right for you to do as a human being. And like my favourite writer Ade Tokunbo will always say...

Be good!" Both says at the same time.

"Ha-ha-ha! He's my favourite writer too. In-fact, am his number one fan," Teemii sincerely says.

"Really?" Professor Kete says.

"Yeah!," Teemii excitedly says nodding her head smiling.

*"That's good but anyway, as I was going to say, I mean; **regardless where you're from or the religion you follow, being good to one another is the only way I see that can bring us together as one.** Without this in mind, I don't think we can ever come together as one. So being good to one another is very important. At least we do that first, and leave the rest to God,"* Professor Kete gives his advice.

"That's right professor. Thank you very much for being with us today. You've been such a wonderful guess," Teemii honestly says.

"Thank you for having me," Professor Kete replies.

"Anytime professor, anytime. I've personally learnt a lot from you today. Hope our lovely listeners also

have. Anyway, it's now time for me to hand over back to Adele in the studio. I should be back on air later-on this evening, to feed you guys more on the whole gist about the festival. I'm still your favourite, Teemii Mah. Bye for now."

Few hours gone past, Teemii - the radio 1 presenter - eventually got to see the various masquerade dances and did join the masquerade at the end of the dance line. She really did enjoy herself, so as many of the people present at the festival. The festival so far is going perfectly well just as Gen. Fahruk wants it to. So far so good, the day is still bright and sunny.

"This is exactly what you want, isn't it? A perfect festive show, this is good. I'm really enjoying myself and I could see the people are really enjoying themselves too. You must have spent a lot of money into this. I mean, the Egungun masquerades were here. I know how much it cost just to bring them to your festive. And not just them, you got some big names international artist performing tonight. A lot of food and drinks are there for people to eat and even to take home. I mean, this is like a perfect day for the people. Is this a way to win their heart over to make them be on your side? I mean...eh....have tried my best to try and win my people over but...eh....their mouth and eye is too wide open. They want to know everything that is going on. I mean... look at you throwing a big big party. No one dares to ask how much you've spent or how much you haven't. Or even dare to say 'he's spending all this money even though the country has nothing to show after 56 years being Independent'. I'm sorry, am not trying to say anything but...eh... I wonder sometimes how you do this. You've been ruling now nothing less than fourteen years and you're still

going pretty strong. I mean... you need to show me the way," Gen. Fahruk's close pal expresses is mind and ask for advice.

"Ha-ha-ha-ha! You make me laugh. You know nothing. You need to consult your spiritualist more often. That's all I can say to you. Ha-ha-ha!," Gen. Fahruk laughs out load while he rests his back on the chair. He lights-up his cigar and then carrying on laughing. *"Ha-ha-ha-ha!"*

The day pretty much went on well as planned. The music, the food, the masquerade dances, and the leaders' luxury gifts to the gods have been the alight of the festival and the Independence Day. It's always been every year but this year, something different happen or was added to the agenda. Just right towards the last minute of the festival, big dark clouds starts to gather up in the sky. A very loud thunder strikes, *"ZZZRAAAA!!!"*

People for a minute went silence. Dark clouds this much has never gathered-up in the sky. The thunder lightning has never been this loud and bright. It's not a good sign. Everyone starts to worry and gets worrier as the dark clouds keep gathering and coming fast to cover over the country and as the thunder strikes get louder as it strikes every two minutes. At this moment on the high table, Gen. Fahruk is nowhere to be found, he's disappeared. His close pal sitting next to him wonders how Gen. Fahruk so quick could have left the high table within a blink. He rub is eyes to see clearer.

"Ha! Where is this man just now? Or is it just me? Or do I need to wear my glasses? Ha! Eh....do anyone know where this man is or as gone?" Close pal looking for his close mate.

"Ha! We don't know where he's gone oh! Maybe is time for us to go back to our various countries," other

leaders on the high table replies

"Ha! Yes is time to go oh! What else are we waiting for? The party is over. We had fun. It's time for us to go. Please let's all go back to where we're from before thunder strikes our head. Please let's start going. Let's start going," close pal suggest to others leaders.

Meanwhile, Musiah at his chilled-out corner also wonder what could be going on. For the very first time he took off his dark shade in public. He brought out a binocular and firstly takes a look at the high table. He zoomed in. He didn't see his father. He saw the other leaders all looking worried and all swiftly leaving the high table heading straight to their various presidential convoys to take them back home. *"Mehn!,"* Musiah shouts out. He then tries to have a look round to see what's going on. He looks at where the stone images of the gods are sited to see that no one has been tapering with the gifts given to the gods because no one normally looks or guides after it. No-one in-fact dares to touch or steal what belongs to the gods, having the belief that – who ever that steal from the gods will suffer. But Musiah just thought he should have a look maybe someone might be tapering with the gifts which might be what's causing heavy thunder striking and dark clouds gathering. Musiah looking closely at the stone images of the gods, he saw Teemii Mah looking suspicious, crawling to go behind the wall where the stone images are sited.

"What de f**k is this stupid b***h trying to do. MUGUN! Go get the stupid b***h off behind the stones. Where de f**k does she thinks she's going," Musiah says and then order one of his boys to go get Teemii.

But meanwhile, Teemii isn't trying to do anything silly. She's scared someone might be after her.

"Oh my God please help. I might have fancied him but not this much. Oh my God. The god of thunder, he could be him this time. Oh my God... I've forgotten what professor told us to say whenever the thunder strikes. Ca...ca...ca....bio...si....," Teemii says trying to pronounce the word – Cabio Sile. *"ZZZRAAAA!,"* heavy thunder strikes as she tried. *"Oh my God!,"* Teemii screams. She then crawls to hide underneath a table behind the stone images. She stays underneath the table shivering and anxious, still trying to remember the words – Cabio Sile - to salute Shango the god of thunder whenever the thunder strikes. *"Cabio....Cabio....Cabio,"* is what she keeps saying until another heavy thunder strikes, *"ZZZRAAAA!"*

As another heavy thunder strikes, a human head drops in front of Teemii. *"Haaaaaaaaaaaaaaaaaaa!,"* she screams. She then tries to run out of where she was hiding. As she gets-out from underneath the table she was hiding, she came face to face with seven dead human bodies'(the prisoner with death sentence) with on heads, hanged on their back onto a giant hook, and six human heads placed on the table she crawl underneath to. *"Haaaaaaaaaaaaaaaaaaa!,"* she screams out load, and then makes a run for her life. *"Haaaaaaaaaaaaaaaaaa! Heeeeelp!,"* she screams as she runs out fast from behind where the stone images of the gods are sited.

Mugun – one of Musiah's boys – the one Musiah sent to get Teemii, was going to stop Teemii but the force and power in which Teemii use to run out behind the stones isn't what Mugun can handle. He got knocked out by Teemii. *"Get off my way!"* Teemii says while she punch-off Mugun off her way. Teemii screaming and running like is the end of time makes the people already panicking from the unexpected dark clouds and thunder striking gets even more scared.

They also started running and screaming, *"Help! Help! Help!,"* people start to scream. Everyone starts to run.

Meanwhile, Musiah still looking round with his binocular can see everything that's happening. *"What de f**k as this b***h started,"* Musiah says. And as he look round and round with his binocular, he saw something intriguing. On top of a mountain in between the forest, he saw some people. He then zoom-in to see clearly who these people are. *"Who are these people?,"* he says. He could see hefty men painted with red stripes on their faces and body. Wearing black head bandana and a red cloth wrapped round their waist, holding a long big hatchet. He's never seen anyone like this before. He wonder who they could be or after. Immediately he calls for his boys.

"Umaru! There's a change of plan. It looks like we got some visitors here with us today. Call-in for the full squad... We're heading to the forest. It looks like we got some friends to play with. Get all the guns out. Everyone should be wearing their protection. Meet me at base-1. Today is the day. Ha-ha-ha-ha-ha!," Musiah calls for full squad which includes the soldiers, the police, and the Cult Boyz, ready to take out whoever that is in the forest or causing all this noise.

As the full squad gather round the forest to invade whoever that's coming in from the mountain in the forest, heavy rain starts to pour. Everyone out for the festival at this time has all gone back to their various homes. No single soul is present or out to see what's coming or what's about to happen. Only the soldiers, the police, the Cult Boyz, and probably Musiah and Umaru are the only people out to fight or stop whatever or whoever that's trying to disturb the peace. *"Go! Go! Go! Go!"* Umaru (Musiah right-hand man) commands the full squad to go get the hefty men Musiah must have seen on the mountain in the forest through his binoculars. While he stays with Musiah his boss by base-1 (a spot where commanders stays and commands his squad).

"ZZZRAAAA!" another heavy thunder strikes, but this time louder. The noise of the thunder is so loud and powerful that the ground starts to shake every time it strikes. And all of a sudden, Musiah lost radio connection to his men and boyz in the forest. They couldn't hear from him neither could he hear from them. He lost full control.

"What's going-on here?" Musiah asks Umaru.

"Sir, I have no idea," Umaru replies.

"Come with me lets go," Musiah says to Umaru. And both in Musiah's Range Rover drove down to see what's really happening on the mountain in the forest.

The whole country feels under threat. No one knows what could be happening or what's about to happen, even Gen. Fahruk. He's nowhere to be found.

Musiah and Umaru drive pass along the hill pathway in the forest to get to the mountain. Still they haven't seen or heard from any of their men.

"Where are these boyz," Musiah says.

"Sir, I have no idea," Umaru replies.

Musiah then decide to park his Range Rover at one corner while it still heavily raining, to have a quick look again at the mountain. He slowly wane down the car window and with his binoculars took another closer look at the mountain. He saw nobody. He then tries to look around. Ahead of them, he saw something.

"Wow! There they are," Musiah says and then zoom-in to take a closer look.

"Oh! Is he still alive or who is this I'm seeing? Have a look," Musiah says and ask Umaru to also have a look to be sure of what he as just saw.

"Wow! I thought he was dead. Or am I seeing a ghost," Umaru says. And both at the same time looked

at each other, thinking, *"Could this be the invasion of ghost attack?"*

The answer is NO. Who they just saw was Solomon, leading the hefty men Musiah saw on the mountain. Immediately, Musiah put his Range Rover on reverse. On reverse, he drives faster than he's ever driven before back to the State House. For the very first time Musiah feel scared. He doesn't know what to do. If it was on a different day then he might think of what to do or not get this scared. But because it's on a day of the festival and according to his belief and warnings from his spiritualist, seeing or experiencing what he had just saw on a day of the festival, is a sign of DANGER.

Chapter Eleven

Solomon Returns

Solomon is back after gone missing for forty days and forty nights in the dark forest. He's back stronger, powerful, and with his own men. He's back to take over.

While the rain still falls heavily all around the country and heavy thunder strikes every two minutes, no soul is outside to experience or wants to see what's about to happen because, what's happening right now (dark clouds gathering, heavy rain-falling, and very loud thunder striking) on a day of the festival sounds creepy and scary. There is silent and no movement all around the country. The sound of heavy rain and heavy thunder striking is the only noise vibrating the whole nation. People are indoors, scared. Only Solomon and his hefty men are outside making their way to the State House. Outside the State House are also fully harmed soldiers, polices, and the Cult Boyz awaiting Solomon and his hefty men. They've already been commanded by Musiah to kill anyone that tries to attack or tries to come-in to the State House.

FIRE!!! - The fully harmed soldiers, polices, and the Cult Boyz awaiting Solomon and his hefty men release fire as soon as they saw a flick of Solomon and his men. But nothing was happening. The bullets weren't harming Solomon and his men. They keep coming closer and closer. Some of the weak or new members of the soldiers, police, and Cult Boyz that noticed nothing is happening or harming Solomon and his men, looked at each other, *"This is not what we sign for. This is beyond our power,"* they thought to themselves.

Immediately, they drop their weapons and ran for their lives. But some that still believes or has faith in the power or charm given to them by their leader – Gen. Fahruk, to use protect themselves against any enemies being a soldier or being a member of the Cult Boyz, stood their ground. They carried-on firing. They have their magical protection on.

"You should never fear or lose faith in this charm when it time for war. It's what's going to protect you and keep you safe," Gen. Fahruk always alert his men on the secret that will make the charm work whenever is time for war.

But what Gen. Fahruk didn't know or realize or might have not thought about is that, just has his father claim to be given a stronger special power by the gods to rule the nation better, and also know the secret to the power behind King Yemojajas', which he uses to conquer and overthrown King Yemojaja and his boys (the Ibakari Boys), claiming they're not using the power appropriately, may have just backfired. Someone else might have just also been given a stronger power to rule the nation better, and might also know the secret to the one of the Agaja's. Solomon apparently, is on his way to prove that.

As Solomon and his hefty men behind him reached the front of the State House, a final heavy thunder strikes, *"ZZZRAAAA!!!."* And all of a sudden, all the soldiers, polices, and the Cult Boyz left outside the State House were stricken to death by the final heavy thunder lightning. Solomon makes his way in with no hassle.

On the entrance of the door, they saw Umaru. Umaru was shooting at Solomon and his men but the bullets were just dropping right in front of Solomon and his men. *"Get him!,"* Solomon orders his men to get Umaru.

Solomon's men - the hefty men painted with red stripes on their faces and body, wearing black head bandana and a red cloth wrapped around their waist, holding a long big hatchet - gets hold of Umaru, and put him on his knee. Then one of them on one attempt swings the hatchet on his right-hand through Umaru's neck. He beheaded Umaru. Instantly, Umaru's head came-off. He died. Solomon and his men, moves on.

They open a door to one of the rooms in the State House to see who's in there; they saw the ferocious military man that took over in 1967 - an Ex Dictator of Egitee - Major General Grunitzky Agaja – Gen. Fahruk's father – Musiah's grandfather - laying on the floor, also stricken to death by the final heavy thunder lightning.

"May his soul rest in peace," Solomon prayed. They move-on.

As they move-on going from rooms to rooms, behind them came Musiah. He's set a trap for Solomon and his men. As soon as Solomon and his men all walked through a door into another room, Musiah shut the door behind them. *"Ha-ha-ha-ha-ha-ha!,"* he laughs out load. He's already set a time bomb in the room Solomon and his men just entered. *"You guys are in for it,"* he says smiling. He then pressed the control button to blow-up Solomon and his men. Nothing happened. The bomb didn't explode. He pressed the button again. Still, nothing happened. *"What the f**k is going on here!,"* he yells. He starts to panic. He then angrily drops the control pad to the bomb and went for his favourite steel chrome plated gun AK 47. *"F**k yaaaaaa! All of yaaaaaa! Haaa!,"* Musiah screams while he shoots at the door room Solomon and his men just entered. And all of a sudden, as Musiah angrily shoots at the door screaming and yelling, *"F**k yaaaaaa! All of yaaaaaa!,"* his head came-off,

158

dangling on the floor. He was beheaded by one of Solomon's men who must have teleported from the room to behind Musiah. Instantly, he died.

"You have got no home training. It's not your fault. May your soul rest in peace," Solomon says to Musiah's dead body. He then looks around, and then, *"Where is his father?!,"* he shouts.

Solomon and his men search the whole house but still Gen. Fahruk is nowhere to be found. So they decided to call him out in the name and on behave of the gods of the land.

"Fahruk Agaja! Fahruk Agaja! Fahruk Agaja! The son of Grunitzky Agaja! In the name and on behave of the gods of the land, I command you to come out now! Come out now! Come out now!," one of Solomon's men did an incantation to call out Gen. Fahruk from wherever he might have hid himself.

Gen. Fahruk couldn't hide anymore. His powerful times are over. Apparently, he went invisible and hid himself in the closet in his office – the president's office. But as soon as they call out his name, there was nothing within his power he can do than to come out to confront justice.

"There you are my very good friend. Or should I just say, bad friend. Oh, or even say brother in-law. Where have you been hidden yourself...? In the dark I suppose? Come-on, say something... Or should I just say the dark has been brought to light. Ha-ha-ha-ha! I'm here for you now, Mr General Fahruk Agaja. No-no- no- no, I must be mistaking. You're not just a General, you're a god, the king of the seas, and the man nobody wants to see his dark side. Come-on, I am here for you now. Why don't you just show me your dark side? I will like to see it. Or are you not ready for me? Come on, say something... 'I am a king. I am a god', is always fun of you to say. Come-on, say

something," Solomon says to Gen. Fahruk.

"I am sorry. Please forgive me, please," Gen. Fahruk says to Solomon, begging for his life while on his knee, surrounded by Solomon and his men.

"Sorry? Is that all you can say? Sorry. Come on, you should know better. Or have you forgotten that **'everyday is for the thieves, and one day is just for the owner'.** *I brought you message from the gods. A reply to what you said to me on the day of the talk show. Can you remember? I'm sure you do. In the pride of your heart you say – I am a god. You sit on the throne of a god in the heart of the seas. But you are a man and not a god. You think you are as wise as a god but not as wiser than me. You miss use the power given to you. By your wisdom and understanding, you gained wealth for yourself and amassed gold and silver in your treasuries. By your greediness you increased your wealth and because of your wealth your heart grown proud. Therefore this is what the gods of the land says; because you think you as wise as a god, they are going to bring the little man against you. He will draw his sword against your pride and wisdom, and slice open your shinning luxury. He will bring you down to the pit and you will die a violent death in the heart of the seas. Will you then say I am a god in the presence of the little man that will kill you? You will be a man not a god in the hand of the little man.* **You were blameless in your ways from the day you were created till wickedness was found in you.** *Through the power given to you, you were filled with violence and you sinned. Your heart became proud on account of your wealth and you corrupted your wisdom because of luxury. By your many sins and dishonesty, you have dishonoured your sanctuaries. You have come to a horrible end and you will be no more,"* Solomon gives his final message to Gen. Fahruk.

"Please! Please! Solomon, please! I will change, please! Forgive me, please! It's the devil, please! I will change, please! Pardon me," Gen. Fahruk begs.

"Sorry..., is too late," Solomon says. He then brought out a sword and says, *"Goodbye my friend. Its good knowing... you will be no more."* He then swings the sword on his right hand. Gen. Fahruk's head came-off. Solomon beheaded Gen. Fahruk. Instantly, Gen. Fahruk died. *"May your soul rest in peace,"* Solomon prayed.

And that was the end of Gen. Fahruk Agaja, in-fact, the **Agaja's**. *"Who's next!,"* Solomon shouts out.

The next day, morning, **9th May, 2002,** Solomon went live on national television;

*"Good morning to you all my fellow good people of Egitee. Yes this might be a big surprise to you all. Yes it is me on TV, Solomon Gondi, the son of Ezekiel Gondi. I'm back again. And this time, powerful and stronger. I have visited the gods of the land and they have given me the power to bring back peace and justice to this beautiful land of ours. I hereby will like to pronounce to you all good people of Egitee that, from now on, things will change, not only for the good but I guess also for the bad. My advice to those that believe in paving their way through corruption, or any sort of crime to live comfortably should STOP because, from now-on, such behaviour will be unacceptable. I am sincerely sorry to come and have disturbed the colourful festival and the memorable Independence Day you all where enjoying in this manner. It was just the right time the gods have set it to be. It's the time we all have been waiting and fighting for. The time for the healing of the wounds has come. **The moment to bridge the chasms that divide us has come.** The time to build is upon us. I hereby, with the power given to me by the*

gods of the land - which I will like to call - '**The Dark-gods**', I make a command to authority; let there be justice for all. Let there be peace for all. Let there be work, bread, water and salt for all. Let each know that for each body, the mind and the soul have been freed to fulfil themselves. Never, never, and never again shall it be that this beautiful land will again experience the oppression of one by another and suffer the indignity of being the skunk of the world. Let freedom reign. And for those of you that haven't heard, the Agaja's family has been brought to justice by the gods. And for those that are still alive and have been part of the misfortune of this beautiful land alongside with the Agaja's, will also face justice. The power I obtain is immortal. It power no man can challenge. It's power from the gods. But if you think you as a man can challenge this power, then be my guest.

I have setup rules for us all to follow. No man, I repeat; no man or soul that lives on this land should dare not break or go against these rules I put forward to you today. I would like to symbolize these rules also as - '**The rules of the Dark-gods**.' The rules are simple and it state as follows;

Hear, O Egitee, the verdicts and the laws I declare in your hearing today. Learn them and be sure to follow them.

You shall not murder.

You shall not steal.

You shall not rape.

You shall not make any sort of assault to your next neighbour.

You shall not by intention hunt the other man.

You shall not be found carrying a gun or knife having the intention to kill or steal.

Whether you are the president, the governor, you are in the military, a police officer or civil servant; you *shall not by any means commit bribery and corruption.*

These are the commands, verdicts and laws I brought to you today. These are the rules from now on everyone will have to follow, whether you're good or bad. Some of you might be thinking how will I enforce these rules to people? Well, before you start thinking far, as you all know, the gods can see everything. With the power given to me, I have created what I would like to call – The Black Eye. A surveillance camera which is now as I speak planted in front of the State House. A surveillance camera that will be able to see all that goes-on on this land. It will be placed on top of a 100ft high gigantic pillar. It will capture all that is going-on in this country. Not only I've got The Black Eye to oversee the whole nation but, I've also in my power form my own vigilante group. I call them, THE DARK WARRIORS. They're different vigilante groups compare to those we have here in the country. They are powerful. They are not just ordinary men. They are men with spiritual intellect. You have been warned. And from now on, other vigilante groups have been banned; only The Dark Warriors will be the vigilante to help assist the Police Force. They will be everywhere to watch over you. You don't have to worry or be scare or fear these men as long as you live by keeping to all the verdicts and commands I give to you today. This new verdicts and law is to help us increase greatly in a land flowing with milk and honey as we always wanted it to. It's time to wave goodbye to poverty. So I suggest that these commandments that I give to you today are to be upon your hearts. Impress them on your children. Talk about them when you sit at home and when you walk along the road, when you lie down and when you get up. Tie them as symbols on your hands and bind them on your foreheads. Write them on the doorframes of your houses and your gates. I'm only saying this because, whoever, and I mean whoever, whether you're rich or poor, that breaks or go against this rules will definitely, I repeat, definitely face punishment. **Do what is right and good. Love your neighbour as yourself.**

However, I will also like to put to your attention that, I, Solomon Gondi, is now the new President of Egitee. By the power given to me by the gods of the land, I have sworn myself in. And as the new President of Egitee, I promise to do everything in my power to make this land a better place for everyone and anyone to live. I'll first focus on five areas that are critical to the future of Africa and the entire developing world: security, opportunity, health, peace, and justice. I understand that there is no easy road to happiness. And I know it well that one can not act alone to achieve success. So therefore, we all must act together as a united people, for national reconciliation, for nation building, and for the birth of a new era. May the almighty God be with us all! God bless Egitee! Thank you," Solomon makes an inaugural address live on national TV. This was broadcast all over the world. Solomon's return became world news headlines.

BREAKING NEWS;

"Solomon returns with the power from darkness!"

"Solomon overthrew with the power of darkness!"

"Solomon is back but this time dangerous!"

"The good man has turned dark. Solomon invades his people with a new power he called 'power from the Dark-gods'."

"Who are The Dark-gods? Where did the power come from? Are the Dark-gods good or bad gods?," headline news all over the world news papers.

The whole world at this point in time is curious. Solomon seems to know exactly what he's doing. He's adjourns every question asked about the Dark-gods

164

that's been ask by world press. He instead concentrates more on putting his country in order. He as been giving blacklist names of people he needs to put to justice by the gods which is what he's dealing with first. They all will be beheaded in public. That's the punishment.

"These people you see here today have undo and over do. The gods are not happy with them. They will be use has an example of what it will be like when one breaks the rules of the Dark-gods," Solomon says to the people before those listed on the black list are being executed.

Those on the blacklist are; some in Gen. Fahruk's government that covers a high post but did nothing but mislead, some high offended criminals that kills and steal from innocent people which includes someone like Mary (Solomon's younger sister), and some high ranks people in the military that involve in crime. Even though Solomon had his younger sister among the people blacklisted, there's nothing he can really do than to carry on with the execution so that people can know how serious he is. *"May their souls rest in peace,"* Solomon's prayer to those executed.

The power Solomon claim he has is what he claimed he uses to create The Black Eye – a higher tech technology surveillance camera device that can see everything that man does on the land whether indoors or outdoors. And if anyone does break the new rules and regulation of the land, whether witness or no witness, he or she will be automatically picked and blacklisted with evidence proof of a video recording by The Black Eye. Then The Black Eye will automatically signal The Dark Warriors to make the capture. The Dark Warriors don't move or walk around. The only time they move is when someone has broken the law. From the minute one breaks the rules; The Dark Warriors will appear and take one away for sentence.

The Dark Warriors only appears to one that breaks the rules mentioned above. And the only sentence that comes with the rules mentioned above is to behead one. Other minor offences are dealt with by the police. The police also work alongside with The Black Eye. If The Black Eye do pick up any minor offences, it automatically send a signal to the police around where the accident as happen or is happening.

Now that everyone in the country knows what The Black Eye can do and the punishment one faces when one breaks the rules, the people of the country or on the land have no other choice than to act, behave, or do good. With the help of The Black Eye, the country is starting to be in order.

Within seven days, Solomon now President Solomon as make a huge dramatic turn around in his country. He's brought all the ex-offenders and present offenders to justice. People now have to intensively think before committing a crime. Solomon setup a new government constitution. He also sent all the armies back to barracks. The only time they're needed is when Solomon as the President of Egitee and as the new Chief Commander of the Army Staff pronounces state of emergency. Solomon made Mr Andrew (the President of the Committee for the Defence of Human Rights) his deputy. He also called for his uncle who lives in the US, Dr Ernest Gondi, his father's half younger brother (the ex-interim President of Egitee - the humble, honest, and naive man Gen. Fahruk and his father plan to put as the interim president before Gen. Fahruk overthrown) to come and be part of his new government. But Dr Ernest Gondi rejected the offer. Gen. Fahruk confronted and threatens Dr Ernest Gondi with a gun to leave the President seat. Since then Dr Ernest Gondi left the country and promise never to come back.

"I don't want any trouble, Solomon. I'm fine here. And besides, what is this power you say you have that is from the dark-gods? You're everywhere on the news; being portray as part of the dark. This is not what our family is about. We are from a good religious Christian background. What has gone into you? When did you start to believe in other gods? Why come this way to rescue your people? You know Christianity rejects indigenous beliefs? You must know where I stand by now. I am a true Christian and a true child of God; I do not get involve in voodooist. I wish you all the best. And I pray you see again the light of Christ. You're on your own now. Bye!," Dr Ernest Gondi on the phone to Solomon. And before Solomon could say anything back; he hangs-up the phone.

"Emmh but I'm not alone. Wait! Listen! Why won't they want to listen to me? I still believe in God. These are only just gods of the land. And, I'm also still a child of God. Or, am I not?" Solomon says after his uncle just hang-up on him.

Not only Solomon's uncle is not happy with him using power from the gods to rescue his people from poverty but also Pastor Nicolas.

"You are a disgrace to Christianity. How could you have gone to that extreme of giving your soul to the goddess? I didn't expect this from you. This is not the plan you discuss with me about. Your plan is to get the people closer to God, not closer to the gods. I thought you're a true Christian. You really have disappointed me. Now I know where you stand. I pray and ask for forgiveness for you from our lord Jesus Christ. May the almighty God be with you? Bye for now," Pastor Nicolas also speaks his mind to Solomon.

"Well is not my fault, what else do they want me to do," words from Solomon.

Instead of Solomon worrying about his uncle and

his pastor not happy with him of his come back to rescue his people, he instead concentrate more on his new post as the President of Egitee. *"My people needs me. And I, as a good one will remain good and serve my people,"* words and thought from Solomon.

Eight months after Solomon as overthrown the authority to become the President and since the inauguration of the Rule of the Dark-gods, things as began to change in Egitee. Everyone is doing what's right for them to do. No one wants to be executed. Everyone has no other choice than to follow the rules. The power is real. People could see and feel the power. The Black Eye and The Dark Warriors says it all. Such power has never been use this way before. Some might have had similar power but never thought of using it this way. King Yemojaja and Major General Grunitzky Agaja are example of those that have been given or proclaim that the gods of the land has given them such power. So it's what people have heard before. But what's new are; The Black Eye, The Dark Warriors, and The rules of the Dark-gods one must follow. Nothing following faith really has change. People still have the choice to choose their faith/belief. Sacrifices are still made to the gods but this time only to honour and pay respect to the gods and it must go through the Dark-gods. Whether one is a Muslim, Christian, or Indigenous believer, one must still follow the rules of the Dark-gods Solomon has set down, which doesn't really affect the Muslims and the Christians because, some of these rules one will find in the Bible and in the Qu'ran. But the rules actually affected some of the indigenous believers that go to the extreme of using human as scarifies to console their gods. 'You shall not murder' is the rule, no matter what faith or religion one follows. It's also now forbidden for any spiritual herbalist (native doctor) to help conjure any spiritual rituals that involves bad/wrong doing or that breaks the rules to the people. Also, all spiritual ritual acts have been banned to be performed in public by Solomon. People now can move freely day and night anywhere and everywhere in Egitee.

"BEWARE, THE GODS ARE WATCHING," words on poster and billboard all around the country.

Not only scary and deep message above is posted on walls and billboards, but also honest messages like; *"LOVE YOUR NEIGHBOUR AS YOURSELF. DO WHAT IS RIGHT AND GOOD. DO TO OTHERS WHAT YOU WOULD HAVE THEM DO TO YOU,"* are all also posted all around the country. It's all Solomon's idea to post these messages all around the country. Solomon intention is to genuinely change his people to be good to one another at all times. He truly believes being good to one another is really the 'key factor' to live a good life.

"Just like my favourite writer will always say, **'Being good to one another is the key factor of a good life',"** words from Solomon.

Ever since Solomon's return, Egitee is shaping up good. But something remains vague. How did Solomon come about this power he claims he has? Where did he go for forty days and forty nights before he came back out not alone but with power from the gods of the land? Being a Christian, why did he end up going to the goddess? And why is he now trying to portray the power from the gods he used to believe as bad now as good? There's something fuzzy going on. Solomon has this entire question to answer to the world. Although, since Solomon took-over and the inauguration of the rule of the Dark-gods, Egitee is gradually changing from bad to good. There is now PEACE in the county. There is no such thing as CRIME so far. People on the land now fears to commit crime or do wrong because, they know if they do, they will definitely face punishment.

However, so far for Solomon, all is going according to PLAN. After sixteen months in power, he's now ready to face the world. He calls for world Press conference. He's ready to be interviewed. He's joined by a senior UK high representative journalist - JIMMY WHITE - at the State House in the capital - Freeland.

"Good morning ladies and gentlemen. My name is Jimmy White. I'm joined here today in the presidential house – The State House - in the capital of Egitee, Freeland. With the man, I will like to say, right now, everyone wants to hear speak. Ladies and gentlemen, he is the new President of Egitee, President Solomon. Good morning Mr. President. It's good to be here with you," Jimmy starts off the discussion.

"Thank you and good morning to you too," Solomon replies.

"First of all, Mr. President; what happened on the night of the campaign? You were gone missing. And sorry to mention, your family were also killed on the same night. What really happened? Please take us through," Jimmy asks his first question.

"Emmh well, if everybody wants to know what really happened, I will tell them. I've got nothing to hide. I'm innocent. First of all, I would like to tell the people the plan I had for Egitee. As you all know this country was getting out of hand. It was just time someone had to do something. No one was ready to step-up to do something or maybe they were scared. But what people don't understand is; it better to die fighting for good than die living in pain and struggle. You might as well don't live. I understand the pain and struggle my people were going through. They had nothing left to hold-on to than HOPE. This is what I

170

*tried to give to them or encourage them not to give-up –
hope. It's good to have hope. Hopelessness leads to
loneliness in the mind. When you don't have hope, you
have nothing. And when you're lonely and have
nothing, you're sad and depress, which isn't good. I'm
a man that has hope. I believe all will get better. I
believe no matter what circumstances or bad times the
country might be facing will soon one day come to past.
Hope and faith is what I had. It's what I could give to
the people then. So I came-up with my own personal
plan. I was sick and tired. I couldn't continue living in
pain. I mean, annoyingly and frustrating, we live on a
land that is blessed with natural resources. Lands that
don't even have half of what we got are doing
incredibly well. But because of some stupid, greedy and
irresponsible people, the country was frustrated with
poverty. I couldn't take seeing my people living like
this; I had to come up with a plan, "* Solomon explains.

"So what was your plan then?" Jimmy asks.

*"Emmh well, my plan first was to use good to get
good, you know, trying to be... should I say, diplomatic.
You know, trying to solve the matter without putting up
a fight. My belief truly was maybe the people including
the leaders are not really truly genuinely good people.
If people are truly genuinely good, then all will be
good, I believe."*

"Absolutely, " Jimmy says nodding his head.

*"I mean, I thought about things. I thought about
things I could do being the Minister of Information at
that time to change the people. To give good
information and good massages to the people was my
idea, which I think is a good idea. Faith was the first
thing that came to my mind. I believe if people have
good faith, they will do good things and do things right.
Then I try to invite Pastor Nicolas James. Luckily for
me, Pastor Nicolas already had a plan of visiting the*

country. He already got a good message to give to the people, which was the Holy Crusade. And apart from the Holy Crusade, I also plan for an interview with Pastor Nicolas live on TV because many times Pastor Nicolas visited the country; his preaching was never shown on TV. So I thought this time not only his preaching will be shown live on TV but also I personally will have a personal discussion live on TV with Pastor Nicolas. It was something I could do under my power. I was trying to use Pastor Nicolas James being a true man of God to help inform or should I rather say, preach or talk good sense to the people and also the leaders. You never know, Pastor Nicolas might have the good power or good massage to help change the people for good. And apart from the good message Pastor Nicolas might have to change the people for good, I also thought of something else that could help change the people for better - education. Don't get me wrong, Pastor Nicolas preaching was educating but just thought the people needs more. Getting educated is never too much. Education is important. If the people know what's good and their right, they will know how to fight and stand for their right and goodness. So I arrange for a campaign to educate the people on corruption and how to live in peace. Which I know it will also be a campaign against the Agaja's regime. And I will like to use this opportunity, once again, to thank the international TV broadcasters that supported the campaign, thank you. Now, me coming to mention, I also had a plan B," Solomon says.

"Plan B," Jimmy repeats.

"Yes plan B," Solomon repeats.

"So all what you've just mentioned was plan A?" Jimmy asks.

"Yes, plan A. My plan B was something different. I would never have wished to go for plan B. It's the idea

of using bad for good," Solomon replies.

"Bad for good," Jimmy repeats.

"Yes, bad for good. The title of my talk show summarise it all. After coming up with a plan, I decided to name the talk show 'Good4Good Bad4Good' to try and make certain people have a clue of what my plan is. But I guess they didn't or maybe they think they can always get away doing bad and living good, not knowing life isn't always like that. Anyway, my plan was if nothing really was changing me trying to use good to get good, then I think I'm left with no other choice than to use bad...

"Bad!" Jimmy says.

Yes bad. I was desperate. Me using bad will be me fighting for good and ready to die for good because, I just couldn't continue living in sorrow. It starts to get really terrifying. I was going to fight whichever way I could or can, whether physically or spiritually. I was ready. And to really clear myself and to be honest with everyone, my plan wasn't to go to the gods to ask for power. I believe more in the almighty God. I believe He's the provider, controller, and master of all. God is good. And whatever that goes against the will of God is what I condemn. It was by accident or should I say, by coincidence I end-up with the gods," Solomon explains.

"Emmh, am sorry Mr. President, before you go into all of that, can you please first tell us what really happened on the day of the campaign?" Jimmy asks.

"Well, on the day of the campaign evening, I receive a phone call from an anonymous lady who called me to inform me of my family in danger. I have no other choice than to put aside whatever I was doing that night and to go rescue my family out of danger. I told a close friend of mine, Mr Andrew, now my deputy, that I will be coming back soon before I left the campaign to

173

go rescue my family," Solomon explains.

"Why didn't you call the police? I mean, you know what to do," Jimmy asks and says.

"Police! That wouldn't be a good idea at that point in time. They were the enemies. The police and the army then, including the Cult boyz are all in one gang. Remember they work for General Fahruk. He's the one behind everything," Solomon says.

"How do you know?" Jimmy asks.

"Of course I know this things, I'm not a kid you know. I know what this man is capable of doing. He wants me dead. Eventually, when I got to the house I kept my family, remember it was heavily raining, and on my way was lot of fire and smoke which I still manage to make sure I make it to the house. I move my family to this house very early that morning before I came for the campaign, believing it's a safer place for me to put my family during the period of the campaign knowing what Gen. Fahruk can do. So when I was told my family was in danger, I didn't hesitate. I immediately run for their rescue. Getting to the house, the house was already on fire. I tried my best to get through the back and front door but maybe because I came too late, there was no way for me to break into the house. I watch my family burns down. There was nothing I could do. The two security men I hired to look after my family were both beheaded and their heads was hanged onto the entrant gate of the house. I start to shout out the names of my wife and my two beautiful daughters even though I didn't want any of the Cult Boyz to see me or hear me, but they did. I heard them coming so I hid myself somewhere I can't remember. But I remember grabbing a long big stick and using it to hit one of the Cult Boyz, it was two of them. Then I started to run deep down into the dark forest. I saw many of them came out from nowhere running and

chasing after me. I was so scared. I said my last prayers. I actually thought I was going to die that night. And the next minute I ran past an enormous tree which 'Beware of the gods' was written on it in white, I think I heard a thunder strike and from then on, I know nothing," Solomon explains.

"An enormous tree and beware of the gods was written on it in white? What kind of tree is it? And did you intentionally run past this tree because you saw words like 'beware of the gods' written on it? Or maybe it was just the only way you could or can run pass," Jimmy asks.

"No! And then again I will say yes. Yes because it the only way I could possibly run through. And no, it wasn't my intention to run past the tree. I don't know what kind of tree it is but, I did see the sign from far and for some reasons, my heart told me to keep running toward there," Solomon replies.

"So what happened after the final thunder stroke?" Jimmy asks.

"I fell into a very big and deep dark hole. I roll over and roll over right to the bottom of the dark hole. I didn't know what happen to me. I must have been too tired. I fell asleep. Me waking-up, I saw an old woman, I mean, very old. She said she was three hundred years old," Solomon explains

"Three hundred years old," Jimmy repeats, surprised.

"Yes, three hundred years old, she said. She also said she's been living in the dark hole for over two hundred years. I started to get panic when I heard that. I didn't know where I was. I was confused but the old woman told me not to worry that the gods of the land are willing to help me. 'The gods of the land?,' I said. 'Yes,' the old woman replied. I try to explain to the old woman that being a Christian I don't believe in such

and don't want to get involve with the dark. The old woman laughs and then said to me in my language, 'you know nothing my son, that's not the problem. The problem is your people needs help and you are the chosen one this time to rescue your people'. I didn't understand what she meant by that. I said to her back in my language, 'if it's something that's against God's judgment and to do with the dark isn't what I would like to be part of'. The old woman then asks me, 'dark as in?' I replied, 'dark as-in evil'. She laughs. She then said, 'my son, evil belongs to man. Is not what we do. The King Sky God is our heavenly Father. All you need to do is believe'. And she gave me a choice: To go back and get killed by Gen. Fahruk. Or go back with a special power to rescue my people. I didn't know what to do. I didn't want to go back without a fight. After all the good efforts I have put to try and put the country in order, going back without any sort of protection against Gen. Fahruk fears me, knowing he definitely wants me killed. So I deeply thought about what to do. And this is me here today as the new President of Egitee. And I have swore with the Bible to serve the nation right," Solomon explains.

"So you still believe in the Bible then?" Jimmy asks.

"Oh yes I do," Solomon sincerely replies.

"Ok. That was a very touching moment indeed. So what did the gods of the land give to you? What sort of power was given to you to rescue your people? And why did you call them The Dark-gods," Jimmy asks.

"Power from God, I believe. I mean, after a deeply thought before making a decision to accept the power, the old woman did a small rite for me before I met the gods. But then again, meeting the gods was through my dream. After the rituals, I fell asleep for three days. In my dream, what I understand to be my meeting with the

176

gods, I dreamt I was in a very dark place where I couldn't see a thing. Then I heard a voice called my name three times, Solomon! Solomon! Solomon! I was scared, panicking. Then I try to trace where the voice was coming from. Getting to trace where the voice was coming from and to see who was calling me, I found myself out on top of a mountain. It was like I walked out of a mountain to come on top of the mountain. Then I saw what I would like to call three huge tall human-like shadow ghostly images, wrapped round in black robes touching from the ground all the way up to the sky. One of these three huge tall shadows, the one in the middle, the tallest one, called my name again three times and then said to me in my language 'you have been given a special power'. It's power from the Almighty. It's a blessing. Go and do whatever it is you want to do. We are right behind you. How and what you use it for is completely up to you. Go now and save your fellow people. You have men waiting for you at the bottom of the mountain'. And that was it really. To me it was like I spent four days in the dark forest, but when I came out, people said I was gone away for forty days and forty nights. Which I have no idea how," Solomon explains.

"So is it this same power you use to create The Black Eye?" Jimmy asks.

"Emmh Kind of," Solomon answered.

"A surveillance camera that can see everywhere and everything that happens on this land even though it's not attached or connected to any physical resources anywhere around the country? I mean, it just this one camera outside the State House that will capture all that is happening and capture anyone that breaks the rules. And is the evidence this one camera gives, you will use to make judgment. Also, mentioning the rules, whose rules were they? And tell us how you come about

making this one camera?" Jimmy says and asks more questions.

"Emm well, first of all, the rules are my rules. Some of it I took from the Bible, and some of it is what I believe will stop crime," Solomon says.

"Good rules I must say," Jimmy says.

"Thank you. And emmh, what can I really say about The Black Eye? It just a new higher tech technology device I created, that's all," Solomon says.

"A new higher tech technology device... What do you mean by that? I mean, you just said the gods of the land gave you power to do whatever you want to do. Are you now saying the gods also gives power to make higher tech technology devices like The Black Eye? I mean, this is my first time of hearing one surveillance camera that can capture everything that is happening indoors and outdoors all around the country without any form of physical resources attach or working along side with it. It's just this one camera working all by itself and nothing else controlling it. It must truly indeed be a new higher tech technology device. Mr. President, enlighten us please," Jimmy says, baffled.

"Well, well, well, I really do not know what to say. It was all my idea but also believe it was with the power I manage to create a surveillance camera that will watch over the country. There's nothing wrong with that, is there?" Solomon says and asks.

"No, no, no, not at all. I was only curious because you haven't actually tell us what this power is and who the Dark-gods are? And if it power believe to come from an unknown source, don't you think it might back fire someday? And I understand there's always a payback whenever the gods do one a favour, is that also true?" Jimmy replies and asks.

"Emmh yes, something always has to go for something. I ask the old woman about this and she said

the gods covers the lost of my family as the payback,"
Solomon says.

"That isn't very nice, is it?" Jimmy says.

*"Yes you're right but that's just the way things go.
And the power, I told you its power from the gods. Or
what else do you want me to say to you? I know what
your problem is but its ok. And let me now tell you what
I really think of technology because you're complaining
and wondering how I come about making The Black
Eye. You see, Africa or should I say Africans have no
idea or knows nothing about the new age technology.
Still we're not complaining even though no one is
teaching or giving us the secret behind it. The nature of
technology has change dramatically in the past
hundred years. Really, the very idea of technology as
we now imagine is pretty much new. To my
understanding, technology was mainly the territory of
craftsmen who passed their knowledge down from
generation to generation, gradually improving designs,
and adding new techniques and materials. But
nowadays, technology had become a large-scale
enterprise that depended on large stores of knowledge
and expertise, too much for any one person to master.
Complex network of interdependent technologies are
developed, such as the suite of technologies for the
automobile. Then your government began to play a
larger role in determining technology through
technological policies and regulations. In the early
nineteenth century, technology referred simply to the
practical arts used to create physical products,
everything from wagon wheels and cotton cloth to
telephones and steam engines. Technology comes from
the Greek – technologia, which is a combination of
'techne' meaning 'craft', and logia, meaning 'saying'.
But nowadays, as the nature of technology changed, it
meaning became vague, leaving room for*

misconceptions that sometimes led to questionable conclusions. I personally believe technology change as somehow disconnected from human influence. Recent technology seems to appear out of the blue. If one could view technology as being outside human control, then these thoughts may have never come up. Think about it. Let me don't say much about technology. Whichever way you want to perceive my power is completely up to you. Power is power. As a leader, you need to have some sort of power to control the people. And to be a leader, you need to have the physical and most especially mental strength to control a nation. Every government got their own way, or should I instead say – system – to run their country. They create a system that will get the people under their control. The western government got powerful strong technology system to put things in order. No one knows how it operates. They use all the power they can to get the nation under control. Maybe my idea is also a system or a way that works for my people. Anyway, let me not go too far on that. I named the gods The Dark-gods because everywhere was dark and they look dark. Also, not to have mention, but if God created me in His own image and likeness, and my skin happens to turn-out dark, therefore I should presume my God to be dark. The word dark doesn't have to mean 'evil'. It's only a colour. I'm not the first to claim to have or given this kind of power but maybe the first to use it this way. I am a good person and I'll use whatever that's in my power to do good. People across the ocean shouldn't be worried. It's all for the greater good. Anyway, technology is technology. The Black Eye I created is also through the influence of technology. Coming back from the dark forest, I thought of something technical that I can do to stop crime. I thought of a surveillance camera that can act as a 'Watch Dog' or 'Crime

*Watch'. So I came up with the idea 'Black Eye'. And to be honest with you, I myself wouldn't really say it power from the gods because, come to think of it now, it all happened like a dream to me but the fact is, when I came out of this dream, I found out that I got this special power, or should I say, got the 'genius mind' or 'genius idea' to do incredible things. Or should I just call it 'magic'. Ha-ha. Anyway, what's most important is, how the power is been use, or the person behind the power. I have sworn never to use the power to go against the will of good. I mean, if am going to be questioned on how I came-up with something incredible like The Black Eye, then those behind technology also need to be confronted because there're some incredible things technology these days can do. A small technical device can wipe-out a whole nation. What do you say to that? Whether it's all man made or not, some of this things do magical things but it all seen as technology, which am not disputing. The man behind technology can also decide to use it to do bad or good. Don't you think we Africans also need to worry about that? But no, the man is from the wests, which are portrayed to be good people, which is good. But now is **the time for us Africans to be seen as good ones too**. Don't you think? Anyway, your time is up. I'm sorry I wouldn't be answering anymore of your questions,"* Solomon speaks his honest mind and decided to stop talking and ends the discussion.

"Well if you say so Mr. President. Thank you for your time. It's a pleasure meeting you," Jimmy says.

"Thank you. It's a pleasure meeting you too," Solomon replies.

"Well, that is it for today. Hope you all have come to conclusion on what you think of President Solomon. I'm Jimmy White. Have a good day," Jimmy ends the conference with Solomon.

Chapter Twelve

The War

After four years or first term, Solomon still continues to be the president of Egitee. No one else seems to fit or has the power/mind/potential to continue what Solomon had done so far to Egitee. In four years, he's turn Egitee Land from being frustrated with poverty, corruption, and injustice to crime free and land full of peace. He's been portrayed as SAVIOUR by his people. There's no one the people could choose or appoint to be their new leader apart from Solomon. To them; he's doing very well. So it seems Solomon will remain as the president for at least another four more years. And by the way, Solomon himself is not looking ready to give-up the president seat.

"I still got a lot to do. The only time I would leave this seat or hand over the power is when we see or find someone genuine to lead the country. But for now, I, Solomon Gondi remains the president," parts of statement made by Solomon going for another term.

It's obvious that many more years to come, Solomon will continue to lead Egitee.

In six years Solomon in power, Egitee classified as undeveloped country as grown to be classify as developing country. And now with the strong oil wealth, Egitee normally rank as one of the poorest countries in the world has been awarded as 'Most Promising West African Country (MPWAC) to be classify as RICH'. The percentage of the population living in poverty has tremendously reduced from 80% to 5%. Corruption is no more tolerated in Egitee. The recent award given to Egitee is no more awards like; the Most Corrupt Country in the World (MCCW), but awards like; the Most Peaceful Land in the World (MPLW). Egitee is no longer cast as BAD internationally. Oil has now proven to be only a blessing and not a curse. And with the help and full power assistant from the government in Egitee, people with ideas and creativity have come together and produce technical devices and machines like; computers, military aircraft, automobiles, motorbikes, and even digital cameras. All made from scratch in Egitee.

Things have really changed in Egitee. Egitee has change from a place one is advice not to visit, to a place to visit. Egitee tourist attraction is nowadays associated with thrilling adventures, exotic natural beauty, and wild safaris. And being close to the Atlantic, Egitee is blessed with beautiful beaches. Not only the beaches are very beautiful but also swimming is exceptionally safe from hygienic point of view. Tests conducted by the Council for Scientific and Industrial Research proved that the sea water of Egitee's beaches is amongst the cleanest in the world. It's also protected by shark nets.

Egitee from nowhere has become huge tourist attraction which has also helps boost the country's economy. The country nowadays is busy full of visitors from all over the world. Sunshine all year means that outdoor lifestyle nowadays in Egitee is full of style and less of danger. No more daily experiences like - killing, kidnapping, gang rape, and armed-robbery but dozens of adventures orientated options to choose from like - diving with great white sharks, climbing up to the highest scale mountain peak, and many more activities such as golfing tours, horseback and camel safaris, big game fishing, hot ballooning, helicopter rides and river rafting. 'The Black Eye' is also an exciting object to see - the one camera that sees everything. Apparently, to make people move freely, The Black Eye only picks up crime activities. Anything else besides crime is purely private and confidential. So people can move freely and have fun to their fullest and enjoy life. And is not only The Black Eye that attracts the tourists, eye-catching natural wonders like The Dark Warriors (heavily built men standing at one point with no top-on, muscles out) also fascinatingly attracts the female tourists. Furthermore, there are also wide ranges of cultural and historical landmarks people can visit, like; monuments, museum, and pyramids that bear testimony to the indigenous and the ancient legacy of Africa along with its colonial past. Egitee presently is definitely a place to visit.

With all the good effort Solomon has put-in to change his country for good in the period of six years, he received a Nobel price award. He's also become the World Most Famous President (WMFP) due to the unexplainable power he claimed he obtained from the gods of the land which he calls 'The Dark-gods'. Westernise countries like the United States and United Kingdom have to give credit to Solomon for the huge turn-around he brought to his country.

On the whole, it's not everyone that has been giving praises or happy with Solomon, some African pastors still criticise Solomon. *"He's one not to trust. He's got power from the dark. It's power from evil. It's not power form Jesus. Be careful of this man called Solomon Gondi. Something bad is yet to happen,"* words, preaches, and statement made by some African pastors.

However, apart from people from all over the world visiting Egitee, Solomon has also been travelling visiting other countries. He's been attending talk shows. The most recent one will be the one with U.S famous and favourite award wining TV talk show of the year 2008; The Talk4Good Talk Talk Show by LADY YOUNG, which at this moment, is live on TV.

"Good evening boys and girls, old and young, man and woman, ladies and gentlemen. Welcome to your TV favourite talk show - Talk4Good Talk Talk Show. The only TV show that talks for good... If you know wot I mean? My name remains Lady Young, and my special guess today is one of the most famous and powerful president in the world today...," Lady Young starts-off the show.

"And I must warn you guys... He's got Voodoo powers," she whispers to the studio audience and then makes a scary face.

"Ha-ha-ha! Ha-ha-ha! Ha-ha-ha!," the studio audience laughs.

"I'm sure you guys already know who that is! Ladies and gentlemen, man and woman, boys and girls, put you hands together for President Solomon!" Lady Young welcomes Solomon.

Applause - the studio audience.

An automatic double doors spread open, it Solomon. He gently walks-up to Lady Young, gave her hug and kisses, while the audience keep cheering and clapping.

"Yes! Yes! Yes! Take a sit, Mr. President. I finally got to meet you. You must be a very busy man. I mean, with all the powers and responsibility in your hands, you must be a very busy man indeed. First of all, I would like to say a very big thank you for having the time to attend my show. Thank you," Lady Young shows some appreciation.

"You're very much welcome," Solomon replies.

"Emmh now, Mr. President. How are you and how are you doing?" Young asks.

"I'm very well and good, thank you," Solomon replies.

"Good. How was your trip flying down here to the United States?" Young sincerely asks.

"Emmh... was boring," Solomon answered.

"Boring?" Young repeats.

"Yes, boring. I don't really like travelling. It's not part of my hobbies. But I guess being a president, you have to travel a lot which am trying to get use to," Solomon says.

"You don't like travelling? That's strange," Young says.

"Emmh... its not that I don't like travelling to see what the other side of the world looks like. I think is just the time one spent while travelling is what I can't stand. It just gets boring. I mean, really boring. If a man can come-up with a teleporting machine that can take a man travel, then I guess I will really enjoy travelling," Solomon says.

"Oh yeah, that will be a good idea. That will make travelling a very easy thing to do. But the sad news is, no man has come-up with that idea yet, and people wanna travel. We can't wait for a man to invent a teleporting machine to take us travel before we travel. The plane is good and fast enough. We don't mind spending the time," Lady Young says and then says to the audience, *"Isn't that so people?"*

"Yeeeeeaah!!!," the studio audience shouts-out.

"You see, we don't mind to spend the time. And am sure the people here in the studio can't wait to have a free ticket to travel to Egitee. They're addict when it comes to travelling. They will travel to anywhere. If by chance people can travel to Hell and come back, no matter how long it might take them, trust me Mr.

President, there will be some that wouldn't mind to go see waz popping, if you know wot I mean," Young says and then makes a funny face.

"Ha-ha-ha! Ha-ha-ha! Ha-ha-ha!," studio audience including Solomon laughs out load.

"You know, just to go have a look before they die. So they can really decide on where to go, Heaven or Hell? You never know, Hell could be the place popping because nowadays, we just don't know," Young says.

"Well, I wouldn't advice anyone to go to Hell. I'll give everyone in here today free tickets including accommodation expenses to Egitee," Solomon says.

"Yeeeeeaah!!!," the live studio audience cheered.

"Egitee looks nothing close to hell but close to paradise. Maybe from there people can decide on where to go. Egitee six years ago was hell or close to hell. And I don't think it's a place anyone would want to go," Solomon says.

"Awww.... That's very nice of you Mr. President, thank you," Young shows some appreciation.

"That's alright, thank God," Solomon says.

"A round of applause for President Solomon, please," Young says to the live studio audience.

Applause - the studio audience.

"Thank you. That's so very nice of you," Young again thanks Solomon.

"Thank God," Solomon says.

"Okay. Now that you mention God, my first question would be; who do you believe God is? Or what is your believe about God," Young asks her first question.

"Thank you, I like that question. To me, I believe **God is good**. *One trying to be good at all time is what I believe or see as putting God first, or doing Gods' will. I believe the story about God is to get people to do good and to be good people. You see, I'm from a very religious Christian family background. My grandfather*

187

owns a church. I was brought up in the church. Ever since I was a little boy, I have always been a good son and always wanted to do what's right and good. My late father believes in me," Solomon explains.

"What about your mum? Is she still alive?" Young asks.

"No, she died of cancer," Solomon replies.

"Awwww… I'm so sorry to hear that," Young says and put on a sad face.

"It's alright. But there's a dramatic story that comes with it," Solomon says.

"Really? What happened?" Young asks.

"What happened? Emmh, at first when my mum felt really ill, the first hospital my dad took her has no clue of what was wrong with her. So my dad decided to take her to a pastor that claims he has power to heal the sick. Taking my mum to this pastor, he told my dad he knows the problem of my mums' sickness is to do with my aunt - my mum's elder sister. Apparently she's a witch. And apparently she's the one that spells the sickness on my mum, so the pastor says. And for some reasons my father strongly believe in what the pastor said. I was present when the pastor was telling my dad about my aunt being a witch and the cause of my mums' sickness. I was confused. I couldn't just believe my aunt to be a witch and could do such to my mum. But anyway, after seven days prayer by this pastor, there was still no sign of healing. And you know in Africa, when a pastor can't solve a problem, there is always an alternative - The Witchdoctor," Solomon explains.

"Oh yeah, the Witch Doctor Who," Young says with a funny face.

"Ha-ha-ha! Ha-ha-ha! Ha-ha-ha!," the studio audience laughs.

"Oh yes the Witch Doctor Who indeed. Or you may

also want to call them - psychics. Because these people also some how claim they can read, predict, check or see into someone's life. Claiming they have mental powers which cannot be explained by natural laws; relating to the mind," Solomon explains.

"Just like what you have," Young says and winks at Solomon.

"Ha-ha-ha! Something like-that. But I don't know how to read into someone's life. And coming to think of it now, its funny how we call such people witchdoctors and over here they're seen as psychics. Hmm... Have just learnt something new today but anyway, let us continue. As I was saying, the witchdoctor, after looking or should I say; reading into my mum's life, he also said the same thing the pastor said to my father that, 'my mum's elder sister spells the sickness on her'. The witchdoctor also claims to have the cure for such sickness, that we should leave my mum with him for another seven days, which we did. And after seven days my mum indeed got better. Fourteen days later, my aunt was stone to death by some local communist claiming to be Christians and fighting against witchcraft," Solomon says.

"Uh, that's unfair, poor lady," Young says.

"Exactly wot I was thinking too. And before she was stone to death by this people, she was forced by torture to confess to be a witch, which I find ridiculously dreadful. Apart from the sad story of my aunt, you will read sad news about how African churches denounce children as witches," Solomon says.

"Noooo... that's not right!" Young says.

"How sad can it get? African pastors accuse thousands of children, leading to torture or death. There was a story I read about a nine years old boy lay on a bloodstained hospital sheet, crawling with ants, staring blindly at the wall. His family Pastor accused

him of being a witch, and his father then tried to force acid down his throat as an exorcism. After so much torture, the boy barely had strength left to whisper the name of the church that had denounced him. A month later, he died," Solomon says.

"Awww... Poor boy. That's a very sad story," Young says.

"Very sad indeed," Solomon added.

"Did that happen in Egitee?" Young asks.

"Never! Not in my regime. Now in Egitee, anyone, maybe you're a witchdoctor, a witch, a wizard, or a pastor that fights over witchcrafts, anyone that breaks the rules will be picked by The Black Eye, captured by The Dark Warriors, and will be punish. No hidden space for wickedness," Solomon confidently answered.

"Wow! I think we need the same tactics here in the U.S. Some people are too arrogant and wicked. Maybe you should install one Black Eye for us," Young says and then winks at Solomon.

"Ha-ha-ha! Install one Black Eye for you? You're funny. Well, your leaders can always put a request for it. And am sure we can always come out with a good deal," Solomon says and winks back.

"I'm sure you guys can," Young says and again winks at Solomon.

"Ha-ha-ha-ha! You're very funny. Anyway, do you then know what later happened to my mum after she was healed by the witchdoctor?" Solomon says.

"Oh yeah, what happened?," Young asks.

"My mum became sick again of the same sickness two months later. But luckily and unfortunately, my dad's younger brother who's a doctor, who at that time just came from abroad, did a medical check on my mum. He found out she had cancer and my mum should have been treated for cancer the first time we took her to the hospital. And before my uncle could

treat my mum, the cancer has already spread. It has been left too late to be treated," Solomon explains.

"So what did the witchdoctor do then?" Young asks.

"Good question. After my mum got better after seeing the witchdoctor, my dad being a Christian didn't really want to take my mum back to the witchdoctor because, I think we were meant to take my mum back after every fourteen days, but my dad instead choose to believe the pastor's prayer on my mum is what later cured my mum. Anyway, my mum later-on died of cancer, which was really sad. She could have been treated on time but instead people worry about what they shouldn't worry about. They instead waste their time thinking my mums' sickness is to do with witchcraft. Sad isn't it?" Solomon says.

"Oh yeah, very sad indeed," Young says and then put on a sad face.

"As a little kid, I didn't just want to believe in witchcraft, or anyone could make a spell on someone. I believe God can see everything going on, just as we were taught in church. So if anybody is doing anything bad, God is surely looking down at them," Solomon says.

"Oh yes, God is definitely watching all ya bad boys doing bad in the hood," Young says pointing at the live camera.

"Ha-ha-ha! He's definitely watching all of ya!" Solomon says also pointing at the live camera trying to be funny impersonating Lady Young.

The studio audience laughs, *"Ha-ha-ha! Ha-ha-ha! Ha-ha-ha!"*

Solomon continue, *"Before my mum past away, even though she was a Christian, she most of the time visits the witchdoctor to ask for protection over evil and wicked ones. She for some reasons believe some*

191

*people are evil and after her. She also encourages me
to believe in the witchdoctor, and always tell me to be
very careful. But as a child growing up in church, my
belief is not to have any reasons to go to the
witchdoctor, which I always try to make clear to my
mum. But my mum claiming to be a Christian and also
goes to church always tell me, 'what do you know you
this boy, what do you know?' I always wondered why
my mum says this to me. As a Christian family, we're
not meant to go to the witchdoctor but my mum always
end up running back to the witch doctor for protection
against evil ones. My mum is definitely not a bad
woman, or a witch,"* Solomon express.

"How old were you then when you lost your mum?"
Young asks.

*"I was only eleven. And growing up in church, they
make us believed there is an evil power somewhere out
there, which is believed to be power from the devil.
They make us believed anything that got nothing to do
with Jesus, is evil. And those days, as a little boy, the
question I ask myself is, 'why can't God just take the
power off the evil, or destroy the devil?' But then again
from young age, I understood God works in mysterious
ways. You have to really understand Him, or personally
get to know Him, I believe, before you see or notice His
blessings. And as a child, it's what I decided to
concentrate on - personally getting to know God. And
now fifty-one years of my life, I've got to learn and
understand more on the ancient legacy of Africa gods,
my tradition and my culture, which have made me come
to conclusion, understand, and get to know more about
the almighty God better,"* Solomon explains.

*"So what about the gods, what do you think of
them?"* Young asks.

*"To be honest with you, I would like to think of them
as Africa warriors with special powers,"* Solomon says

smiling.

"*Ha-ha-ha-ha! Africa warriors with special powers indeed,*" Young says also laughing.

"*I'm only joking. I will like to think of them as God's descendant. That's what the story says about them anyway. Also, the story of the gods comes from how we Africans believe earth was created, or how life started. But then again, this story was condemned and portray as wrong. Making us believe there should be only one story, and there is only one God, which I now kind of disagree. I believe there is only one God but, there are many different stories about God. I believe God as appear to us all differently. And why that is? Only God can answer to that. We all are different people from different cultures and backgrounds. We all have our own different way of life. Which should be normal, and which makes life much more interesting. I mean, we all can't act the same or be the same, can we?*" Solomon says.

"*Definitely not. I am very different from you, Mr. President. You don't even like to travel. I loooove travelling. Ha-ha-ha-ha,*" Young says with a girly attitude and laughs.

"*Oh yes of course, we are not the same. What am trying to say is that, it could possibly be that maybe God himself was the one that sent all these various leaders, prophets, or gods to these various roots or backgrounds to show, preach or prophesise His good wisdom and power. I remember my pastor telling me that, the Bible tells us that 'God has revealed Himself to every one of us in various ways.' If you notice, most religion preaches about one thing - GOOD,*" Solomon says.

"*Do they?*" Young says.

"*I think so… I mean, what I'm trying to say is that; why condemn region that preaches about good and* *against wrong doing? It will never be possible for us all to follow one religion, never, no matter how good a religion might portray itself. But **it could be possible for us all to be good people in our own ways.** I personally believe there's good in us all,"* Solomon says.

"That's right. But I also personally believe there is evil in us all too," Young added.

"Absolutely yes, you're right. Or you can say, 'there's God in us all, and there's also devil in us all,'" Solomon added.

"That's right Mr. President, that sound much better," Young says nodding her head.

*"I also personally believe the mind is open to good and evil. That's when religion comes-in; to entice people to follow the good side of their mind, which is possibly the best way to get people to be good. You see, in most cultures you will find a religion, or some sort of belief. Culture in other words, is a way of life, background, belief, and tradition of people. So I presume someone from one particular culture, or that follows one particular culture should follow the belief that comes with that culture. I believe most religion is set-up or formed from the belief of a particular culture or set of people. We're all different kinds of human beings. We should have different beliefs. It's part of life. It's part of us. It's normal. It's what we notice about life. We all are meant to be proud of our cultures, so as religion, unless one wants to condemn his or her own root to follow another man's root. There is nothing wrong in us sharing and learning from one another cultures and beliefs. But what I'm against is, some people trying to make one abandon one for another. It's wrong. **We're meant to learn from each other and not go against each other.** It's annoying and disrespectful for one man to condemn another man's*

belief. That's why you see or hear about religion crisis happening everywhere around the world. I mean, from my own point of view, a man that truly has the wisdom of God should have the understanding that God has come to us in various ways and in various forms. The people that claim to be religious people are the ones to lay good examples on how to be good people. Not the ones showing people on how to go against one another. I mean; in the Bible, it says, 'love your neighbour as yourself', not discriminate and condemn. Discriminate only generate hate and separate people. Your neighbour doesn't have to be like you, or follow the same religion as you before you show them love, or what's good. As long as they're good people, I do not see what the problem is. I personally believe no matter what religion or belief one follows, we're still all one under God," Solomon expresses his feelings on religion.

"Oh yeah, I believe so too," Young says nodding her head.

"Sometimes I think religion is set up to be; who has the most followers? Whose religion or culture is the best? Who is the closest to God? It's like there is a competition going-on. What I'm trying to say is; no one has the right to condemn other people's beliefs, culture, or religion. Sometimes I wonder why I have to condemn my own tradition to adopt another mans' tradition. The reason why I'm saying all this is because, growing up in church, I was taught to think against other beliefs or religion as wrong and not the way. They also teach and make us to believe Jesus is the only way. But now that I've personally met the gods, and old enough to make my own decisions, I...," Solomon expressing.

"Emmh before you continue Mr. President, do you still see yourself as a Christian? You still retain your Christian name," Young asks.

"Ha-ha-ha, that's right. I don't think the Christians will even consider me as one. But I personally will not condemn it. My uncle and my pastor have already disowned me," Solomon replies.

"Disowned you! Why?" Young asks.

"Because I accepted power from the gods, which is forbidden being a Christian. I don't really understand what's going on but, all I know is that, God is in control no matter how powerful I might want to think I am. It wasn't my intension to meet the gods. Things happen for a reason," Solomon explains.

"Don't worry Mr. President, they're only jealous because you got special powers and they don't," Young says.

"Ha-ha-ha, you said so, I didn't," Solomon says laughing.

"Ha-ha-ha, am only joking," Young says also laughing.

"Hope they see that as a joke. Anyway, with my Christian name... Emmh... I think I will keep the name for now. Think am too old to be changing names. But it will be better representing with an African name. I will look into that later. I might change it to Kuntakunte," Solomon says.

"Ha-ha-ha! Ha-ha-ha! Ha-ha-ha!," Young including the studio audience laughs out load.

"Kuntakunte! I remember that name, not bad," Young says laughing.

"Not bad at all, ha-ha-ha," Solomon says also laughing.

"Anyway, what religion or faith would you now say you follow?" Young asks.

"Emmh obviously am sticking to my culture and tradition. Almost fell apart from it, but thank God am back on it. Emmh am actually thinking of coming up with my own religion too, that goes with my culture and *tradition. You see; our first leader King Yemojaja, who actually didn't keep his Christian name, started his own religion – The Eeyemojaja Followers - because he didn't like the one of the Anglican and Methodist missionaries. He wanted to keep to his root. But anyway, if am going to come up with a religion, I will call it -* **True Believers. Good Followers***,"* Solomon says.

"True believers. Good followers…? That sound pretty much of what I am. Ha-ha, am only joking. When you say true believer, good follower; what do you mean by that? Or what philosophy will the religion base on?" Young asks.

"Believing in good, obviously. Believing its all good no matter what condition you're in. Like I said earlier, God is good. My intention will always be good and nothing else. And to make myself clear to people, I'm not just pretending to be good to deceive people that I'm good. My only intention of being good is because I have fear for God, and I believe God is good. I also believe to live well and to live a good life; you just got to keep it good. No hate, just pure loving and caring. That's the only way you can be a qualified True Believer and a Good Follower. **Genuinely being a good minded person. Never one day try not to be good.** *No room for hate. You got to keep it real good.* **Treat the other human the same way you will like to be treated.** *And leave the rest to God,"* Solomon explains.

"That will faithfully be a good religion," Young says.

"Oh yes! It will be the best," Solomon says.

"Competition!," Young says. Reminding Solomon about what he said about religion groups being competitive.

"Ha-ha-ha-ha!," Solomon including the studio audience laughs out load.

"There you go, you're being competitive yourself. You just said your religion will be the best. Anyway, let's move-on. So what about the power from the gods? What would happen to that?" Young asks.

"Emmh, to be honest with you, fifty-one years living this life, I personally believe there is power on every land to be use and this power is not power from the devil but from God. Power for man to use to get life to it very perfection God wants it to be. Power I would like to see has a blessing from God. The power given to me, which I believe is power from God, will only be use to get things better. That's what the power is there for, to get things done. But then again, out of selfish ambition or vain conceit of some people, they use the power only to get things done for their own benefit. It's up to the man behind the power whether to use it negatively or positively. I mean; back in those days of Moses and Jesus, men had these special powers to do incredible things. First, Moses turn a stick into snake, and then partition the red sea into two to make way for his people to escape. Another person was Jesus; he wakes the dead, heals the sick, walks on water, and also turns water into wine. These things are spiritual things, or should I instead just call it 'miracles', or 'magical'. I mean; most people believe is through the help and power from God these people were able to perform such miracles, or magic if that's what some people wants to see it as. I'm not saying am one of these people but, this power is there for man to use, I believe. Just as God gave Moses power to rescue his people, God did the same to me, maybe in a different way. Or should I instead say, just as God has given some people in Israel, or in the middle-east, or any other land God has given some people special powers, God also did the same in Africa. People just need to understand that. I don't understand why the power

found in Africa is portrayed to be evil, or witchcraft, or from the dark. Any magical thing in Africa apart from the miracles the pastors performs is seen as power from evil and also called black magic. But any other magical thing that happens anywhere else is seen as magic or miracle. Why is that? I mean; I believe in Jesus and I also believe in my ancestors. I believe in any religion that makes man believe in spiritual power because God is spiritual. And, I also believe in the devil," Solomon expressed.

"The devil?," Young says.

"Yes the devil. If you believe there is a devil, then you should believe there is a God too because, the story about the devil comes from the story about God. It's not that devil comes from Africa, and than God comes from Europe, or from the Middle East. Anywhere there is God, there is devil. And anywhere there's devil, there's God. God is everywhere, so as the devil. And to make something clear, hope people do understand that even the devil's power is believe to be power from God. But the devil being devil, use his negatively," Solomon explains.

"True! True! True!" Young says nodding her head.

*"And to be honest with you Lady Young, I personally now think there is **no such thing as evil power,** if it's God that gives devil his power or that gives power. Also, the power that one can use to do bad could or can also be use to do good. Or the power one can use to do good, also can be use to do bad. **Power is power**. It's up to the mind choice the man behind the power makes. For example; a man that has the talent, which is believe to be special gift from God, to do good, can also use the same talent to do wrong, bad or evil. And even though I was given a power to by the gods, or from the dark, my mind is still open to good and evil. But I've choose to stick to the good side of my mind.*

Whether you're a pastor, a leader, a saint, or even the devil, **everyone's mind is open to good and evil**. People should understand that. So truly, it's really up to who's behind the power that matters," Solomon expresses his mind on power.

"That's right. That's another way to look at it," Young says.

"You know wot I mean! Even the powerful Holy Bible that is use to pray for people is also use to swear and make curse on people. People don't go around saying the Bible power is evil power, do they?" Solomon added.

"I see wot you mean," Young says.

"Now that I mention the Bible, I would like to talk about the Bible. I know the Bible is filled with wisdom and guidance on pursuing an enriching responsible life but, there are some parts I read in the Bible that I really didn't understand and I would like to understand because, this life is a learning process and we all are still learning and trying to understand," Solomon says.

"That's right Mr. President. Go ahead, what is it?" Young says.

"Thank you. Recently before I came to the U.S, I decided to read my Bible from the beginning to the end all by myself this time because people are always reading it out to me. Reading from Genesis, I came across some questionable issues. I know we are not meant to ask question but how do they want us to understand to know what we're learning. But anyway, as I was reading through Genesis, after God made the wild animals according to their kinds and all the creatures that move along the ground according to their kinds, and God saw that it was good - Genesis 1:26 'God then said, 'Lets "us" make man in "our" image, and in "our" likeness'. My question is; if there's only one God, who is God referring to as "us"

200

or "our"? Us as in, us Gods? Also, another issue I would like answers for is, when Cain killed his brother Abel, Cain said to the Lord, 'my punishment is more than I can bear. Today you are driving me from the land, and I will be hidden from your presence; I will be a restless wanderer on the earth, and whoever finds me will kill me'. The Lord then said, 'Not so, if anyone kills Cain, he will suffer vengeance seven times over'. Then the Lord put a mark on Cain so that anyone who finds him would not kill him. So Cain went out from the Lord's presence and lived in the land of Nod, east of Eden. The story then carries on saying 'Cain lay with his wife, and she became pregnant and gave birth'. My question is, if Adam and Eve were the first human God created, and Cain and Abel was meant to be their first only children according to the story in the bible, who are the ones that Cain is afraid will find him to kill him? Or who are the ones that will suffer vengeance seven times over if they kill Cain? Who are the ones he will be showing the mark God put on him? And also, who is Cain's wife? Where did she come from? So these are questions I would also like to have answers to, if they really want to know who really the Dark-gods are," Solomon asks the questions bothering his mind.

"I reason with what you're saying, Mr. President. You sound very intense about this issue. But sorry I can't answer any of your questions, maybe a priest can," Young says.

"Oh yes, this religion issue is very intense. I did spoke to an African pastor back home to give me answers to these questions. The answer he gave to me about who God was referring to as - us, he said, 'God meant "us," as-in; God the Father, God the Son, and God the Holy Spirit', which comes as one, and which is called or means Trinity. For me it didn't sound like a genuine answer or make any sense because, if there's

201

God the Father, God the Son, and God the Holy Spirit, then we have three Gods. Or why would God be talking to himself, or referring to himself as us, if He's one? He must be talking to other Gods. And also when God was making the wild animals, why didn't He refer to himself as us? Why is it that, when God was about to make man was when He uses the term "us"? To me, the term; the Father, the Son, and the Holy Spirit is not convincing enough to describe God as I know or understand He(God) to be. But it can be use to portray a man. For example, as a man; I pray to my heavenly Father whom I see as God. I believe I have a spirit in me which you can call the Holy Spirit. And we're all children of God, which makes me a son. Except they want to say we're all Gods," Solomon explains.

"Wow, you're just like Jesus," Young says and then makes a funny face.

"Ha-ha-ha-ha!!!," everyone in the studio including Solomon laughs out load.

*"I'm definitely not Jesus. But I'm definitely trying to be a good man like Jesus. And not only me, everyone and anyone can use it for themselves too. But with God, who will God call His Father? Does God have a spirit in Him? God being the son, who is His Father? What about the mother? Is she not important? We can't just have the father and the son and not have the mother. Or is Mary the mother? There is something wrong or missing. I personally don't know God to be all of this. I only know God to be one big Supreme Being. But if the Father, the Son, and the Holy Spirit is what some people wants to see God as, then no problem. I'll learn from it and try to understand that, **God as appear to some people differently**. Anyway, that is that. Cain's wife is meant to be his sisters, so the pastor says. And those that Cain is afraid would kill him; the pastor has no answer for it but, he promise to get back to me. And*

also, something just came to my mind; am sorry to go into what am about to say but, if you don't understand and you feel confuse about something crucial in your life, it is always good to ask, or do something about it to find out. So what I want to say is; they say Jesus died for our sins, right? Because I remember Pastor Nicolas telling me Jesus died as a payment for our sins," Solomon says and asks.

"That's right, that's what they say," Young answered.

"And they also say we need to repent from our sins, right?" Solomon says.

"Right...that's what they always say," Young says.

"Now, my question is; if Jesus really has died for our sins, or my sins that I have no clue of committing if am going to be honest, then why do we still need to repent from our sins? Why do every morning when we wake-up we still ask God for forgiveness for our sins? Why do people still go to church to ask for forgiveness? On judgement day, we're all still going to be judged against the sins we commit, which is what will determine whether one will end in Heaven or Hell. So what sins exactly did Jesus actually die for us for? Because I just don't seem to understand and find it really hard to figure-out the sins Jesus actually died for me for. If Jesus really has died for my sins, then I should have no sins. I should be sinless, a saint, and not a sinner if him dieing for my sins is to wash away all my sins. I shouldn't have any sins to repent from. I shouldn't even bother to ask for forgiveness when I wake-up every morning. Instead, I just rejoice and praise Jesus forever for dieing for my sins, which is what I think they want us to do. I shouldn't also even bother or worry about judgement day, there are no sins to be judge against; Jesus has died for it all. Isn't that's how is meant to be? Or is it just me? Or did Jesus only

die for half of our sins? I'm actually putting myself forward; I want to know the sins that I commit that Jesus Christ died for me for. And am not saying am not a sinner, or I have no sins, no. What I would like to know is, which of my sins did he actually die for? Is it the sins I commit when I was younger? Or the sins I commit when I was older? Or the sins I commit before I came to life? Because you never know, I might have committed some crazy sins before I came to this life or the life before, you never know, things happen. Which of my sins, I would just like to know? Did he die for all of the sins I will commit as I live my life? Oh! Now I remember. I also remember Pastor Nicolas saying something like; Jesus died as a payment for our sins and now God can now offer forgiveness and reconciliation to all those who come to Him. But I still don't get it. What sins did we commit that Jesus has to die before God can now offer forgiveness to us? Does Jesus have to die before God offers forgiveness to the ones He claimed He loves and cared about? I mean, what exactly did we do wrong that God has decided not to forgive us not until Jesus Christ died on the cross for us? So if Jesus Christ didn't die for our sins, we're all going to Hell fire? Because I just don't know, I don't understand. I wasn't even alive during these days that Jesus Christ died. What sins? I would honestly like to know. Am in my right to know, right?," Solomon says and asks.

"Well, I don't know. But what you're saying kind of make sense," Young says.

*"It's the truth! **The truth is bitter but it's got to be told**. You can't just come to my land all the way from yours to convince me about a man from your land is my God and just expect me to just accept that without asking questions. Why should I give another man from another land that got killed by his own kind of people*

204

*many years ago my life? Telling me he's my God that I should worship him and give my life to him. Telling me he died for my sins. What sins, am asking. What about God that we know before introducing us to Jesus? Dump Him in the bin and then give my life to Jesus? I don't thinks so. And please, I don't want them telling me the sin Adam and Eve commit is the sin Jesus died for us for? Because if you remember the story; after Adam and Eve ate from the tree, God said to Eve that, 'I will greatly increase your pains in childbearing; with pain you will give birth to children. Your desire will be for your husband and he will rule over you'. To Adam, He said, 'cursed is the ground because of you; through painful labour you will eat of it all the days of your life. It will produce thorns and thistles for you and you will eat the plant of the field. By the sweat of your forehead you will eat your food until you return to the ground, since from it you were taken; for dust you are and to dust you will return'(Genesis 3:16-19). Which is what is still happening to man and woman today. Whether you're a born-again Christian or not, women still go through pain before they give birth and man still have to struggle and work hard to survive. And the sad news is, we're all still going to die. So Adam and Eve's sin can't be the sin Jesus Christ died for us for. They put the fear in us and make us feel if we don't accept Jesus has died for our sins, and that if we don't commit our life to him, things will go wrong for us, or things won't be good for us, and that we will end in Hell. Well, today, I've broken that fear and release myself from bondage. A good God is kind to everybody and not just certain people. One doesn't have to give God anything to see His blessings. I personally believe one doesn't even have to believe in God before one sees His blessings. That's why **God is worthy to be praised.** God cares about everybody and not just only the Christians.*

*I mean, the God I worship cares about everybody and not just only me. If Jesus only cares about Christians or one have to be a Christian or should I instead say, "born-again Christians" before one sees his grace, then one can't go around saying Jesus Christ cares about everyone, if that's the case. We'll never all be Christians. That's part of life, that's human beings. So if Jesus Christ truly really cares about every human being, born-again Christians shouldn't be the only ones on his list. And to be honest, according to the story I know about Jesus, when Jesus Christ was alive, he cared and showed love to everyone. It wasn't about the religion you follow, to him. He was so kind that he even forgive his killers. He was merciful. That's why people compared him with God. That's what we know God to be - kind and merciful. So why would Jesus Christ be so kind to everyone when he was alive and all of a sudden after his death, he's now only coming back to save born-again Christians? Is like Jesus doesn't care about everybody any more, which doesn't sound like Jesus. 'You have to be a born-again Christian before Jesus Christ saves you' is false prophesy about Jesus, I will like to think. Anyway, what I know and believe is, I'm a good soul and I deserve good and to end good. I don't need to give my life to no man to end good. God will not make my life hell, or put me in Hell because I didn't follow or believe what these other men are saying to me. I definitely understand and know God not to do that. God will definitely not put me in Hell because I've decided not to follow other peoples believes or religion. God is good. And there's nothing good about putting one in Hell because one is different from the other. God cares about everybody. **God has created us all to be different.** Anyway, if they really want me to be a follower of the Bible and to be born-again into their religion, I need reasonable answers to this questions* *for me to understand because, already not reading too far, am already getting confuse. Another question I would also like to ask is; if everything we need to know is in the Bible, why are the answers these pastors give not in the Bible? Is there something they're hiding? Where are they getting their answers from?,"* Solomon expresses his mind about Jesus, the Bible, and Christianity.

"God? Or from Jesus?," Young says and makes a funny face expression.

"Ha-ha-ha-ha!!!," everyone in the studio including Solomon laughs out load.

Young then says;

"I'm only joking. But I reason with what you're saying, Mr President. The question I would like to ask, and this is just a simple one, is; how did man know or so sure about how God created earth and man? Was any man there? Anyway, like you said Mr. President, this life is a learning process and we all are still learning to understand. But anyway, the question I was going to ask you is; would you advise anyone to worship the Dark-gods?"

"You see Lady Young, before I answer that question, and to be honest with you. The reason why it might seem like, or sounds like am against Christianity is because; some African pastors have gang-up against me to point at me as an evil one," Solomon says.

"Why will they do that? Have you done anything evil?" Young asks.

"They say I have power from evil. They say and preach to people not to trust me, that I'm a pretender, and that people should be careful with me. But what these pastors don't understand is, first; these pastors say to people that; if you know Christ, you'll have no crisis in your life. They also say; if you have Jesus, you'll have peace. And if you know Jesus, you'll know

*good. You see; statistics shows that recently these African countries that these pastors preaches has the highest population of people that goes to church and strongly believes in Jesus. They believe Jesus would return in their lifetime and also believe in Heaven and Hell. This statistics also proves that these pastors are really putting up effort to draw people close to Church, which is a good thing. Now, what these pastors don't understand is that; it's been over hundred years these people have been going to church and waiting for Jesus. It's been over hundreds years these people have been with passion calling for Jesus; for peace, no crisis, and for good things to happen to them. If it true gospel these African pastors that call themselves true man of God preaches to these people, why are most of these people yet to find peace? It's like most of these people don't know or yet to find Jesus. Most of these people hardly know what being good is. Most of these people live in crisis. In these African countries with high population of people that goes to church to serve Jesus, people don't trust one another, people hate on one another, there is corruption everywhere, and all sorts of assaults. Even countries that don't believe in Jesus are doing way better than them. If these African pastors are really doing their job right, these people should really know what to do. They should be living in peace. They should have no crisis. And most of all, they should know what's good. Something must be wrong somewhere. It looks like these people are lost or they just don't understand what they're doing or learning in church. Or maybe the teachers are not very good teachers, or the students are not just ready or willing to learn. This is also part of the reasons why I went to call for an international genuine pastor to preach the real gospel to the people. I remember Pastor Nicolas telling me that; **people shouldn't just listen to the word of***

God but also practice it. *Maybe this is what these pastors need to tell their followers more often. You see, Egitee six years ago like I said, was hell. But now with the power they call power from evil, I have used it to bring peace to my people. There is no such thing as crime, corruption, crisis, and most importantly the people now know what's good. They have no other choice than to act/behave/do good. I have used what's in my power to lead them good. People run away from these other African countries that so much believe in Jesus to live in Egitee or other westernise countries that people over there don't really go to church or call Jesus, to find peace. Also in these African countries with highest population of those that believe in Jesus, all that matter is money. One can be bad and still be praised and credited for doing nothing. As long as one has money, one really is the boss. This is the mentality of most of these people. It's not really about whom you are but how much money you have. That's not meant to be good people's mentality. Good people take people for who they are and not what they worth. I know people that do negative things to get money and then go to church to oppress and praise Jesus for it. Pastors know very much about such people that come to their churches. They say nothing but praise Jesus along with them. I mean, these Pastors that claim they have power from Jesus are meant to use this power by all means to bring good to their countries. It's not by just starting-up your own church and just preaching to the people. It involves more than that if they really want to change the people for good. Jesus said in the bible; **'Watch out for false prophets**. Not everyone who says to him, 'Lord, Lord', will enter the kingdom of heaven, but only he who does the will of the Father, who is in heaven. Many will say to him on that day 'Lord, Lord' did we not prophesy in your name, and your name drive out* demons and perform many miracles?', which would sound something like what some of these African pastors that always accuse and denounce children as witches will say to Jesus on that day…"

"Ha-ha-ha! Ha-ha-ha!," Young including the studio audience laughs out loud.

Solomon continues, *"Ha-ha…is the truth. Jesus then went on saying, 'he will tell them plainly, I never knew you. Away from me, you evildoers!' So really, people also need to watch out for these fake African pastors too and not just me. Anyway, I have decided to leaved these pastors judging me in God's hands because, Jesus also says that; 'Do not judge or you too will be judged. For the same way you judge others, you will be judged.' Jesus also says; 'you hypocrite, **first take the plank out of your own eye, and then you will see clearly to remove the speck from your brother's eye.'"***

"That's right," Young says nodding.

"So that's all I have to say to these African pastors that gang-up against me and trying to judge me. They need to understand that this life is a learning process and we all are still learning to understand. To know something or have an answer to something, you must have understood it all to know it and for you to then be able to give answers to it. But with this life, no one knows or has a genuine answer for it. We all are still learning to know what this life is all about. We have learnt so much so far from the days of Adam and Eve to this present day. And yet, this life still needs understanding. The more we keep-on learning, the more we keep-on understanding. And the more we keep-on understanding, the more we keep-on knowing what this life is truly all about. Anyway, emmh now, coming to your question of whether I would advise anyone to worship the gods. You see, in Egitee, people

*are free to do and follow whatever belief or religion they want to follow, just like in the western countries or over here in the U.S where people understands that people can have different beliefs. If some people in Egitee believe the gods can get them closer to God spiritually, then so be it. But when they come out to public, they have to understand and have no other choice than to behave good. At this stage we have reached in life, I presume people should by now understand that, **it's not about the religion they follow that makes them a good human being but where they stand in their mind. Anything can happen to anybody,** and **anyone can be lucky**. It doesn't really matter what religion you follow. In every religion, there is good and there is evil,"* Solomon explains.

"That's right, I believe so too," Young says nodding.

"In Egitee, people can always make sacrifices to the gods just to honour them being our ancestors. But it has to be on anything that will not break the legal rules," Solomon explains.

"Okay, now that you just mention the rules, what is it like to the people binding to these rules? Rules like; you must not steal. When I was a little kid, I use to steal meat from the pot which I believe is common among kids. I also know friends that do the same. Does stealing meat from the pot apply to this rule? I mean; stealing is stealing, that's what my mama will say," Young says.

"That's right, you shall not steal is the rule. Children are warned before taking meat from the pot they should inform their parents or the person responsible for the cooking. This is a way of training our kids not to get to the habit of wanting to steal. This is also a way of teaching them and making them understand that stealing is really not a good behaviour.

Let me tell you a short story that happened to one family that came to Egitee for holiday," Solomon says.

"Go ahead Mr. President, tell us." Young excitedly says.

"A little boy, age seven, you know, out of curiosity he wanted to see what will really happen if he did steal. You know, some kids think they are smart, think they could or can always get round things...," Solomon telling a story.

"Oh yes, that sound like me when I was a kid. I always do or go for things my mama doesn't want me to know or warn me not to go for. I don't know why, am just a naughty kid," Young says.

"Oh yes I could tell you will be very naughty as a kid," Solomon says.

"Really," Young says.

"Oh yes really. You look naughty," Solomon says and then winks.

"Ha-ha-ha! Ha-ha-ha!," the studio audience including Lady Young laughs out load.

"Ha-ha, am only joking. You look beautiful," Solomon compliments.

"Awww.... Thank you Mr. President. What a beautiful thing to say. Woo, am blushing," Lady Young girlishly says twinkling her eyelashes.

"Ha-ha-ha! Ha-ha-ha!," the studio audience including Solomon laughs out load.

"Anyway, continuing with the story about this kid, this kid thought he could sneaky steal from the sweet shop, and normally theirs is no one watching over the sweet shop. You pick the amount of sweet you want and then drop the money in a box that is boldly written- please pay here - left by the sweet shop owner because the sweet shop owner knows no one dares or even have the interest to steal. Also, there is a sticker in front of the sweet shop that boldly says – All criminals are

prosecuted. Don't steal - Rules of the Dark-gods. But the little boy instead ignores that, thinking he's superman and went ahead to pick-up the sweets. He looks left and right, I know this because there is a video recoding of this incident, and then put the sweets in his pocket, then ran out of the sweet shop without paying. On his way back to his parent, he was stopped by the dark warriors. 'Give the sweet you just stole' The Dark Warriors said to the kid. The kid was shocked. He started crying, crying for his parent. Meanwhile, his parents are having fun by the sea side. The dark warriors handed the boy over to the police to take the kid back to his parent. The boy's parent was shown the video of their son stealing sweet," Solomon tells.

"So was the little boy prosecuted?" Young asks.

"Not at all. We don't prosecute children age under fourteen that breaks the rules. We hand them back over to their parents, warn the parents to carefully watch over their kids unless they will be the one prosecuted, as in, pay penalty charges," Solomon replies.

"So for example, if I was a kid even though my mama wasn't around and I want to, you know, take extra meat from the pot, I have to call her up before stealing... sorry I wanted to say take the meat from the pot. Ha-ha. So I will be like, mama can I take an extra meat from the pot please. And she will be like, no you aren't gonna take no extra gat dem meat from the pot, because if you do, I will myself cut your head off and use it to cook diner for your papa. I don't wanna be paying no gat dem penalty charges to no gat dem government man!," Young says and again does her funny face.

"Ha-ha-ha! Ha-ha-ha! Ha-ha-ha!," the studio audience laughs out loud including Solomon.

"Trust me, my mama is like that. She herself doesn't like the idea of stealing. Things were hard those days.

213

She couldn't afford me taking extra meat apart from the one am having for dinner. Anyway, Mr. President, is like my time is up. You've been a wonderful guest and before I wrap this up, do you have any massage for the people watching you right now?," Young says and asks.

*"Emmh... I would say, be good, have faith, and always belief in yourself and where you're from. And also, be understanding. I really just notice that **understanding really matters**. You understanding is you educating yourself. This life is a learning process and we all are still learning, and the only way we can know is us understanding it. We learn new things everyday. Some of these things might seem wrong but we just don't know yet until we learn it all. If some people are not trying to understand life, then how can they know what this life is all about? People really need to open-up their mind to understand all these differences about life before they can come-up with a conclusion of what life is. There is no genuine answer yet. People just need to keep-on researching and keep-on learning. Maybe one day we might know and be able to do the working-out for us to reach or arrive at a good result,"* massage from Solomon.

"That's right, Mr. President. Thank you so much. It's been a great time spent with you. And I do hope, maybe, one day we'll know the working-out to arrive at a good result. Thank you once again Mr. President, thank you," Lady Young says, thrilled.

"It's a pleasure to be here," Solomon says, tired.

"So that is it for today's segment. Join me same time next week. I will be joined by another character. Who that is? Stay tune for the next segment to find out. I'm still your favourite Lady Young. Ladies and gentlemen, boys and girls, man and woman, old and young, stay bless, and bye for now," Lady Young ends

her show.

The TV went off.

"I see," the President of United States says. He's been watching Solomon on Lady Young's talk show in his office in the White House. He then picks up the phone to make a call. *"Hello,"* he says.

Solomon getting back from the United States after attending the Lady Young's talk show, he has two things in mind he needed to rectify. First – the penalty that comes with the rules, and secondly - the GUNS.

After six years of the strict rules, Solomon thought there should be no need to behead one that breaks the rules. He thinks, *"For anyone at this point in time that breaks the rules, that person should be mad, not well, stupid, or mentally ill."* Because he believes for one to be aware of the penalty that comes with one breaking the rules and one still go ahead to break the rules, then that person seem not to be alright. So instead of one losing his/her head, they will be first taken to a mental home to check if he/she is perfectly okay before then sentence to prison.

Solomon changing or stopping the behead penalty was no hassle. But for the guns; Gen. Fahruk being a man of war during his time has loaded and make a constant supply of guns and ammunitions from the Americans up till today which Solomon now sees as waste of money and not needed. So he decided to call-up the Americans to make a stop to the supply of guns and ammunitions to Egitee.

"Why do we need guns? We are genuinely good people. We have no intention of killing and shooting at one another. We're all children of God. We are covered by His power and His grace. Egitee is a peaceful land

and not interested in war. In-fact, I have burn down and destroy all weapons, guns and ammunition. If any tries to bring war on us, they should be ready to fight against the gods of this land. I'm very sure it will only take few minute with the power the gods has to wipe out any country that tries intervening," parts of statement Solomon made when calling-off the supply of guns and ammunitions deal with the Americans.

A week later after the cancellation of the supply of guns by the Americans, Solomon is in his office in the State House flicking through the channels on TV. He came across a programme that interests him – The Lady Young Talk4Good Talk Talk Show with special guest, Solomon's favourite writer – Ade Tokunbo.

On TV; *"Anyway, Mr Ade Tokunbo, is like my time is up. You have been a wonderful guest. And before I wrap this up, do you have any massage for the people at home watching you right now?"* Lady Young asks Ade Tokunbo.

"Oh no! I've missed! It's almost the end of the show," Solomon says. Not happy missing the interview by Lady Young with his favourite writer.

On TV; *"Emmh, I would say three things. One;* **be yourself.** *Two;* **do the right thing.** *And three;* **be good,"** Ade says.

"Can you please express more on that?" Young says.

"Emmh well, we're all here to live a life. Only you can live your life. To live your life, you need to **be yourself.** *And to be yourself, you need to* **know yourself.** *And to know yourself, you need to* **find yourself** *to know what kind of person you are and what you represent. And the only way you can find yourself*

is to **always be yourself.** So it's very important to always be yourself, it's a right thing to do. And in this life, there are two ways one can go; right or wrong. No one wants to go the wrong way or get things wrong. So to prevent that, you try your best to do things right. You **do it right,** you **get it right**. And if you **do it wrong**, you will **get it wrong**. Life is as simple as that. And to become better and the best at what you do, you need to first start as good," Ade explains.

"You mean; life goes as far to be good, better, best," Young added.

"That's right. You first have to be good at wot you do before you get better and then your better becomes best. I mean; it's the right thing to do if one wants to be the best of them selves. I remember in school, we were taught a short poem, it goes;

'Good better best
I shall never rest
Until my good is better
And my better best'

It's the first thing we say every morning the teacher walks-in to the classroom. It's a real good massage. I took it in from young age as part of my life plan; to first be good at everything I do, then work harder to get better, and then my better becomes best," Ade express.

"Definitely a good plan to set to live a good life, I'm speechless. Thank you so much for the good messages. It a great time spent with you. May God keep blessing you? Thank you," Young gratefully says.

"You're most welcome. Thank you," Ade sincerely replies.

"So people, make sure you go out and buy the new story book by Ade Tokunbo. It's a good book with very interesting storyline and lots of good massages for you to go through or bypass life. Ladies and gentlemen, it's Ade Tokunbo!" Young cheerfully says.

"Heeeey!" the studio audience cheered and applause.

"So that's it for today's segment. Join me, same time next week. I am still your favourite Lady Young. Ladies and gentlemen, boys and girls, man and woman, old and young, stay bless and bye for now," Lady Yong ends her show.

Solomon switched off the TV. *"Yes, that's my boy,"* Solomon says. Then the phone rings, *"RINGS!"* He picks up the phone. *"Hello,"* he says. It's a call from the United States government over the issue of Solomon cancelling the supply of guns and ammunitions to his country and wanting to use the power from the Dark-gods against other nations. The conversation with Solomon on the phone cannot be said. It's strictly private and confidential.

However, from the conversation over the phone with Solomon, the United States government will be sending UN weapon inspectors to inspect what type or kind of weapon or power Solomon have to fight against other nations.

UN inspector coming to Egitee isn't a problem for Solomon. He has nothing to hide. As far as he's concern; *"No matter what the United Nations might think of my power, I will still keep to what I believe will rescue and save my people,"* words from Solomon.

Two weeks after the phone conversation, the UN weapon inspectors arrive to Egitee.

"Welcome to Egitee, the land of the Dark-gods, welcome," Solomon welcomes the UN inspectors. From there, they went ahead to the meeting room in the State House in Freeland, to have an intensive final discussion on weapons a country can hold or have to use in battle against other countries. Weapon of mass

destruction is certainly unacceptable. But now that Solomon has destroy all weapon and also stopped the supply of guns and ammunition to his country by the Americans; the UN weapon inspectors wants to know what Solomon will use to defend and protect his people should in-case another country brings war on them.

"Well, if any one tries to bring war on us, they will definitely be fighting the gods. The gods themselves told me to destroy all weapons. They told me we don't need it. The power of the gods is powerful enough to conquer any nation, so they say, not me. I just have to listen and follow to what the gods said. I don't know why you bother yourselves. It's not that I'm going to use my power to conquer the world. I'm a good man for crying out loud," Solomon explains.

The UN weapon inspectors weren't thrilled or convinced with Solomon's statement. They reply; *"We understand you're a good man, Mr President. But the gods, who are they? Is there any chance or chances we can speak to them? And besides, can we please see what's in your laboratory? We understand your ex-leader – late Gen. Fahruk - the man you executed, is a man of war and he has weapon of mass destruction; both chemical and biological weapons, in violation of UN demands. Also, we were informed he bought aluminium tubes useful in a uranium plant. Such a plant could produce the highly-enriched U-235 required for making an atomic bomb. We really don't know if you still keep such weapons. Could you please show us round, if you don't mind."*

"Sure, why not. But before I do that, I will like to make something clear. Like I said inspector, only I could or can communicate with the gods. They are just the gods of the land. They're our ancestors. But if you really want to speak to the gods, then you have to do a simple sacrifice and ritual to enable you to speak to the

gods. And for the weapons, I have destroyed all weapons. I ordered destruction of all chemical weapons. All weapons – biological, chemical, missile, nuclear – were destroyed. There is not a single missile left. I only kept the blueprints and moulds for production, but all the missiles were destroyed. But if you insist you want to see the laboratory, this way please," Solomon says. He then took the UN weapon inspectors to the laboratory in the State House. On the front door of the laboratory, it's label – The Dark Lab.

"Welcome to the dark lab. Here is also a place I use to communicate or meditate to the gods. You don't have to be scared, it safe. But be careful of what you touch because some of the things in here is not what you might really want to touch," Solomon says and then, *"You might disappear,"* he whispered to the chief UN weapon inspector. He then laughs, *"ha-ha-ha."*

"Don't worry Mr. President; we will be much more careful. And for your information, we don't do rituals and scarifies to any," the Chief Inspector (CI) says back to Solomon.

The UN weapon inspectors went ahead to give the lab a thorough search. They have their full boom detective wear on. Of course, searching for weapon of mass destruction isn't what the inspectors "really" are looking for. They want to know what exactly is behind Solomon's power. They search and search and search, nothing to do with weapon of mass destruction was found. The UN inspectors were about to leave then one of the inspectors found a dead rotten human body hidden in one of the laboratory cabinet. The body has no identity. Solomon was shocked. He has no idea of how a dead human rotten body was kept in the lab.

"How will you explain this, Mr. President? A rotten human body found in the State House. Any

explanation?," the Chief Inspector says to Solomon.

"I know nothing about this. This must be a set up. Fahruk should know about this," Solomon denies the allegation.

"But Gen. Fahruk is nowhere to be asked question, is he? You killed him," Chief Inspector says.

"No. I didn't kill him. I put he that did wrong to justice! And I know nothing about this dead rotten body." Solomon says looking and sounding very angry.

"Well, in that case, we're going to take this body along with us to our laboratory. To find out the identity, and find out when exactly the dead body was dumped. You don't mind us doing that do you, Mr. President?" Chief Inspector sincerely says.

"No! Not at all! You can do whatever that you want to do with the body. I'm pure. I have nothing to hide," Solomon agrees with the Chief Inspector.

"In that case Mr. President, see you on the judgment day," Chief Inspector says and then smiles.

The UN weapon inspectors obviously didn't find any weapons of mass destructions but a "dead rotten human body." This is not a good reputation for Solomon. The UN inspectors went with the body and then two weeks later they found out the identity of the body and how long the body is been dumped in the Dark lab. According to the scientific test on the rotten body, the test shows that the body was dumped in the lab four years ago. Which proves and shows that, the person was killed four years ago. It's been more than six years Solomon as been the President of Egitee or has moved-in to the State House. So according to the UN inspectors, Solomon should know about the dead body. It's the body of Alora – Gen. Fahruk's "hot" girlfriend.

What Solomon and the UN inspectors don't know is; when Gen. Fahruk shot Alora on her forehead on the day of the campaign for calling Solomon, he hid her body in the lab, and then sprayed her body with some liquid substance to keep the body fresh for at least two more years. Why he did that, nobody knows. Now Solomon is the one to face the consequences. Now the UN inspectors have something to hold against Solomon.

Two years later, the American government have decided on what to do base on the so called "power from the Dark-gods" Solomon have decided to use against other countries should in case of war. So they called for an immediate remover of the "dark power" over international affairs.

"It's not power that we know or neither power that we believe-in, nor-either know the source of the power. You have to take it off. It doesn't go with the rules. You can't use power no one knows to wipe out nations. How do you expect other nations to defend themselves against your dark power? You have to fight physical like everyone else. But since you have resist and going ahead using your dark power against other nations, we have no other choice than to make a force remover. Such power used as a weapon is classified or rated to be weapon of mass destruction," phone conversation from the U.S government to Solomon over the issue of his "power."

As the United States government forwarded statement of force remover against Solomon's power, they also at the same time inform the G6 leaders on Solomon's plan on using his so called "power from the dark-gods" to wipe out other nations. The U.S government also at the same time call for an urgent assistant of the western countries to join and help support remove the power from dark Solomon plan to use. Apart from the power from dark Solomon might have or want to use to wipe out other nations, which worries some nations, he's also being portray as a "suspicious one" by the U.S government base on the dead rotten body found in the State House; Which then makes the matter worse. People starts to get inquisitive and anxiety about this issue and Solomon.

" 'What could this be? Is President Solomon trying to take over the world with his so called power from the Dark-gods?' 'Maybe the African pastors are right about him'. 'Or is this just another invasion of the U.S government on other country over matter that's not met to be issues?' " comments and thoughts from people all over the world. People really don't know what to think. Rumour has spread all over that Solomon is trying to use his power from dark to wipe out nations.

" 'But why would President Solomon want to wipe out other nations? He's known to be a good man and a saviour by his people.' 'If the U.S government wants to bring someone down, they always make that person looks bad.' 'But then again, why would President Solomon want to fight other countries with supernatural power no one knows about? That's unfair and scary. We don't want to start worshipping or be ruled by some dark-gods,' " thoughts and comments from some other people around the world.

While everyone all over the world try to figure-out what's going-on, the president of the United States – PRESIDENT GEORGE FORREST, and the Prime Minister of the United Kingdom – TONY BELL, at the same time at their various countries went live on TV to make a public announcement speech;

"My fellow citizens, issue over President Solomon Gondi and his so called power from the dark gods have now reached the final days of decision. For more than two years, the United States and other nations have pursued patient and honourable efforts to disarm the

dark power without war. We have passed more than a dozen resolutions in the United Nations Security Council. We have sent hundreds of weapons inspectors to oversee the disarmament of the power from dark on international affairs. Our good faith has not been returned. Instead, we found a dead rotten body in his resident...," President George Forrest speaking.

"And I tell you honestly what I fear; my fear is that we wake up one day and we find that this man that so called himself a good man but also retain a power from the dark, and a dead body found at his resident, decide to use this power he claim to be from the gods and we get sucked into a conflict with power we have no idea of it source...," Prime minister Tony Bell speaking.

"The United States and other nations did nothing to deserve or invite this threat. But we will do everything with our technology to defeat the power from dark. Instead of drifting along toward tragedy, we will set a course toward safety. Before the day of horror can come, before it is too late to act, this danger will be removed. The United States has the sovereign authority to use force in assuring its own national security. That duty falls to me, as Commander-in-Chief, by the oath I have sworn, and by the oath I will keep," President George Forrest speaking.

"This brings us to how we make the rules and how you decide what is right or wrong in enforcing them. The UN Declaration on Human Rights is a fine document...," Prime Minister Tony Bell speaking.

"The United States, with other countries, will work to eliminate the dark power over our heads. If we have to challenge the gods, then so be it. We believe in one God, not gods. Whatever that the power from dark might be, our good God will stand by us. Good night, and May God continue to bless America," President George Forrest ends the speech.

France, UK, with some other UN countries will join hands together with the U.S government to force remove the supernatural power Solomon plan to use over international affairs.

Since Solomon have destroyed all the physical weapons his country can use to fight other countries, he has to show the western countries what his country will use to fight should in-case there is war. Well, one is about to start.

Solomon is left with two choices; first, he can agree to take-off the idea of using his so called "power" from the dark-gods over international affairs and then reactivate back the country's gun and ammunitions supply contract with the Americans, to prove his innocent. Or secondly, he can reveal to the west the real source or secret behind his supernatural power, to save conflict. Solomon himself at this moment doesn't know what to do.

"First thing first, there is no way am allowing guns back into this land. And secondly, there is also no way to prove my power, only if they're ready to face the gods. I don't know what exactly they want me to do. Well, if they're coming for war, then it war," words from Solomon, ready for the worst to happen. He then decides to make a national TV appearance to his own people too.

"My fellow citizens of Egitee, I hereby call for a state of emergency. Do not get scared or panic. Everything is under control. The west are coming to force remove me from power, claiming I have got power equivalent to weapon of mass destruction. I don't know why this is an issue but all I know is, I'm innocent. I want every single one of you, both young and old, man and woman, including with the animals, please till further notice, evacuate and stay away from this land to avoid BLOODSHED because, I don't know

what's going to happen when the west arrive. All I want is the safety and protection over my people. I will also like to use this opportunity to ask my other fellow Africa countries to please accept my people because, right now, life on this very land is in danger. May the gods of the land come out themselves to prove their innocent? And may the almighty God be with us all? Have a good life ahead. Wish you all the best," state of emergency announcement made by Solomon to his people.

As the people of Egitee are gathering and packing all their belongings preparing to evacuate off the land, the western troops are gathered and parked with all the weapons they could or can possibly lay their hands on, prepared to go to war on Egitee.

WASHINGTON DC, Military Headquarter;

"Sir! The soldiers are ready. Ready to go," second in command – Command Sergeant Major TONY says to his boss – first in command – Sergeant Major of the U.S Army, via TV transmission.

"Good. Make sure you make very good use of the weapons and your men," the first in command - Sergeant Major of the U.S Army says to Sergeant Major Tony.

"Yes sir! I have given the Egite military units clear instruction on actions they can take to avoid being attacked and destroyed. But in-fact, the president has instructed his people including with his military men to evacuate from the land, left only the Dark Warriors to fight," Tony explains.

"So you have only the Dark Warriors to fight?," the first in command asks.

"Something like that, sir. But our mission is to make sure the power from the dark is disarm," Tony answered.

"So you could also be facing the gods of the land?," first in command asks.

"Yes sir, if they are truly about sir," Tony answered.

"If they are, have you got the weapon to fight against them?," first in command asks.

"Not exactly sir. Our technology weapons are the only thing we depend on, sir," Tony replies.

"Technology weapons?," first in command repeats.

"Yes sir!" Tony says.

"I suggest you carry a Bible along with you when you're going. Anyway, you can always get in touch if help is needed. Don't let us down. You will be leading the UN coalition. It's right about now, all in your hands. Go and safe the world from the power from dark. I give you my command," Sergeant Major of the US Army gives his final order.

"Yes sir! I promise not to let you down sir!" Tony makes a promise to his boss, then salute.

He then disconnects the TV transmission to his boss.

"Sir, I know who we can take along instead of you carrying the Bible along sir," RISKY– also a Sergeant Major – Tony's assistant in command makes a suggestion. He was standing behind Tony while speaking to their boss.

"Who?" Tony asks with annoyance.

"Pastor Nicolas James from the UK sir. He's a true man of God. He's also a good friend to President Solomon. It will be better for us to have a true man of God around than you holding the bible. You don't even believe in it or even believe in the existence of God," Risky (Tony's assistant) says to Tony.

"Well, I'll see about that. First of all, let me see the list of weapon we're going with?" Tony asks Risky.

"Here sir," Risky gives Tony a paper that shows list

of weapons they're going to war with.
On the list;

Bolt-action   Rifles Sniper Rifles   Semi-Automatic Rifles   Sub Machineguns

Assault Rifles   Pistols Light Machineguns   Anti-tank weapon

Hand Grenades   Light Mortars   Flamethrowers M1 Garand

MP43   Colt M1911   Bazooka   Panzerfaust

AC-130 Gunship   F-22   JSTARS U-2 Aircraft

UAV   E-8 Joint Stars Aircraft   F-15

The F-22A Raptor   MQ-1 Predator   REDCAP

B-1Bs Bomber   B-52s Bomber   B-2s Bomber   F-16C1

…and many more

"Good. I wonder what the gods will have or use to defend and fight against all these super power weapons," Tony says and then makes a big smile.

"Why don't we test them first sir," Risky comes up with an idea.

"Oh yeah... That's a good idea," Tony says.

Meanwhile, as Tony and Risky try to come-up with a plan on first attack to see what will happen, outside the Military Headquarter, more than 100, 000 protesters flooded Washington to demonstrate against the U.S led war in Egitee. And more than 15,000 protesters marched out in the City of Westminster, London, UK, to also protest against war on Egitee.

Meanwhile, back in Egitee, people are already making their way out of the land to various West African countries close by. There are a lot of people to evacuate the land. The only way people could or can go is by land, which there isn't. They have to cross River Ijogun to escape off the land. Another way to leave the land is by air and at this moment in time, no one is there to work or fly a plane. The only plane flying is the UN plane that comes to pick-up their people that came for holiday or living in Egitee.

People are rushing to evacuate the land before the west arrives. There isn't enough boat or canoes to cross everyone over. People start to panic. It's been almost eight years the people have been living in peace. And now, it looks like what could or can be the end of peace and the return of revulsion.

More than a million people are waiting by the river side to cross to the other side. People have to wait for the first set of boats and canoes to come back before they can cross over. No one dares to swim across River Ijogun because of it reputation ever since the story of the Nigerian informant that tries to swim across but never made it and was never found.

All of a sudden, Solomon was signal by the US force about the E-8 Joint Stars Aircraft coming to attack. *"What am I going to do? The people,"* Solomon thought to himself.

Next thing, Solomon appears on an electronic advertisement board along the river side to speak to the people.

"Do not get panic. Everything is under control," Solomon says to the people.

He waited for the first set boats and canoes to reach the other side before he again shows off his supernatural power. He did a miraculous wonder that as only been done by a character in the bible – Moses. He pointed his finger forwards via the electronic advertisement board and then all of a sudden, the river start to split open into two, making a pathway for the people to cross over to the other side before the arrival of the E-8 Joint Stars Aircraft coming to attack.

"Woo!" The people yell, surprise and happy to find a way out. They gave Solomon rounds of applause for his miraculous wonder.

"Hurry, they're on their way. Don't get panic, just move slowly. Go, go, and go now. May the almighty God guide you all?" Solomon calmly says to his anxious people.

Meanwhile, as the Egite people cross along the split open river to the other side, the E-8 Joint Stats Aircrafts arrives in the sky, flying over the people. The people start to get panic and started to rush, both the old, young, man and woman. The E-8 Joint Stars Aircraft surveys hundreds of miles of the country at a time. The aircraft's crew can see the people crossing to the other side. *"Sir, sir, sir, we can see something...miraculous or... magical happening here on this land,"* aircraft crew radio back to the headquarters to inform Tony and Risky on what's going-on.

"What is it? What's going-on? Tell me, tell me!" Tony's desperate to know what's happening.

"Sir... the river sir!," aircraft crew reports.

"Yes, yes, what about the river?" Tony asks.

"Emm... I don't know but I think the river is partition into two, to make a pathway for the people to escape off the land sir!," aircraft crew reports.

"A river partition into two..., how?" Tony says. And then looks at Risky. Risky looks back with a face expression that says - *what de f**k!*

"Ok, I see wot he's playing at. Never mind. Release

the missiles on the Black Eye," Tony gives an order.

"Ok commander, we shall do so," aircraft crew obeys.

The E-8 Joint Stars Aircrafts then went-on to fly over the Black Eye which is just right in front of the State House where Solomon is. They release the missiles.

Meanwhile by this time, all the people in the country have already crossed to the other side, before the river then closes back. The only people left on the land are Solomon and The Dark Warriors.

Ten minute after the missiles was released on the Black Eye, normally the missiles were suppose to explode as soon as they touch the ground but ten minutes since the missiles touches the ground, no explosion has occur.

"Sir, it looks like something is wrong with these missiles. They're not exploding!," aircraft crew radio back to Tony and Risky.

"Not exploding! Release more. Come on! Release all you have," Tony says, not impress.

The E-8 Joint Stars Aircrafts release all they have but still nothing happened.

"I think is really time for us to go there and face this man," Risky makes another suggestion.

"That's what I like to hear. That's why you're my boy. Ok, gather everyone together. It's time to make a move," Tony says.

"Yes sir!" Risky replies. Both ready to go to war.

The whole western troops gather together including Pastor Nicolas, ready to go to war against President Solomon and his men, and maybe the Dark-gods.

(Live on international TV)

"This is going to be big. Teemii, what do you think?" Andre Morgan asks Teemii Mah.

"Emmh... I honestly don't know what to think or expect. This is my country we're talking about; I don't want any war in my country. But if the leaders have decided to sort it out through war, then I have no other choice as a broadcaster than to broadcast the show. What do you think?" Teemii Mah replies, now working for BBTV as their Africa news correspondent along side with Andre Morgan, broadcasting the war live on international TV.

"Well, as you said, we are just broadcaster ready to update people and ready to take live courage of the show, if that's what you want to call it." Andre and Teemii live at the western military head base.

"Well for me, it's going to be a show. I can't wait to see what's going to happen and how the west is going to force President Solomon remove his dark power," Teemii says.

"Well, I can't wait to experience that too. So people, as you can see, today the 30th of March, here at the western military head base, behind us, the western troops are making their way to this one land, that is believe or portray to be the land of the dark-gods, to force remove the so called power from the Dark-gods that President Solomon Gondi have decided to use over international affairs. With me today, am joined with Teemii Mah, to bring to you live on how is all going to go down," Andre reporting live.

"Oh yes, we'll be bringing you the recent of the latest news. But first of all, we have here with us, the head commander, Command Sergeant Major Tony. Good morning sir, how are you feeling today, ready for the war?" Teemii asks Tony.

"Oh yes! As an army, you always have to be ready," Tony replies.

"Of course yes. But do you have any idea of what to expect when you get to the land?" Andre asks Tony.

"No idea. We are fully loaded. And beside, we aren't fighting real soldiers but ordinary men with no war experience. I think is going to be an easy battle," Tony replies.

"Well, if you say so commander. Thank you for talking to us. We wish you all the best," Teemii says.

"Thank you," Tony replies.

"Let's go! It's time to move," Risky shouts out to the troops as soon as he saw Tony finish talking to the press.

The western troop makes their way. All in big war ships heading straight to Egitee Land.

Meanwhile, back in Egitee, Solomon seem anxious, he doesn't know what to do or how to combat this war. He has no weapon. He's only relying on the Dark-gods. He has no idea of what's going to happen. He still wouldn't change his plan of fighting spiritually or using his powers. "If is what that can save us, then this is the time we know," Solomon thinks.

Few hours later, the western troops are about to arrive, coming through the Atlantic, about 5 to 10 miles away.

"Well, is this the land," Tony says while he looks through his binocular from one of the war ships.

"Yes sir, there is the land. The land of the Dark-gods," Risky replies.

"Oh really? Where are the so called Dark-gods then? Are they not going to come out to fight," Tony says.

"Emmh, why don't we just wait till we get there sir, before you start...you know," Risky carefully says.

"Come on Risky, if this people have good war strategy, they should have made a move or an attack by *now,"* Tony says.

"Sir, maybe they got another strategy," Risky says.

"Another strategy? This must be a joke. I want to see how they're going to fight back without any sort of weapon. All the Dark Warriors have is only long ass cutlasses. Imagine only trying to fight with long ass cutlasses. This guy they call Solomon must be a joker. I think he's a man that seeks for attention. No problem, we got his time. A man like that makes our job worthwhile. What do you think Risky, enh? What do you think? Or do you think is risky to go to war against this man? Ha-ha-ha-ha! Risky my boy, come-on don't be scared. This is going to be an easy ball game, don't worry. You just sit back, relax, and enjoy the show. Ha-ha- ha!" Tony says laughing, for some reasons, excited.

"Sir... I just think you should let us get there first before you start blowing you trumpet," Risky sincerely says.

"Blowing my trumpet! Come on Risky, the trumpet has been blown already. Like I said Risky, there is no risk or what so ever on us fighting this war. If anything, we're the goods ones. Don't forget the saying that says 'the good will always end good and the bad will always end bad'. This battle is going to end good for us, believe me Risky, believe me," Tony says, boasting.

"If you say so commander. You are the commander and your wish is my command," Risky says.

"That's what I like to hear," Tony says. *"Ha-ha-ha-ha!,"* he then laughs.

And all of a sudden, dark clouds start to gather round the land.

"ZZZRAAAA!," heavy thunder strikes.

Tony and Risky looks at each other. Then heavy rain starts to pour.

"It's only a rain! Get the men out of the ship! Let's

get ready to invade! Do it now!" Tony shouts at Risky. The noise of the thunder striking is too loud, and it's heavily raining.

"Yes sir!" Risky shouts back.

The troops then start to jump off the war ships into the water, in the rain, ready to attack or for attacks.

"God be with us on this very day," Pastor Nicolas prayed and then did the cross sign.

"Oh yeah, it seems the troops are ready to go onto the land as you can see," Andre and Teemii reporting from a special protected army helicopter flying above the land, viewing all that is happening.

As the troops touch the land, the heavy thunder and rain stopped. Then the troops stopped, and all of a sudden, the ground start to heavily shake like earthquake wants to occur.

"Get back to the ships! Get back!" Risky order the troops back to the ship.

"What's going on here?" Tony asks.

"I have no idea sir," Risky replies.

"Did you check the weather?" Tony asks again.

"Oh yes sir. It says bright and sunny," Risky replies.

"Bright and sunny! Is that all? Why is the ground shaking then?" Tony asks.

"I have no clue sir," Risky replies.

"Ok I know what to do. Send one of the F-22 Raptor," Tony commands.

"Yes sir!" Risky obeys.

The F-22 Raptor is Air Force most advanced weapons system, ready for combat. The F-22 Raptor takes off from one of the war ships, ready for operation use. The Raptor did what it could do but yet still no explosion. Instead, the ground stopped shaking.

"I wonder what's going-on with these machines," Tony quietly says to Risky. He then picks up his

binoculars too view the land. He zoom-in and all he can see behind the tropical trees are the Dark Warriors, still standing and not moving. *"They're just there, standing, not moving. What kind of creatures are these? Ok, I know what to do,"* Tony says. He then decided to wait for a while to see if they're going to be attacked. They waited few hours, still no attack from Solomon or the Dark Warriors. Meanwhile, Solomon is in his office in the State House watching all that's going-on via the Black Eye. As they waited for Solomon to attack, another strange thing happened; for the very first time in West Africa, it starts to snow heavily.

"Snow! In West Africa! Risky are you sure we are at the right location or direction?" Tony says, surprised to see snow falling.

"Sir, this is surprising for me too. I have no clue on what's going-on," Risky says.

"Ok, make sure you get the men to keep warm because very soon, we're going in! And also, get the Pastor ready," Tony gives orders.

"Yes sir!" Risky obeys.

"Oh my God, snow in my country. This is wonder happening. I should take some pictures," Teemii says.

"But we're filming," Andre says to Teemii.

"I know. I mean..., personal picture for myself and maybe to show my kids in future," Teemii says.

The heavy snow fell for half an hour before it later stopped. Then the dark clouds came back out. This time no thunder striking or rain falling, just very dark cloud which makes everywhere looks really dark.

"Sir, it looks like is getting late," Risky says.

"No, it's only 2pm. Turn on the oxygen light on the ships, get the men ready and lets go," Tony says, ready to make another move-in.

Tony and Risky with the coalition including Pastor Nicolas eventually got off the ships to make their move-in. As they touch the ground, again the ground starts to shake and heavy wind start to blow.

"Don't move and don't go anywhere! Stay where you are! It's a trick!" Tony shouts-out to his men.

"Jesus!" Pastor Nicolas shouts.

The ground is shaking heavily, making the entire troops/coalition stumble.

"Oh why are they making us do this?" Jack - one of the British soldiers says.

"I seriously don't know" Dwayne - a US soldier replies.

This two soldiers are very good friends. They met and became friends when they were sent to Afghanistan to fight.

After twenty minutes the ground stops shaking. Solomon then appears again on a very big electronic billboard that is normally used to inform people on safety along the sea side of the beach.

"There he is," Risky says pointing to the billboard.

"Oh there you are. What have you got to say now? We're here for you, enh?" Tony says to Solomon.

"I'm sorry but I have a confession to make," Solomon says.

"What? A confession to make!!," Tony, Ricky, and Pastor Nicolas all says at the same time.

"A confession!," so as Teemii and Andre says and also Jack and Dwayne.

"I knew it! I told you he's dodgy, I knew it! You should always listen to me," Tony says to Risky.

"Go ahead! Confess to the world and let the devil be ashamed!" Pastor Nicolas says to Solomon.

"Well people, the president is about to make a confession," Teemii reporting.

"Emmh... first of all, I'm so sorry to have caused all this commotion," Solomon says.

"Now you're sorry. Is this a game plan? Well if it is,

you've already lost," Tony says.

"No, this isn't a game plan. And this isn't what I plan for. This isn't what I want either. War is the last thing on my mind," Solomon explains.

"Then why didn't you do as you were told?" Tony says to Solomon.

"I think **is time to stop the world pushing us Africans around. It's about time we don't do as we were told but do as we want to do. It about time we stand for ourselves as Africans**. *You don't tell us what to do on our land. We do what we believe is good for us to do,"* Solomon express.

"Yeah that's right. But not giving your soul to the darkness. Children of God stay away from darkness," Pastor Nicolas says.

"It depends on what you see as darkness pastor. If you mean darkness as-in bad, then my heart genuinely belongs to the light, Pastor." Solomon says.

"I'm not sure about that. Not after receiving power from the goddess," Pastor Nicolas says.

"Pastor, why are you not getting my point? Why are you finding it hard to let go, why? Why have you decided to portray me as bad, whereas you know I'm not," Solomon says.

"Not anymore. You need to be born again," Pastor Nicolas says to Solomon.

"Be born again? Why? How many times do I need to be born again? My life is already in God's hand. Or are you now telling me to abandon my belief as an African to be born again into yours or another man's belief? Or you're telling me being African and trying to follow my root isn't a good thing? I just don't understand why you so much want me to abandon mine. Why don't you abandon yours to follow mine? You will definitely find good or should I say 'God' in it!" Solomon says to Pastor Nicolas.

"You two should stop there! We are not here for reconciling. Pastor, you should let it go. He doesn't want to be a Christian anymore. We are not here for you to change people to be born again. That's all you pastors know; born again! Born again! I don't know how you expect a grown man to be born again. Kill himself and go back into his mother's belly? Come-on pastor," Tony says.

"No. Not at all. All you need to do is give your life to Christ and accept him as your Lord and personal saviour," Pastor Nicolas explains.

"Christ as my lord and personal saviour! Come on pastor, you talking about Jesus, right?" Tony asks.

"Yes, Jesus Christ of Lazarus," Pastor Nicolas answered.

"So I should give my life to Jesus, why? I understand he was just a simple man like… you know, I was gonna say like me but I'm not perfect," Tony says.

"Exactly pastor, do you now want me to take my life off Gods' hands and give it to Jesus? I mean, why should I abandon God that I already know for Jesus? You wouldn't give-up Jesus for no one else, would you?" Solomon says and asks.

"Never," Pastor Nicolas answered.

"So why do you then want me to give up mine? God has appeared to us in different ways and I am not giving-up my way to follow another mans' way, just like you wouldn't. My life is saved and safe in Jaja's hands, thank you very much," Solomon says, sticking to his words and belief.

"Can you three please stop?! We are here for something else and not this!" Risky screams at Pastor Nicolas, Solomon, and Tony.

"Yeah, someone was making a confession. We're listening to you, Mr. President," Tony says.

"Like I was saying, there is no need for this war. It's

a set up," Solomon confessing.

"A set up! Is this man kidding me? Set up by whom?" Tony asks.

"The gods obviously," Solomon replies.

"The gods....!

.....The gods!

The gods....!"

—Everyone present at this scene — the coalition, Andre and Teemii, the camera man and even the people watching live yells.

"Yes the gods," Solomon repeats.

And all of a sudden, *"ZZZRAAAA!,"* another heavy thunder strikes. Again, the ground starts to shake.

"Don't move! Stay where you are! Stay where you are!" Tony shouts-out to his men.

Right in front of the coalitions, something never seen before starts to come-up from the ground;

"Oh my God! Is the camera man filming this? This could be the gods, or should I say something like three huge human-like shadows looking ghostly images, wrapped round with black robes, coming out from the ground, growing taller and taller. Oh my God, this is incredible! Wow!" Teemii says, excited for some reasons.

"Wow!" again everyone present at the scene says. All surprised.

"ZZZRAAAA!" another heavy thunder strikes.

"Jesus!" Pastor Nicolas shouts out.

"Don't get panic! Let see them do their worse!" Tony shout-out to his men.

"Who are you guys? Are you the gods of the land?" Risky asks.

"Yes who are you? We're not scared of you. We're good soldiers fighting for peace. And I'm the head commander that leads this... (He looks back at his men, all looking scared) *...lot! If you are the gods of*

the land then you need to speak to me or else," Tony says.

"Sir, we have nothing to fight the gods." Risky whispers to Tony.

"We have no weapon but we have good faith. Let them do their worse. We need to know the source of this power," Tony whispers back to Risky.

"Yes come on! Do your worse!" Tony says to the three huge shadows.

And all of a sudden, a heavy wind blows away Tony back into the sea.

"Woo...!

....woo!

Woo...!" - Everyone says.

"Sorry commander, sorry, I got you, I got you," Risky says to Tony while he tries to drag Tony out of the water.

"I'm alright. Leave me alone," Tony says while he struggles out of the water.

He then walked straight back, alongside with Risky and Pastor Nicolas behind, to the front of the troops who are still by the edge of the seaside. The three huge shadows are about 100m away from the edge of the seaside.

"Is that the worse you three could do, is that it? Let me show you mine. Release the missiles!" Tony says and then commands the release of missiles on the land.

A USAF Stealth bomber fires a "bunker buster," the latest variant of the B61, still no explosion;

"Ok, now I see your move," Tony says.

"Sir, I think is better we talk than doing this," Risky suggest.

"Ok then, let's talk! Can you please first of all tell us who you three shadows or whatever you guys might be, are?" Tony asks.

"They're the gods of the land," Solomon answered.

"Are this the ones that gave you dark power?" Tony asks.

"Not dark power, but yes, they are the ones that appear to him in the dark forest. They are the ones that plan for this war," Solomon replies.

Then the ground stops shaking.

"What! How?," Risky asks.

"It's a long story. The gods and I have a secret together," Solomon confessing.

"Secret together! I thought you have nothing to hide?" Pastor Nicolas says.

"Yes I have nothing to hide when it comes to me being a genuinely good minded person. It was part of me trying to make things all good that causes all this commotion. Before I was given the power, I was told there is going to be BLOODSHED on this land after seven years, which is like a week according to the gods' time," Solomon confessing.

"BLOODSHED!!!," everyone yells.

"Yes! I was told after seven years, my people will carry guns to kill each other, which is the last thing on my mind I will want to see happen to my people. This was going to be as pay back for receiving the power not the lost of my family. But then again, I believe I could or can change things round," Solomon confessing.

"Woo…" everyone yells.

"My plan was to destroy all guns and ammunition before the time comes. At least, if there isn't anymore guns and ammunition, then there will be no guns for the people to carry to cause bloodshed. That's the reason why I decided to cancel the guns and ammunition supply and then destroy the once we already stored. I was able to exceed the gods time planned for the bloodshed. But then again, I've come to realise no one can change the agreement or plan one has with the gods because obviously, the reason why you lot are

242

here is to cause bloodshed," Solomon confessed.

"No, the reason why we're here is to take out the dark power," Tony says.

"You shouldn't have taken the power at the first place. I told you about my dream, didn't I? I told you I see bloods on your hands, didn't I? Now see what you've cause for yourself and your people, you see!" Pastor Nicolas says to Solomon.

"I was desperate Pastor. My people needed help. I truly believed I could change things round. I didn't know it was going to end this way. My belief was, if I never do any bad with the power then I expect nothing bad back. I apologise to my people for the inconvenience I might have cause them to evacuate the land," Solomon explains.

"Well, now, what's going to happen? Are the gods got something to say or do? Because now that we all know their plan is to cause bloodshed, we're going to drop down all our weapons and see what they got for us. What do you think Risky?" Tony says.

"Sir, I think that's a good idea," Risky replies.

"With the Holy Bible on my hand, I command every bad or evil spirit, destroy!" Pastor Nicolas says. And then, *"ZZZRAAAA!!!,"* another heavy thunder strikes.

"Jesus!" Pastor Nicolas screams.

The thunder was so strong and powerful, everyone takes cover. Then the eye of the "middle huge tall shadow" among the three opens.

"Oh my God! One of the gods has opened his eyes…
Yeah I know," Teemii and Andre reporting.

"Ok, say something then. Gods, shadow, or whatever that you may be, at least, say something," Tony says.

"ZZZRAAAA!" another heavy thunder strikes.

"We are the gods of this land, the ancestors. Who are you? And why are you here?" the huge middle

shadow says.

"*Who am I? Are you asking me who am I, and why we're here? This is a joke. Ok, no problem, I will tell you since you guys don't know who am I and the reason why we're here. First, let me introduce myself to you; I am Commander Sergeant Major Tony... and this lot behind me... are my soldiers. We are here to take you out! I mean, your dark powers,*" Tony says.

"*Our dark powers. How and why?*" the middle shadow says.

And then the other two shadows (gods) open their eyes.

"*With the power of Jesus we will take you out!*" Pastor Nicolas shouts out.

"*Take us out with the power of Jesus? How and why? Pastor Nicolas James,*" the middle shadow says.

"*How did you know my name?*" Pastor Nicolas says.

"*We know everything that goes-on on this land. This land belongs to us,*" the middle shadow says.

"*No, the land belongs to the Almighty,*" Pastor Nicolas says.

"*Oh yes, but personally located to us. You got your own land don't you?*" middle shadow asks.

"*Yes we do but we're here to make peace,*" Tony answered

"*Peace! But the people on this land were living in peace before you decided to bring war on them,*" middle shadow says.

"*Not on the people obviously. We're here to stop the bad one. To bring whom that's bad to justice,*" Tony says.

"*So who is bad that you're bringing to justice?*" middle shadow asks.

"*You guys obviously. You're the once poisoning the mind of the people. You belong in the darkness,*" Pastor

Nicolas says.

We guys? We belong in the darkness? What do you mean pastor? You don't even know us. Are you here again to mislead the people? To make them turn their back on themselves, making them misunderstood the power they could or can find in themselves, just to follow you and be slaves to your people. Because we don't understand why you say we belong in the darkness. Darkness as-in, to rot in hell? Are many years of slavery not hell enough for this innocent people? Or you're just wishing us bad. Not a very good way to think of your next neighbour, isn't that so pastor? If you ask us who is poisoning the mind of the people, we will blame it on people like you because, before people like you came to this part of land, people on this land have their own way of life and blessing from the Almighty. The people then might not be wise enough to understand the use of their blessings but then again, life is a learning process. A religion was set on our behalf to guide the people on this part of life just as you got that book you're holding to guide you...

"*Ummmh,*" the other two shadows says.

"*But then again, the whites, also known as the wise ones, came alongside with this same book you're carrying, which represent people from another land, to poison the mind of the people on this land, making this innocent people that didn't really know much turn their back on themselves. Portrayed us as evil ones, mixed things up, and took some of the people away to be slaves to them and for sell. They mix the people up to make unity impossible, all in the name of God. Not very good way of behaving, isn't that right, pastor?*" middle shadow says and asks.

Pastor Nicolas didn't say a word.

"*Some were brought to this very land which humans are not even meant to live on,*" middle shadow says.

245

"*Really?*" Tony asks.

"*It's a land reserve for the gods, which is us,*" middle shadow says.

"*Ummmh,*" the other two shadows says.

"*We try to make the wise men realise people are not meant to live on this land by spreading a disease but the wise men wouldn't give-up. We understand a wise one hate not to know the problem of a cause, so we decided to play along by showing them the special power people from this part of land can have through one of our chosen one,*" middle shadow says.

"*Ummmh,*" other two shadows says.

"*The power was portrayed as dark and called black magic. We wonder why?*"

"*Ummmh,*" the other two shadows says.

"*Not only on this land will one find such power in people but also major lands. We're the first set of human sent to this part of land or should we say, life,*" middle shadow says.

"*Ummmh,*" the other two shadows says.

Given a special power to build the land but then again, some of us, out of joy, were too happy to be part of the first set and then got drunk on palm wine…

"*Ummmmmmmmh…*

…ummmmmmmmh," the other two shadow says.

It leads to disaster. And then the Almighty - He that sent us wasn't happy with our set and then put us behind the scene to help assist the next set with the special power given to us. We try our best in our power to show, guide, and open up the mind of the chosen ones or those that believe in us, the power they could or can find in themselves…

"*Ummmh*"

"*But obviously, some men finding out their power and it potential, used it wrongfully. And pastor, we are not to blame,*" middle shadow says.

"So why give power or open the minds of the ones you know will misuse the power?" **Risky** asks.

"Yes why?" Tony also says.

"Very good question, you must be a wise one. Not you, but him. First of all, everyone deserves a chance. Secondly, we don't give power, the Almighty does. And thirdly, every man will be judged by their own actions. The Almighty has already blessed us all. It might seem like we give power but really, our job is to help assist man with our power to reach his peak of his power. Some men don't need us to find the power they have in themselves. Whatever power man obtains or has is completely up to man on how he uses it. We are just here to guide. The people on this land got it all wrong since the very day the wise ones appear. The ones that have power have nothing good in mind. They become greedy. They want all the luxury things the wise shown to them. So they use whatever that's in their power against their fellow human beings just as the wise men show to them on how to get luxury. People from this part of the world need to be wise. Trying to be like the wise abandoning their ways is not going to lead them far. They have to be themselves to be a wise one of their kind because, at the end of the day, the wise one is only being himself and following his roots. Learn from the wise, don't act like them."

"Ummmh," the other two shadows says.

"The wise men know this. But because of what they want or after, wouldn't make them do the right thing. They were all after treasures. So as most man at that time..."

"Ummmh," the other two shadows says.

"Yeah but we the wise ones of this day are not greedy. We have grown far ahead of that. Our forefathers might be greedy but not us. We have learnt so much from the past. We support nothing that got to

do with greed. The only reason why we're here is to make sure there's good protection over the world. We have to come here to confirm if really the power that he has, is not dangerous. But talking to you guys, you sound convincing. And I think this will be a great opportunity to say a very big sorry to you guys and your people," Risky sincerely says.

*"No, no, no, that's alright. It's no one's fault. Up till today, man is still finding his way to get life to it perfection. Those days were ways man believed he could or can find good. Even some of us are not pure. As ancestors, my advice to people will be; keep discipline and not get carried away by the joyfulness of life. Always follow the good part of the mind. Be good people as much as you can. **Show the same respect you will want for yourself to your fellow human being. Support one another. Understand one another** and do what's right for you to do,"* the middle shadow says.

"So is it right for you gods to do something and then wants to take blood as pay back?" Pastor Nicolas asks.

"Good question pastor. Our pay back is part of the rules set with life. It's to make man realise the impact and damages that will cost life if one tampers with the free will of life or tries to use shortcuts. Man is fully aware of the consequences that come with the wrong use of the power they obtain. But out of selfish ambition or vain conceit of man, they still use it wrongfully. It's also a test to see how far a man will go to get good. Man is meant to work hard to achieve good life. But when man decides to go the shortcut, then some thing has to cover the long space. Even though man was given a power to make things easier and quicker, is still mans' responsibility to apply some creativity to it. To create is the main purpose of the power because, at the end of the day, we all are sent here to create and develop life to perfection. So we think and so we

248

believe. The power is there, is up to man on how the power is to be used..."

"Ummmh," the other two shadows says.

"But there's a problem; one of us directs traffic along the road of life. That's his job. He carries compliance to the gods, questions to the spirit world, and messages to any living things. With his connections, he can be a powerful one. He's also a god with a sense of humour and often likes to cause confusion to keep life interesting. You will always find him on the bad side of the mind. So you humans really have to be careful and not take him seriously, not make any connection with him, or act like him. To us, he's a joker. Stay strong on the good side of your mind, its will prevent you from getting deceived by him. And the war today is something we plan for since the very first day the wise brought slaves onto this land. We were not impressed with the way our people were treated and deceived. It reminds us of the bad behaviour of one of us. He was part of what made the Almighty put us behind the scenes. And we believe he's also got something to do with the behaviour of the wise towards the people on this land. We didn't want the same way we got deceived by him happen again to the people on this land because, during our days, he was seen as a wise one too, not knowing he is only a trickster god. The rest of the gods, with our powers, came up with a plan on how to even things up, if you know what I mean," middle shadow says.

"Ummmh," the other two shadows

"By the way, we're not meant to be seen this way, but because you guys ask for it, we have to come out this way."

"Ummmh," the other two shadows

"Solomon is genuinely a good man. He as used his power wisely. The bloodshed issue is to test on how

249

he's going to react and use his power to prevent bad coming. Solomon did the right thing. **Man does not need guns and ammunitions to control life.** *But then again, because men are still against each other, peace will never be found. Man needs to show more love and respect to each other more often than condemning and not trusting one another."*

"Ummmh," the other two shadows

"Anyway, our time is up and we have to go now. We promise never to appear in this manner to man again. We are the gods of this land and may peace be upon you all? The Almighty has blessed you all. Be happy and carry-on creating. Have a good life," the middle shadow ends the conversation with man.

"Hold-on, don't go yet! We haven't finished what we came here for. Hold-on! Wait... We might be sorry but we still haven't come-up with a strong agreement of the power not being use wrongly. Or come-up with a plan to put the power under good control. Am right, Risky right?" Tony enquires.

"Oh yes sir, you are!" Risky replies.

The three huge tall shadows didn't say a word back to Tony. Slowly they go down back into the ground. Again, the ground starts to shake and thunder again start to strike, *"ZZZRAAAA!"*

"Oh! It seems the gods are going back down. It's been an ingenious moment spent with the gods, don't you think so Andre?," Teemii reporting.

"Oh yes, sure. So what's going to happen to the land now?," Andre reporting.

"Well, there is nothing else to fight. The coalitions have to go back to theirs, and then we the beautiful people of Egitee will come back to our beautiful land. Yeah!" Teemii excitedly says.

"Hold-on, hold-on, it looks like the President got

something to say," Andre reporting.

"Well, there will be no need for any strong agreement on how the power will not be used wrongly, or coming up with a plan to put the power under good control," Solomon says.

"Why?" Tony asks.

*"Because today is when my contract expires with the gods, I'm probably now powerless. But I would like to use this opportunities to give a strong massage to my fellow Africans. Please, please, and please, as you can hear the gods, we need to be more of ourselves to be wise ones of our kind. We need to teach ourselves more on how to love ourselves. We are Africans. That's the only creature or human we can be. Embrace your own culture. Don't abandon yours to go for another man's'. Be more of yourselves. Do what's right for you to do. Be discipline. Be understanding. Be proud of who you are and where you're from. We can't keep on understanding other people's traditions and not understanding ours. We need to be united. We need to be wise, to be useful, think positive, be civilised, be advanced, and be creative. **Respect yourselves and respect your neighbours**. That's our culture, and that's part of our belief. Let us be the good people that we are. We don't like to have bad names for ourselves, so why create one. It's time for us all to come together and lift Africa up. Please, please, and please, let us for the sake of our heavenly Father that we believe in as Africans; be good. It's the only way forward. We can't continue being seen and portray as bad ones anymore longer. It time to change for better. If you're a leader, lead your people right. Be the man you say you are. Don't be a coward. **Do what's in your power to do good.** Be responsible. Care for your people. Be truthful and faithful. Show more interest on making life better for your people. Think less on money and the luxury*

things you could have. Instead, think more of the kind of person you are or represent. Stop the killing. We are all one. Africa, united we shall stand! God bless Africa!," final and last message from Solomon.

And as Solomon ends his strong massage to his fellow Africans, the dark clouds that gathered up in the sky starts to clear as a full sun set shines upon the land. And all of a sudden, the missiles and bombs dropped by the western troops earlier on the land starts to release and explode. *BOOM!!! BOOM!!! BOOM!!!*

"What's going on? What's going on?" Pastor Nicolas says.

"Oh my God! Sir, the bombs are starting to release," Risky says to Tony.

"Really! We have to leave now! Come-on, get everyone back onto the ships, hurry!" Tony commands Risky.

"Back to the ships!," Risky screams.

"Oh my God! The bombs are exploding. Oh my God! Our beautiful land is destroying. Noooo! This is odious! Why? God why? Noooo!," Teemii screams out, and then started crying.

"It's alright my dear, it alright. We will look after you. I am sure the western governments will surely help the humble good people of Egitee develop back their land. It's alright darling, it's alright," Andre tries to console Teemii while she cries.

Every single one of the coalition/troops made it back to the ship. Only Solomon and the Dark Warriors still remain on the land while the bombs keep exploding. The whole land starts to get blown-up.

"Oh my God, we should have rescued him," Risky says to Tony while they're back on the ship looking at the land destroying.

"He's a strong man, he will find his way," Tony says.

"May the almighty God be with him," Pastor Nicolas prayed for Solomon.

The whole land got destroyed. The bomb thrown by the western troops was to powerful, it wipes out the whole land. The whole land sinks deep down into the Atlantic Ocean.

"Oh my God! It looks like the land is sinking," Risky says while he looks at the land sinks through his binocular.

"May his soul rest in perfect peace," Pastor Nicolas says, did the cross sign, and then quietly went back inside into the ship holding-on tight to his Bible.

"Well, what as happen, as happened. What can we really do? It's what the gods have planned. They took back their land," Tony says.

"But what about President Solomon, we could have saved his life," Risky says.

"Well, if the gods really wanted him alive, I think they know what to do. He might even come back after another 40 days and 40 nights. You never know. Nowadays, s**t happens. So, let just go back in, we are not in a position to decide on who is wrong and who isn't. All I know is; one just needs to be good at all times. So, be a good boy, son. That's all you need," Tony says and then went inside, leaving Risky all alone.

"Well, God... Allah... Jesus... Jehovah... Jaja..., I know people call you different names... I don't know what to call you... but all I know is, you're up there somewhere, looking over us. I know we all have done wrong and bad. If you're truly there, please, forgive us all, guide us, and lead us through the right path," Risky says looking up to the sky. He then quietly went

in to meet the rest of the troops.

At the end of the war, Egitee as a land or country is no more on the surface of the planet. The whole land got destroyed. Since then, from the new diagram of the planet to start a new decade, Egitee as a country got erased off the Africa map. The Egite people spread all over the world to find peace. And ever since the end of the war, one man still remains in the heart of everyone – Solomon.

"Is he dead or alive?" the whole world is curious.

Some people say, *"He died when the land got destroyed."*

While some people say, *"He's probably gone with the gods to a special place."*

No one really knows what happened to Solomon. His body was never found. However, to know what really happened and where Solomon Gondi could be, turn to the next page.

Hi, I am Solomon Gondi. Hope you enjoyed my story. And hope you learnt something from the story. Thanks for the time you've spent to read my story. And to my Egite people, I'm very sorry for the loss of our beautiful land. I'm in another life right now telling the people our story.

God bless you.

THE END

The Good Message II

GOOD should never fear BAD.
BAD always look out for GOOD.
No matter what circumstances the good and bad gets-
in, the good will always ends GOOD and the bad will
always end BAD.
So my dearest brothers and sisters;
Let us for the sake of ONE LOVE and for GOODNESS
sake;
Put BAD to DARK and bring GOOD to LIGHT.
God bless you.

...be good.

Message from
Ade Tokunbo:
Crown from across the sea.

The Good Message III

No human wants BAD to happen to them. But for those "humans" that involve in BAD, whether in a form of; Hate, Kill, Violence, Abuse, Racism, Dishonesty, Disrespectful, Untruthful, Unkindness, Steal, Bully, Rape, Jealousy, Greed, Selfishness...etc, help to join promote BAD happening.

You do not want it to happen, so why promote BAD?

You can always STOP BAD happing.

So my dearest brothers and sisters;

"Do nothing out of selfish ambition or vain conceit, but in humility consider others better than you. Each of you should look not to your own interests but also to the interests of others." (Philippians 2:3-4)

Treat the other human the same way you will like to be treated.

God bless you.

...be good.

Message from
Ade Tokunbo:
Crown from across the sea.

Questions

1. What part of Africa is Egitee?
2. What is Egitee official name?
3. Who found the land and named it Egitee?
4. Egitee is a small land demarcated round by a river called….. and named after whom….?
5. Egitee was named after a young black beautiful woman (one of the slaves). What's her name?
6. What year did Egitee gained Independence?
7. What's the name of the capital of Egitee?
8. Who was the first leader of Egitee?
9. Who kill the first leader of Egitee?
10. Who is Gen. Fahruk's father?
11. How will you describe Gen. Fahruk?
12. Who did Gen. Fahruk overthrew the power from?
13. Who gave birth to Musiah?
14. The name Musiah means or given to sons that is….?
15. Who is Solomon and how will you describe him?
16. What was Solomon's post when he was part of Gen. Fahruk government?
17. When and why did he resign from his post?
18. Who killed Solomon's dad?
19. What is Solomon's dad's name?
20. What is Solomon's grandfather's name?
21. Who is Solomon's uncle?
22. Who is Solomon's sister?
23. Who is Tina and how will you describe her?
24. How many kids has Tina got and what's their names and age?
25. What is Gen. Fahruk "hot girlfriend's" name and who killed her?
26. What killed Tina and her kids?
27. Who did Solomon believes he can call for rescue to save his country?

28. What country did Pastor Nicolas first visit before going to Egitee?
29. What country is Pastor Nicolas from?
30. Who is Mr. Thomas?
31. How did Mr. Thomas die?
32. Who is Gagman?
33. Who killed Gagman?
34. What part of Egitee is Yemojaja village?
35. What's the meaning of Yemojaja?
36. What does Jaja means?
37. What does Eja means?
38. Who is Solomon's favourite writer?
39. Who is Teemii Mah and how will you describe her?
40. Who is Teemii's favourite writer?
41. Where is Professor Kete from?
42. At what age did Professor Kete lost his parent?
43. How did Professor Kete parent died?
44. How old was Professor Kete on the day of the festival?
45. What happen on the last minute of the festival?
46. Where did Solomon go for forty days and forty nights?
47. What year did Solomon overthrew the power?
48. Who is Lady Young and how will you describe her?
49. Who is Umaru?
50. Solomon as the leader or president of Egitee, what is the prosecution given to one (someone) that breaks the rule?
51. Why did the U.S government decided to go on war with Solomon?
52. Who is Tony and who is Risky? Including their ranks.
53. Who do you think the Dark-gods are?
54. Are the Dark-gods good or bad gods?

55. Who do you think is bad or need to be stopped?
56. What do you think went wrong or who do you think is in the wrong?
57. In one word, describe Solomon.
58. What would you do differently if you were to be Solomon?
59. Where do you think special/magical powers come from?
60. Did you learn anything from the full story? If yes, what did you learn?